Two Unlikely Souls

Two Unlikely Souls

The Mysteries of
Bella Rose Estate
Book #5

Phyllis Dewey

Copyright © 2022 Phyllis Dewey
ISBN   978-1-7364347-8-9

If nothing more,
we will always have
The Pineapple

J.C.S.

Relationships

Strangers meet
Friendships develop
Closeness begins.

Changes come
Differences show
Questions rise.

Love grows
Love fades
Friendship stays.

Life continues
Friendship grows
Love blossoms.

Phyllis Dewey

Dedication

Two Unlikely Souls is dedicated to adventure and the many people I met along the way.

To the open roads that took me through beautiful areas that so many never see or others take for granted.

May you each find your open road to your adventures of life.

Prologue

So much to do in such a short amount of time. What had happened to the simple, carefree life that Terri had imagined she would have when she moved to the quaint town to start her life over? Yes, she had her own business, made several new friends, and fulfilled a few of her dreams. She had also put her past life behind her. Would it come back and interfere with her future?

What she had not expected or planned was to fall in love. She thought that was behind her. She had given it a college try years before. Then again, recently. Neither had worked—until Adam. Now life seemed complicated again. Was it time to withdraw again? Time to crawl into her shell where she repeatedly found comfort?

The Bella Rose family continued with its own mysteries. The more they tried to be a normal family running a business, the more family history came to life. The kids were growing up, and business was growing. Could the family closeness continue its success? Or was it time for more change? Would the family discover truths that would tear them apart? Would a normal life in the small town become boring?

What was the key to happiness, success, and love?

It was time for:
Two Unlikely Souls
A story of –
Friendship, Love, and Personal Discovery
All within the Bella Rose Estate Mystery Series

Chapter One

Blurred Vision

Sunlight filled the bedroom as Terri awoke. She felt the ring on her left hand as she moved her arm underneath her pillow. Terri smiled briefly as her joy was replaced by the recollection of the dream she had just woken from. She kept her eyes closed as she tried to retrieve the full-color play in her mind. Another smile formed as she opened her eyes. The dream was her perfect wedding. She closed her eyes, trying to see more details. She searched the photo in her mind.

Why could she not see Adam standing at the stage at the end of the aisle she was preparing to walk down? The figure she saw was not distinct.

She shook her head and blinked her eyes. She pulled her arm out from beneath the pillow and looked at her hand. At least the engagement ring was real, and the diamond was clear.

She rose from the bed and spent the next couple of hours avoiding thoughts of her dream. Normally she could never recall any dream she had. Why was this one so clear while also being fuzzy? What was going on with her? She decided not to share her dream with anyone – especially Adam.

~~~~~~

When Adam proposed to her, she was sure of what she wanted. She knew she wanted to spend her life with him. He made her happier than anyone ever had. What had shocked her was how quickly her feelings had formed for Adam.

They initially met when he answered a call to bid on remodeling her café. He had drawn up the plans, made the adjustments she wanted, and quickly was hired. They developed a friendship almost instantly. Adam soon spent hours after his workday was finished just talking with her. He often lent a hand to help her clean up and prepare for her next day at work.

It did not take them long to expand their friendship and begin dating. Terri learned his background and his history. She accepted it as a part of who he was, and she was thrilled that he was no longer that person. He was open, honest, and loving. He loved her, and it did not take long to feel love for him.

Their intent was to have a small intimate wedding. All too easily, more people heard about it and wanted to attend. While they originally planned to have their wedding in the Café where they met, with the larger guest list, they relocated the ceremony to the little chapel and the reception to the event hall at Bella Rose Estate. If the weather cooperated, the ceremony would be outside.

While thinking of people to invite, Terri began thinking of people in her past. She had so many wonderful memories of all that she had done. She hoped that life with Adam would add to her cherished memories.

She smiled when she thought of the summer a few years earlier when she went on the trip of her lifetime. It was a location she had always dreamed of going to, but it became much more than her dream. It was with Jay. It was a time neither of them would ever forget. How could they?

Terri smiled as she remembered her time with Jay. She gave her heart to him, waited for him, and was there for him. And for a while….. Love filled their days and nights.

Now her new future lay ahead of her. But before that was fulfilled, she needed to revisit her past. Something was calling her back. Like her blurred dream, she was uncertain of the force beckoning her.

Chapter Two

Life Adjustments

A year had passed since the last time Terri thought about her adventures on the West Coast. She was first reminded of them when she met Steven and hired him on the spot because of his connection to her favorite stop on her vacation there.

She was reminded of that area again when she met Adam. He had a connection to the same place. Her courtship with Adam had grown quickly. Something about him drew her to him the minute they met. Once the work was complete on the Café remodel and he asked her out, she knew life as she knew it would change. Their first hug on their first date sealed the deal in her heart. Their connection was real. Their love was intense.

Life had thrown her for a loop a couple of years before. It had taken her heart and filled it with love. One that she did not want to forget, so she had written about it. She wanted to treasure her journey and Jay. She wanted to remember their beginning. It had not turned out the way she had hoped it would. As her life was about to change again, she wondered about her last love. The best way to remember it was to reread what she had documented.

Before locating her travel journal, Terri thought back to the beginning with Jay.

It was all her sister's fault. Her little sister, Angela, introduced her to Jay. He was in town working on an assignment with his job, and Angela thought it would be nice if Jay learned about the area from someone who had been there a while. The first person she thought of was her sister. Terri had been single for a while; maybe it was time to get into dating again. If nothing else came of it, at least

Jay and her sister could have a good time together while Jay was assigned to photograph that area for her magazine.

On the night of the date with Jay, Terri had been nervous. It had been so long since her last date. She was not expecting much to come of it. She knew Jay was only in the area to photograph and write about the town's history. Maybe a good friendship would come of it. That was all she expected.

Instead, after the nerves of the first night out to eat with Jay, she found herself intrigued by him. He was different than any man she had known before. He was quiet initially but opened up after a glass of wine. He told her about his past, corporate job, and how he had fallen into photography. He told her he liked being on his own and enjoyed the quietness and beauty of nature. She learned that even when he was not on a work assignment, he had his camera gear and always found things to photograph.

He showed her a few photos on his phone, telling her the best ones had been taken with his camera. He invited her to his hotel room to look at some of them, but she declined that first night.

The days and nights that followed found them together as much as possible. Jay soon was given another short assignment, and Angela permitted him to combine it with some vacation time and suggested he and Terri go on the trip together. Angela sensed how close the two were getting and wanted to help their relationship grow.

Terri shook her head as thoughts of their beginning landed on their trip West. The beginning of the ending, as she referred to it. She cleared her mind and recalled how Jay came into her life and the story of his past.

Jay had finished at the top of his high school and college classes. His father had dreams for his son, and Jay followed the leadership his father gave him. His father had worked in the corporate world all his life and retired early with a great pension. That was what Jay wanted – early retirement.

His dreams ended when the company folded after being in business for over seventy-five years. No one dreamed such a thing could happen. And yet, he and his colleagues sat without their chosen career, looking for work.

Luckily for Jay, he not only received a good severance package that would hold him for years, but he had also saved money from day one, which would help carry him even longer.

While he sat in his tiny apartment for the last night, he realized how little he had done in his life. He had spent it all devoted to his job. On the rare weekend he took off and the even more rare vacation he took a few times, he had picked up the camera his mother had given him and would capture nature as he walked the local parks.

He always dreamed of what else was out there beyond the city limits but never took the time to travel that far. Now was his chance.

He had shared a few of his photos with colleagues and friends over the previous years, and they all told him he had a natural eye for capturing beauty. A few offered to buy his prints. He always told them he did not need the money and just gave prints away.

Now, he reached for his camera. It was the last thing he needed to pack. It was also the key to his new life.

Tomorrow he would climb aboard the jet headed East to his new life. A life he knew little about. A life he would learn as he went. He was grateful for his best friend, who admired his photography so much that he put him in touch with another friend. That friend wanted to hire a travel photographer for her magazine. She hired Jay without so much as an interview. His photos spoke for themselves.

His first assignment was a little unincorporated town in The Smoky Mountains of Tennessee.

He had never been far from his home city, let alone to a different state. He was nervous but excited. A new world awaited him. Jay was thankful to be single and to be able to pick up and go. So many of his former colleagues had families to consider and were lost after losing their jobs.

He placed his camera inside his backpack to carry with him on the plane. He knew never to leave it out of his sight. He also knew a photo opportunity could show itself at the least expected moment.

When Angela hired Jay, he was suspicious of her magazine's legitimacy, "Unknown America, Its Beauty, People, and History." He had never heard of it. But, he realized he had led the elite's sheltered life for so long that he barely noticed anything else. Unless he had his camera.

The next afternoon he gathered his luggage, strapped the backpack to his back, hailed an Uber to the airport, and never looked back. His other belongings were already headed by truck to his new apartment. Which, according to some of his friends, seemed to be in the middle of nowhere.

After arriving at the airport and gathering his luggage, he called for an Uber driver to drive him to his new dwelling. Several miles of curvy roads and hills later, the driver pulled up to a tiny house surrounded by woods. A small pond occupied a portion of the side yard. Overgrown bushes framed the fence to the walkway. Jay was certain there was a mistake.

"This is it," The driver said as he opened the door for Jay. On the trip from the airport, the driver learned a lot about Jay. He smiled when Jay talked about the wonderful cabin his boss had provided for him. It soon would become evident that wonderful meant full of wonder.

Jay looked out the window before he twisted his body to climb out of the van. This had to be the wrong address.

"Are you sure? This does not look like the home of a world travel photographer. This looks like something I would photograph for the before view on a total remodel. I am here to live and photograph the area and the nature, not a rundown shack."

The driver insisted it was the correct address and verified it for Jay by comparing Jay's documents with the faded address painted on the damaged mailbox by the road.

"May I have your cell phone number to call you when I need to bail out of here?" Jay smiled.

The driver laughed and handed Jay his business card."

"Ah, at least they have the internet here to order cards."

"No, I printed these myself. You will find the closest internet connection three miles down the road at the post office, slash coffee shop."

Jay closed his eyes and shook his head. What had he gotten himself into? "They do have phone lines here?"

"Oh, yes. I am sure there is a landline inside for you. I am not sure you will have cell service with all those trees surrounding your … cabin." He hesitated to call it a cabin. Jay had been more precise; it was a shack.

As the Uber driver lifted Jay's luggage from the back and carried it to the front porch, Jay slowly looked around at what Angela had done to him. He could not wait to call her and ask if it was all a joke. Then Jay remembered there may not be any cellular service and doubted the landline was hooked up. He sighed and followed the driver to the front door.

Jay reached into his backpack and pulled out the key. Inserting it into the front door, he turned it and pushed the door open. Little did he realize how much his life was about to change.

Soon after he settled into the inevitable life he was introduced to, Jay began photographing the area as he was assigned when he spotted a small overgrown park. He walked to an old bench to rest and just take in the scene before him. He knew Angela had an office nearby but did not realize she was in the area on his first day of shooting. Until he heard his name being called.

He looked around and noticed Angela walking toward him. By her side was another lady. He assumed it was her assistant or some other office worker.

When Angela reached him, he stood to greet her. She shook his hand and introduced him to Terri, her sister.

~~~~~~

That was the beginning. Terri remembered how quickly she and Jay formed a friendship. The more she learned about him, the more she questioned why she liked him. He was different from anyone else she had ever met. He was so much not her type. Even Angela shook her head at the relationship they formed. Angela even commented that they were the most unlikely souls to connect she had known.

Jay was shorter than Terri and more sophisticated than her due to his corporate upbringing. He had different opinions on major topics than she did. Yet, somehow they worked around it. They agreed to disagree or not even discuss certain things. Terri came from a bad relationship, and Jay's last one broke his heart.

Together, they made it work –at first. Terri's memories of their beginning now had her wondering. Then she remembered more.

Now she wanted to find and read her journal, look through the photos she had stored, and understand where her heart lay. The wild thought of finding Jay again came to mind. She wondered where he was and what he was doing. Had he gone on with his life? Was he happy? She shook her head at the thought of wondering if she was even happy and would be happy being married. Should she marry Adam if she was having thoughts of Jay? And why was she having thoughts of Jay after all this time? Or was it just a case of wanting to know her past was behind her? It would not be fair to be married to one man and still feel some feelings for another. Feelings she didn't know she had.

What was she feeling? Her heart must be playing tricks on her.

Yes, oddly, she felt something. Maybe it was the need for complete closure. Maybe there was something still there. If that was the case, she needed to address it soon. It was not fair to Adam to be holding the slightest thing back from him. He deserved her all and all of her best. Not just a portion of herself and her love.

Terri took a day off work, telling Adam she needed a day to breathe before making more plans for their wedding.

Adam didn't ask for details. He had learned enough about Terri that there were days she needed to be alone and escape. Adam sensed something was not complete with their relationship and wondered if that was why she needed this time alone. His love was true to the end, and giving her time was the least he could do to make her happy. He silently hoped and prayed that if she addressed what was bothering her, she would be able to give her all to him.

Terri remained in her nightshirt and slippers as she poured herself another cup of coffee and curled up on her sofa with the notebook of notes she had placed in a safe-keeping locker. She skimmed through her notes.

Her eyes lit up as she read. She shut out the world against the sounds around her. Terri focused on the pages before her. She hoped it would answer her internal questions. After skimming the loose pages, she decided it was time to read the full journal she had written.

She sipped her coffee and sat with her slippered feet tucked under her on the sofa. She blocked out her current world of reality, then opened her journal to the first page.

Chapter Three

The Journey Begins

He said he wanted a travel companion.
  I said I would love to go.
    We had only known each other for two weeks.
    What would become of us beforehand,
    What would happen during our travels,
    Would we change afterward—
    Could we make it that far?

It was a trip across the country.
  A dream we each had.
    My dream since my teen years.
    His dream for several years.
      Neither one had ever made it that far.
      Until now.
      Together.

A friendship many didn't understand.
  A connection that amazed us.
    Common interests.
    Common goals.
      Matching collections.
      Equal thoughts.
      Friendship.

Would this adventure make or break us?
Would it answer any questions?
Would either of us reach our goals?
Would our friendship endure?
Would it teach us anything?
Would we listen?
Would memories be of the journey?
Would the destination mean more?

This is my story of Jay and me. This is the story of us willing to put ourselves out there with each other, not knowing how anything we face would turn out. Unknown to us stood the distant future as each new day dawned. Together we pushed on.

Two souls learning to live life to the fullest—on a trip of our lives.

Wow! What can I say? The dream of my life is coming true. Not only true for what I have wanted since I was a teenager but much more!

My dream for so many years ago? To touch my feet in the state of California! That's all. To be able to say, "I have been to California." But, my life got in my way. My relationships, work, and family had stopped me before I could even plan the first thing about traveling that far away from home. No one wanted to go with me. I had no money to go. I never had enough time to make the trip. I realized that I would never make it there. I would walk the streets of gold in heaven before I ever made it to the state of the gold rush of so many years before. All excuses I thought were reasons not to attempt my dream adventure.

14

Then Jay entered my life!

Little did I know that my answer agreeing to have dinner with this man I barely knew, would completely change my life. I wonder how this trip would change it even more. Would spending every hour of nine days alter what we had become? And what were we? WE were great friends. We had become great friends in a short amount of time.

Soon after our first date, we talked of his desire to take a trip West to drive the Pacific Highway. Then he added that he would like a travel companion. A Travel Companion! I was IN! My dream was to come true after all. Even much more than I had dreamed.

People thought I was off my rocker agreeing to go with Jay. Some knew him and questioned me about the two of us being together. Others were worried because they did not know him and imagined him being a serial killer. I knew in my heart that he was a good man. And the more we talked, the more time we spent together, the more I liked being with him. We did a lot in the first few months of hanging out together. We could talk to each other about anything from day one.

As time passed and Jay talked about the trip more, he agreed we could travel together. We spent hours mapping out our trip, booking the airline flights and the hotels, and making a list of the places we wanted to experience. As we made plans, we both wondered if we would even be together when the day came to leave. We each wondered if we would be friends at the end or want nothing more to do with each other when the last plane landed, and we returned to our homes. We were filled with uncertainty, determination, faith, hope, and a desire to make it work.

So, with bags packed, paperwork in hand, and nerves set aside, I walked away from my home one last time as I waited for Jay to pick me up after he finished his last photo assignment. He was going home to shower and change

15

first, so my wait was slightly longer than I expected, but that was okay.

Before our trip, Jay said he would not treat it as his job. Instead, he was going to enjoy it as a vacation. I wanted to at least write about it. So I started writing a few notes as we went. I hope if I don't get to write it as we go, I can at least have enough notes to write the details later. I also feel that he will be taking more photographs than he realizes.

Jay and I spent the night before our flight at his place. We loaded his car as much as possible before calling it a night. Our flight was scheduled first thing in the morning, so we went to bed early and went straight to sleep.

Morning—early morning! It was still dark when we left Jay's house for the airport. We had slept, but getting up and going was a forced action. Coffee was needed, and Jay made some good coffee to wake us up.

It had been so long since I had flown that I followed Jay's lead in boarding the plane. Once we were on the plane, it felt surreal to me. I felt a tear forming as I looked out the window while the plane taxied for takeoff. I was going to see my dream come true!

I looked over at Jay as the plane took off. His smile was small on the outside, but I could sense how happy he was inside, knowing his dream would come true. It made me happy seeing him happy.

I wondered what was on his mind as we flew. Was he anticipating anything? Was he worried about anything? Was he relaxed? I was not willing to ask him. Not yet, maybe not ever. I didn't want to ruin how I felt. I was excited, nervous, and hopeful. Excited to be on this trip, nervous about not knowing what was to come of the journey, and hopeful that our relationship would grow.

Even though we were on this trip describing ourselves as friends and travel companions.

Landing in Dallas was amazing. I remembered the challenge of getting to the correct gate for my next flight when I had previously flown. This time, with Jay, it was easy and quick. He seemed to take it in stride, getting us where we needed to go. I had no worries with him in the lead. I knew which gate number we needed to reach, and he knew how to get there. So far, our trip has gone well.

How do I say what is occupying my mind during this initial part of our trip? I am on a cross-country flight and road trip with a man I have only known for five months! Who does that? I do. I had gotten to know and trust Jay enough that I was willing to join him even when he first mentioned needing a travel companion. Did I know how it would work? Did I know if we would still be friends by the time the trip came? No. But I am glad it has worked out so far.

San Francisco. What a nightmare it was at first. Our luggage was hard to find, and the car we rented took longer to get than we expected, but it all turned out great. The car was perfect for us. And before we knew it, we were headed to our first destination! Luggage in the car, cameras at the ready, Jay driving as he does best. And so many things to observe! Pier 39 was our first goal. So many things to see even before we got that far, but so worth it when we finally arrived; I was mesmerized as we stepped onto the pier and began to walk among the crowd—so many iconic places to take in.

As we walked the pier, I realized I could spend hours taking in the scene. We walked to the end of the pier, where the bay was in front of us. In the distance stood Alcatraz. Jay was amazed—he didn't realize it was there. I decided that was the best place for our first selfie. So, with Alcatraz in the distance behind us, we posed and took our first selfie on our trip. It was our beginning.

Before reaching our first hotel, we had another destination to visit, so we soon put Pier 39 and San Francisco behind us and drove to the Golden Gate Bridge. An amazing bridge that I can now say I have been across. I think part of my trip will be places I can mark off my bucket list if I ever write a list of the places I have seen or visited. So far on this trip, and it's only the first day—I can mark off California, San Francisco, The Golden Gate Bridge, Pier 39, seeing Alcatraz. Even though these last two were never a part of my original list. I would mark off Point Reyes – my first lighthouse, and Fort Bragg, CA, by the end of the day.

Jay had places he wanted to see on this trip. One was Port Reyes Lighthouse. The drive there took a lot longer than he anticipated. Then the last stretch of the road was closed, and we had to walk farther than expected. It was my first lighthouse and worth the extra time. The drive away from the lighthouse had some beautiful views of the water. I felt like I was living a dream. I didn't pinch myself for fear I would wake up. I knew it was real. I was experiencing the trip plus of a lifetime.

Nighttime was falling when we finally reached our hotel for the night in Fort Bragg. CA We were both so tired. All we wanted to do was unload the car, crawl into our beds and sleep until morning. Instead, we were welcomed to our room by a wet floor, an industrial fan blowing on high, and a bad feeling about the place that seemed so beautiful when we booked it online. But, alas, we were so tired we didn't bother to complain to the lady at the front desk. We unloaded the car, put our slippers on while walking on the floor, and went to bed. I listened and wrote as Jay drifted off to sleep.

I smile as I write this. We survived our first day, our first twenty-four hours together. I wonder what tomorrow will bring? I'm too tired to think about it. I may not be writing a book, but I am writing my journal, so I don't forget the sights, the sounds, the emotions, and the friendship. May the morrow bring more peace, beauty, and emotions through our experiences with the places we see, the people we meet, and each other. Good night.

Chapter Four

Memories Made

Day Two:

We survived being together so far. I find myself watching Jay when I hope he doesn't realize it. His patience through the city traffic, dealing with crowds of people, and being so easygoing on this trip does us both well. I hope the rest of the trip goes as smoothly. If it does, I may be in love!

Today we began our day with Jay locking the keys in the car's trunk! Not a good thing to happen so early on our trip. Thanks to my AAA, we got the car unlocked, and we were soon on our way. While we waited for AAA, Jay and I walked around the parking lot and enjoyed the garden area. We took photos of their unusual plants, and we talked. He was upset about locking the keys, and I told him not to worry about it. We left there and went to breakfast at a place called Dave's.

Dave's was a local favorite. We could tell this by how the waitresses interacted with those who were obviously regular customers. The waitresses knew the 'usual' breakfasts the people ate and how they took their coffee. As Jay and I looked around, we felt that hometown touch of the place. So often, we are treated like just another customer when we eat out. Here we were treated like family.

After breakfast, we drove to the local grocery store at the other end of the large parking lot of Dave's. Inside, we found food for our lunches, healthy snacks, a biodegradable cooler to hold the food, a few water bottles, and the bag of ice we needed. With a sigh, we began our day of travel. Later than planned due to the locked keys, *but as I have always accepted, delays happen for a reason. What that reason was for us today, literally, God only knows. We could speculate, but I wasn't going to waste my time. I wanted to continue on our trip. Places to go and a big new world to see.*

We stopped at a beach not too long after leaving the grocery store. We walked to the sand and the edge of the water to watch the waves roll in and breathe in the sea air. It was the first time I ever saw the beach on the Pacific Ocean. I was overwhelmed with the beauty, sound, air, and the fact that I had not only made it into the state of California but also the West Coast and the ocean! The emotion of it all brought tears to my eyes. I momentarily forgot I had my camera or even my phone with me. I was living my dream.

One of the stops today was at Mackerricher Park. We parked the car and walked on the short trail. We were met by squirrels who were not afraid of people. Instead of running away or chasing us, they let me get close to them with the camera on my phone to capture cute photos.

After walking the trail, we sat on the benches overlooking the ocean. We didn't say a word for a while. Both of us were mesmerized by the area around us. I scanned the area and kept taking photos. In this little oasis above the ocean and the shore was a view that brought tears. Driftwood lay to the right of us, with native plants in the foreground. I captured the contrast of the gray wood against the greens and orange colors of the plants. I hoped the photo would be a good one to keep. I had always loved driftwood, and if I could not take this piece home with me, I at least wanted a good photo to cherish. I watched as Jay also captured the beauty as we traveled with his camera. He focused on beauty for beauty's sake and not related to his work. Being careful not to duplicate his artistic talent, I photographed things he may have missed.

As we drove, we were met by a T in the road. We could have turned left and continued on to our next destination. Instead, we read the signs, then looked at each other. We smiled, and Jay turned right. There are times in life when no matter what you have planned, you need to take time out of life and go see something God puts before you.

We headed to Legget, California.

We had seen some redwood trees as we drove. The sign said there was a redwood tree we could drive through. What the heck. We arrived, and sure enough, there in front of us was the choice to pull up and park or drive through this huge Redwood tree. Jay drove slowly through it! Then we parked the car and went into the gift shop. Inside we each bought a coffee mug. He also bought a t-shirt and a puzzle.

Jay collected coffee mugs from most of the places he had been. I had a few at home but began collecting them when Jay and I started dating and going places together.

We both enjoyed putting puzzles together. The one he bought would be one we could work on together when we returned home and had downtime.

By evening we had reached our destination. A new day, a new town. As we drove along Hwy 1 today, I could not get over the beauty of the ocean to my left and the trees to my right, followed by a sudden change that surrounded us by trees and forest. The road wound around so tight that sometimes we felt we may meet ourselves on our way around the corner. I had lived in the mountains half my life, but this was nothing like I had ever seen. There was another piece of beauty and heaven to see with each new turn. I have only been on this trip for two full days, and I already want to stay forever. I hope that the rest of the trip is as magical.

Our second night in this state was spent in Crescent City, California. So many people talk negatively about the state. I agree the prices may be higher than in other parts of the country, and if you dig into the politics, not everyone will agree, but the beauty is beyond imagination. Crescent City seemed like a small town. The road had four lanes, but traffic was light. The harbor was across the street from where we were staying. The hotel was beautifully decorated with lighthouses in the lobby, lighthouse artwork on the walls, and lighthouses painted on the elevator doors.

Jay and I spent time this evening talking about what we had seen so far and making plans for tomorrow. We realized that there were things on our list that we wanted to see that we would not have time to visit. Crossing things off our list was heartbreaking. Having only a limited amount of time and with the drive taking us longer than either of us had anticipated, reality set in, and we had to reset our goals. And, like one of my favorite poems says, 'We saved the rest for another day, yet knowing how way leads on to way, I doubt I'll ever be back.'

So, how was I feeling about my time with Jay so far? I was glad he had invited me along as his travel companion. I was still amazed. All our doubts before we set foot on the first plane were squashed in the reality that we had made it. Our friendship had grown over the few months since he first asked me out on our first date to where we are now. Did I wonder where we would be by the end of the trip? Of course. Was I trying to figure out where I wanted us to be by the end of the time we returned home? Yes. Did I have any idea what the truth would be? No. The more time I spend with him, the more I like being with him.

On our second night together, I fell asleep, exhausted but happy. Friendships do last. Friends can travel together. Friends are the best.

Day Three:

We awoke early with no alarm. We had places to go, things to see, and coffee to find. Yes, we love our coffee, so *it is usually the first thing we think of when we wake up—coffee!*

We walked down the street from the hotel to a local restaurant called The Fisherman's Restaurant for breakfast. The four-lane highway was deserted, allowing me to stand in the middle of the road and capture a photo of how 'busy' it was there. The moment we opened the door to the restaurant, the lady standing behind the counter greeted us and told us to find a seat anywhere. The service was awesome, and when we mentioned what we were doing and that we were searching for lighthouses today, the waitress brought us a thin book with a map in the center of the local road. She pointed out where the local lighthouses were for us to see as we drove that morning. We could only see one of them, but we were thankful for her help.

We drove the road along the coast as we left town. We agreed it was a very friendly town and wished we could have stayed longer.

We changed our original plans before boarding the plane to head West. Now, just a day into our trip, we realized we would make several more cuts in our plans. There was just too much to see and do. I don't think either of us realized how much we would want to talk with the local people and get to know the area in some of the locations we stopped to spend our nights or even stopped to eat. Everyone has been so friendly and willing to share and help us out.

Day Four:

Leaving California today was bittersweet. As much as we wanted to keep going, we had to fit so much into a limited number of days, but we would miss California. I would miss it because it had been my life's goal. I had succeeded. Everything past this time was beyond my dreams.

We said goodbye to one state and drove into another. We entered Oregon and stopped at the sign that welcomed us. Jay had been in the state before but not to the area we would visit. Most of this trip was our trip. Places neither of us had experienced. That was a word Jay liked to use— experience. Life to him was more than seeing things; it was taking them in, feeling them—experiencing them in every way possible.

The sign into Oregon was a must-stop for a photo to prove we were there. I also used it to set a date and time when we were there to gauge where our photos were taken. I often see tourists in my town taking photos of things I see daily and wonder why. Now I understand.

The views today continued to catch us with all the beauty. As much as I was supposed to look with my eyes and feel in my soul, my camera was usually in hand every time Jay stopped the car. I was impressed at how often Jay did not take any photos. He told me he was not going to work while we were away. So far, he is staying true to his word.

Each stop that led to the beach also led us to collect stones. Now I wonder what we missed seeing by looking down so much. But I know we will continue to look for rocks to take home for lasting memories.

We missed some famous views because of the dense fog over the ocean. The fog in itself was beautiful but hid so much. It often makes for some unusual photos.

Lunch today was a picnic lunch at Bandon Marsh. A secluded spot overlooking the marsh. We had stopped at a store after breakfast and bought food to make sandwiches and healthy snacks. We sat on the bench, made the sandwiches, and shared an apple Jay cut and the cheese I cut into pieces. We continued to do our best to eat healthy on this trip. Very few sugary snacks and no fast food stops along the way. I appreciated that about Jay. He appreciates food and especially good food.

I had wanted to stop in Coos Bay, Oregon, but we drove through it. The harbor lay to my right as we drove. Pictures would have been nice, but there is only so much time each day.

I watched the beautiful land as Jay drove. The scenes are ones I know I will never see again. As he drove, I watched him. I wondered if he knew how much I did watch him. We were friends. We were travel companions. I hope he knew I wanted more. I wanted us to be in a relationship. He said he wasn't ready. So I didn't push him. But watching him made me smile. Watching him as he watched the world go by and we made our stops and experienced our trip made me smile. I loved watching him enjoy life and living.

We made a stop in Florence, Oregon. We walked through town, stopping in a few shops, including an ice cream shop, for the first ice cream of our trip. It was also the first small town we walked through. We had walked in San Francisco and around our hotel stops or near the places we had eaten, but this was the first small town to walk through it. It was a nice break. As we sat by the water, watching the birds and viewing the bridge, I felt close to Jay. This was our time. No one else that we knew was on my mind. Just Jay.

We talked about the bridge. How each one we have come to has been so different. Some elaborate, some simple. We wondered why some were built as fancy as they were when there was no need for it that we could tell. Even the Golden Gate bridge—why was it built that way? Questions that will never be answered. We talked of traveling the country to see as many bridges as possible. Then realized that would take a lifetime. I smiled at the thought of spending our life together traveling. I wondered if he had any thoughts even close to that. I knew we never would see more bridges than we would see on this trip. At least, that's what I tried to remind myself.

We wanted to stop at a few overlooks and scenic areas today, but the fog was so thick over the ocean that we drove past many sights. One was Cape Perpetua. Known for its forty-mile views, we were lucky to see forty feet in front of us when we reached this location. We were both disappointed. The way our trip was planned, we had little time to wait for the fog to lift. That could take all day or longer.

This realization of time was hitting us more each day. We adjusted what we could do as we traveled. The only thing that was not changeable was our flight home. The rest of the time we had could be changed. This ability to change plans as we went was difficult for me. I like plans. I like to know what I am doing and what time I am doing it. Being with Jay is teaching me that it does not always matter. I am learning to go with the flow of where the day takes us. He is learning that some things do take planning. We are reminded that we make good travel companions because of our differences.

Our original plans involved far more things to see and do than we had time to do. A few things we had to omit were a disappointment to us. We quickly wished we had more time to spend on our vacation.

We reached our destination of Lincoln City, Oregon. That night at Whistling Winds Hotel was memorable. The rooms were rustic cabin décor. Smaller than most hotel rooms, we had enough room. It was a block off the beach, which was nice. We did not walk to the beach from our room as there were other rentals on the ocean side. We drove into town to find someplace to eat. We decided on the Chinese place, but we turned right and parked on the ocean side across the road. The sun was just beginning to set and was the first good one we had seen on our trip. We delayed eating by walking the beach, taking photos, and experiencing the romance of dusk along the water's edge.

A girl can dream. A walk on the beach. A man by my side. We watched the sunset. I watched him. His thoughts were on the beauty of nature. The colors of the sky. The crashing of the waves. His smile was from his heart. His emotions ran deep. He knows how to experience life and living.

I was learning to do the same. It was easy to do on this trip.

Dinner that night was too much food. It was good, but my heart was not into the food. My heart wanted more.

~~~~~~

Terri took a break from reading her journal. She gazed out the window of her living room, where she had been reading. She remembered how she felt that night. She remembered how she felt during all of their trip West. She remembered agreeing to be just friends and his travel companion. Early into their relationship, that was their agreement.

They had spent so much time together planning that trip. She smiled as she remembered the dinners at his place, followed by looking over maps, making notes, and researching where he wanted to visit. Jay had been West before. This trip was more his idea and his dream than it was hers. She simply wanted to put her feet in the state of California. She had never had the inkling to travel Highway 101 and Highway 1. When she learned of his dream, she immediately wanted to be part of it.

Now she realized that in the beginning, he was her chance to travel and fulfill her dream. Nothing more. Yes, she could travel with him. No matter what it took, she would make their friendship last at least until they returned home.

Then she remembered starting to have feelings beyond their agreement. She was falling for him. She ignored the issues he had. She ignored all the signs and his words telling her not to get involved. She ignored her head and felt with her heart.

Her heart had gotten her in trouble in her earlier years. She thought she was more mature than she had been. After all, she was a lot older. Jay was older. Looking back now, she saw how her heart was getting her into more trouble. She had done her best to hide her emotions.

She smiled as her mind jumped ahead to what she knew was on the journal for the rest of their trip and future. She stood up and poured herself a glass of wine. Good wine. The kind Jay had introduced to her. He knew good wine, good food, and good fun. He also knew her, as she would find out later.

She picked up her journal, took a sip of the Pinot Grigio wine, and continued to read.

Chapter Five

The Roads

Day Five:

We woke up early again to start our next day. Vacations were supposed to be laid back. Ours was full of places to go, people to see or meet, and no time to relax.

Before leaving town, we had breakfast at Pig and Pancake. Jay said he would eat healthily. Then ordered banana pancakes with pineapple sauce. It looked delicious. But I stuck with my omelet. And, of course, coffee.

After breakfast, we drove to the ocean a few blocks away. Jay held his cup of coffee as he walked the beach. I walked behind him and videotaped him. He had told me earlier that one of his dreams was of walking the beach while enjoying morning coffee. I could not resist capturing that moment for him. It may remain one of my favorite videos in my life. Viewing it has so many untold stories within it.

The dreams of a child running along the beach. Maybe with his dog chasing him. The longing of a young adult to walk along the beach with a cup of coffee, contemplating life and the next step. The reality of a man who finally could live out his dream of early morning, watching the sunrise in the sky while he walked with the love of his life by his side. Okay, maybe that was not the case with the love of his life by his side. Maybe that was my part of the dream.

While we walked on the beach and looked around and down, I noticed jellyfish. Clear globs of jelly-like substance. Hence their name is jellyfish. I was not brave enough to touch any of them. I did capture photos.

31

We left the beach to head to a place Jay always called the Bone Store. This section of our trip is one where he had been before. It held memories for him. I hoped his memories of this place would include me this time.

The store was open by the time we arrived. Inside were some beautiful pieces of rock and fossils. Some I would have loved to have but were out of my price range. Jay did buy a t-shirt to remember the place.

From there, we were headed to Aberdeen, Washington.

It was our last day to spend in Oregon. Suddenly it felt like we had not spent much time in the state. I felt we had missed a lot along the way, and in reality, we had.

We had missed whale watching. We had missed the Oregon Dunes. We had missed what was supposed to be the best fish and chips on the coast in California. We missed the Sequoia Park Zoo. When we reached Oregon, we realized that we should have spent more time in San Francisco. There was so much more to see there. We merely had a glimpse of what the city had to offer. Maybe one day we would be back. –Maybe.

On the way to Aberdeen, we stopped in Tillamook Bay and toured the Air Museum. There was a lot less inside the museum than we anticipated, although it was interesting. From there, we stopped at the Blue Heron gift shop. There were so many things to see and wish we could purchase and take home.

There was a side trip that we would have made if we had had time. A place called the Blue Agate Café. Jay had been there on a previous trip and wanted to return. We never made it there.

We stopped along the road and captured the sights of large rock formations in the ocean. Cannon Beach with Hay Stack Rock was one of many.

Again we did not take the time to stop in Mananetta to tour a winery or see Rock Away Beach. So much to see, so little time. I know I repeat myself, but it is true. We rounded a bend in the road and looked back to see a beautiful sight of the ocean reaching the shore. The light was perfect for it to look reflective. We both took our time taking a lot of photos of the scene.

We reached Astoria and had to stop. It was the last stop in Oregon. Situated on the Columbia River, it was a busy town. We found a Mo's Restaurant to eat seafood. It was a long wait, but we stood outside on the deck and watched the fowl swim and eat in the water a short distance from the walkway. Our meals were worth the wait.

From there, we drove across another beautiful bridge into the state of Washington. There was no sign to welcome us there. As soon as we crossed the bridge, we were met by a T in the road. We turned left, hoping to find a welcome sign as we drove. There was no sign. People would have to believe us at our word that we were there.

We drove along the river for a while. So massive. So beautiful.

We arrived in the town of Aberdeen, looking for our hotel. We located it tucked back a little from the rest of the area at the end of town. I walked inside the lobby and waited for the desk clerk. Jay joined me when it took a while. We waited several more minutes until the man finally arrived. He checked us into our room and gave us the key.

Our room. We were located right beside the outdoor ice machine. The area did not look like the safest place, but we made the best of it. We unloaded the car and drove into town. It was an interesting area, but none of it looked great. We stopped for supper and then returned to our room. We planned our trip for the next day and made it an early night. We were coming to the end of our trip. There were three more major stops for us to make, and this location was not one of them. It was just a place to lay our heads.

In the middle of the night, we both woke up to the sounds of yelling. We lay low and just listened. When we *didn't hear any gunshots, we knew all was okay. We did hear a fight going on and furniture being turned over. Two men, most likely drunk, having a brawl. Oh, the joys of staying in some locations. We would not recommend anyone stay there and noted that if we ever got back there, we would never stay there again.*

Day Six:

Our next stop was to stay a night with a classmate of mine and his wife. I had not seen him in maybe ten or twelve years. Luke and Brenda lived in an airstrip community. Luke also owned a ranch in Texas. Able to be retired early in life, he and Brenda enjoyed life to the fullest. That was all I knew about their current situation.

We had a National Park to explore before arriving at Luke and Brenda's. Olympic National Park!

What a day it was for us. Jay and I loved hiking. We loved to walk in the woods at home. This place was nothing like we had at home or anywhere either of us had been.

We stopped at a pull-off, not realizing what it would lead us to see. We thought it would be a quick stop until we noticed a sign that pointed to the left to take a hike. True to being who we are, we rebelled, turned to the right, and started walking. The fog was heavy and beautiful, with the sun trying to fight its way through. The trees were so tall I swear they reached the sky. We found the largest Hemlock tree in the country and stood at its base. We looked so tiny in comparison. We walked on and found a small waterfall. We made the trail loop and marveled so often along the way. The beauty that God put on this earth. Even the downed trees were interesting. They gave us insight into their age and life. If trees could talk, I often wondered what they would say. The storms they had survived. The storm that took them down. The people who had walked passed them when they had stood tall. The people who had stopped to wonder about them after they had fallen. We had stopped. We had touched. We had marveled.

We drove off in silence for several miles after that experience. Our next stop was a small country store that seemed to be located in the middle of nowhere. We could not help but stop. We bought food for our lunch and coffee mugs to keep as souvenirs. There was only one mug on display, and we both wanted the same design. Two of the three ladies working there stopped what they were doing and went to the storage area to look for another mug. It took them a while as they searched through totes and boxes to find what I wanted. Jay bought another puzzle. We talked with the ladies who ran the shop. They told us of a road to take to experience more of the area. Being the adventurous people we were and having a little extra time, we headed down the road the ladies had suggested.

The paved road soon turned into a dirt road with the beauty of the woods surrounding us on both sides. After a while, the road seemed like it would never end. We debated turning around a few times but thought it might be a short distance ahead until we were on the road we needed to be on, and the road behind us would take us forever.

Then we came upon a beautiful waterfall. We stopped to admire it, climbed around the base of it, and took photos.

~~~~~~

Terri set the journal down. She raised her head and gazed out her window without focusing on anything. Her mind drifted back to the bottom of the falls. She remembered them as though it was yesterday.

Two men were taking professional photos of the light reflecting off the cascading waters of the falls. They had noticed her and Jay and offered to take their photo. She had welcomed the offer. Jay was reluctant but agreed.

So with their arms around each other's back, the taller man snapped a few photos. Terri remembered how she felt with Jay's arm around her. She only hoped that it would mean something to him towards her one day.

Terri sighed. So many fond memories from that trip with Jay. Her journal was a good reference to her experience but did not hold a candle to the emotions. While reading it, she could feel the emotions that were not written. There was no way to write how they affected her actions that summer. Everything rushed in as she closed her eyes to feel it again.

She looked down at her journal and wiped the droplet that had fallen from her eye. She smiled as she remembered.

Jay had so much love to give. She had felt it from their first date. When he asked her to travel with him, Terri had not hesitated. She was still glad she had said yes to him.

Terri took a deep breath, and as she began to read again, she noticed that she had not written about Jay holding her except while their photo was taken. She thought back to the reality of that day. Yes, he had his arms around her for the photo, but not after the camera's focus was taken off them. She then remembered her feelings at the time and that they did not match the ones he was expressing.

Chapter Six

Nature's Beauty

After Jay and I finally turned off the dirt road to nowhere, we wound our way back to the road we needed to be on. We found a pull-off along the way that led to more hiking trails, with a picnic table at the beginning of the trail. Jay parked the car, and we got out the food to have a picnic. We did not have time to go for a hike but did enjoy a fairly quiet meal. We had a visitor who wanted some of our food, so we fed him. A Blue Stellar Jay. A western Blue Jay. It was not the first one we had seen while out West, but it was the closest that one had come to us.

After the picnic, we continued on our trip farther north. We pulled over along the road at Calawah River in Forks, WA. The sun was casting a reflection on the water that created the effect of a field of diamonds. The diamond-covered water was mesmerizing no matter what angle we took photos from.

It was soon time to start heading East. Our trip was beginning to head us home. I don't think either of us wanted it to end. Thankfully, we did have a few days left to enjoy the area.

Our next stop was the Elwha River. There was a parking area at the river with hiking trails. Instead of hiking, we chose to walk to the river and hunt for more unique rocks.

I had a knack for finding rocks in the shape of a heart. Jay had a knack for finding truly unique rocks. He had proved that with the ones he picked up on the beaches along the coast.

Speaking of the coast. I missed the ocean already. It had been beyond my dream to set foot in the Pacific Ocean, and *now that I had, it was a part of my history. I wanted to go back.*

We do certain things in life that we wish we could do more often. Or things that we wish would never end. Being at the Pacific Ocean was one of those memorable things in my life I will never forget. Maybe it was because of who I was with. Maybe it had nothing to do with him. I just knew that I missed being near the ocean.

Not all of the stops we made would hold the memories this River did. It was beautiful. Maybe it had something to do with the fact that we had stopped and were standing on the rock bed in the shallow water. Maybe it was that we were together, standing in it. No, the memory was because as Jay walked from rock to rock, searching for the perfect stone to take home, he lost his footing and fell into the water. At first, I made sure he was okay. The water was not deep where he fell, and he caught himself from falling into the deeper water. Once we knew he was not hurt, we both laughed. Here we were, two adults, acting like kids. That is the great part about life. Staying a kid as long as we can.

We found our way to the river's edge and climbed up the short bank and back to the car. Jay changed his shorts before getting into the car.

From there, we headed to spend the evening and overnight with Luke and Brenda.

The road to Luke and Brenda's was long and winding as we made our way a little farther north before turning East. I was a bit saddened when Jay made the turn facing home.

Yes, this turn was a turning point. It was the northernmost location of our trip. It was nearing the end of our trip. I was still hoping it was the beginning of something more.

Jay turned onto the last road toward Luke and Brenda's home. I had little knowledge of what or how they lived. Until we made that turn. Jay and I looked at each other and raised our eyebrows. Before us lay beauty. Large homes, well-maintained yards. Mountains in the distance and flat land in front of us.

We pulled into their driveway and took a deep breath. It was time to relax for a while. Luke came out of the house and greeted us. I introduced Luke and Jay and hoped they would find something in common to talk about. Little did I know they had a lot in common.

Brenda was waiting for us inside. It was good to see her again. She was busy making dinner for us, and as soon as we had our luggage placed in our rooms, I offered to help. She thanked me but said she had it all under control. So I sat, and we talked while she finished preparing the meal.

Jay and Luke were already busy talking about birds. I had no idea Luke was a birder. More of a birder than Jay was. I knew it would be an easy visit.

We gathered around the table for dinner. Luke said he and Brenda decided to make us a home-cooked meal so we would have something other than fast food. Jay and I looked at each other and laughed. Then I told Luke that we had not stopped at any fast food places on our trip. And that we rarely eat fast food at home.

After dinner, Luke took us for a walk to the edge of their home's development. We stood looking out over the water at the edge as we watched the sunset. It was the most beautiful sunset of our trip. We stood there until the sun was below the horizon as if it had sunk into the water.

When we returned to the house, we all stayed up for a while. Luke and I talked of all our classmates we still had contact with or those we at least knew something about. Jay was impressed at how many I knew details of that were current friends. Luke was also impressed. He only knew of a few of them.

We enjoyed breakfast with them the next day and headed to our last stop.

Seattle, Washington, USA

Chapter Seven

Reflection

Our last hurrah. A ferry ride. And memories.
This was going to be our last stop before flying home.
We had set aside two full days to enjoy this city.

--- Seattle ---

Terri looked up from her reading.

Seattle.

She wondered if she was ready to read her journal of those last few days. It was those days that changed her life. She smiled as she visualized what had become one of the most memorable times of her life. She decided to take a break from her reading, and instead of reading, she thought back in her mind and remembered what she could.

She felt a smile form. Then she sighed. And then she, no, she was not going there. Not yet. She knew reading her journal would take her there soon enough. Those last few days certainly had been a mixture of emotions for her. And for Jay as well, now that she thought about it.

Seattle.

The city that would always hold her heart.

The entire trip had been a matter of firsts for Terri. Not her first time flying, but the rest of the trip, yes. Mostly firsts. Dreams came true that she never dreamed of. Life had a funny way of doing that to people when they let it. She quickly scanned over her life. Yes, the times when she had let herself go held the best memories.

She shook her head as a few memories arose, and she realized that not all things were the best to remember. Yet, somehow they had played an intricate part in her life. Each one had led her to where she was now.

Ah, now. Where was she? She reviewed her life and decided what her future would be... again. It was time to read more of the journal and understand what had brought her to where she was. She wondered, though. No, now was not the time to wonder. Now was the time to read and then move on. If she could.

Suddenly she remembered the phone call she had received just a month before. One that had prompted her to find the journal and to read it. A phone call that she had not answered. One that she waited for the caller to leave a message. What a message it had been. One that tore at her heartstrings. A stronger pull than she ever thought possible after the last two years. What had taken him so long? Why now? She never returned his phone call. She listened to his message several more times. And then let it go.

Seattle. The days that changed her.

Terri settled down in her favorite chair, this time to read and reflect. His voice was fresh on her mind as she had been reading. His message was just a reminder. The truth was on these pages. The truth—

Chapter Eight

Pineapple, Burgers, and Sangria

After leaving Luke and Brenda's, Jay and I drove south to meet the Ferry. It was another first for me. I had only watched videos of ferry rides as large as this one was. I had taken a smaller ferry ride several years ago. This was nothing like I remembered.

Jay had ridden on them before. I was repeatedly grateful for Jay on this trip. We each had our former personal travel experiences. We had compared them in our conversations. Some were similar, others different. We decided that maybe one day we would take a cruise and take other trips together – Maybe. Someday.

We arrived early at the Ferry and were near the front to board when it was time. We took a short walk around after parking our car in line. It was a breezy day. Or maybe it was because of being near the water that the wind felt strong. We had our jackets. I was fine with the weather.

We had been fortunate this whole trip. We had one day of thirty minutes of rain. The rest had been sunshine or clouds. God had blessed us.

The call came to get into our cars and drive onto the ferry. I felt a feeling of claustrophobia set in until we parked, and Jay said that once we were parked, we could get out of the car, walk to the front of the ferry, and watch as we rode across the river. I was better then.

Several people got out of their cars and walked to the front. I realized quickly that those that stood in front and watched were most likely visitors to the area. Those who lived on one side worked on the other or often did this, sat in their cars.

43

I became emotional as I gazed out upon the water and heard the engine start to move the ferry forward. I shed a tear. Jay had warned me that I would shed tears on this trip. I had noticed he shed a few from time to time too. I looked over at him as he stood quietly and watched him wipe his eyes. Yes, emotional.

The view of the approaching city of Seattle – words are hard to find. It is just one of those things each person should experience at least once in their lifetime. Magical? Beautiful? Impressive? Breathtaking? Take your pick and add your own.

The city looked so tiny from across the water where the Ferry started. Slowly we moved across the water. The buildings became larger. The iconic buildings stood out. And then there was Mount Reinier! We wanted to have time to visit that mountain but doubted we would.

Again, a Robert Frost poem came to mind. We saved that for another day. Yet we doubted we would ever be back. Life was like that. I have learned this year to take advantage of all the opportunities you are given if at all possible. This trip with Jay was a perfect example.

I remember when I was a teenager and was invited to join my girlfriend and her parents on a trip West to the Grand Canyon. I asked my parents if I could go. My mother had the wisest words beyond yes. She said, "Go. You may never get to travel again like this." And so I went. Somewhere I may still have that journal. Maybe not. Little did my mother know what direction my life would take. Little did she know all the places I would get to travel to in my life. I am grateful for her words when I was so young. Sometimes I forget her words of wisdom and miss what could have been. But, such is life. We tend to forget the wisdom we are given sometimes.

The ferry docked and turned off its engines. Jay and I had walked back to our car before the ferry stopped so we would be ready to get off and drive to our hotel.

Our hotel. We decided when we were making our reservations that we were going to splurge at one hotel. Jay had picked this one for us. We hoped it would be as special as it seemed on the internet. First, we had to navigate the streets under construction and find our way through all the traffic. I missed the rural countryside we had just left behind as we drove through this city. I'm a country or small-town girl at heart. I dreaded if we had to drive a lot while we stayed here. We would see.

We found our hotel, parked our car, and went inside to register. Oh my God! The hotel is known as The Pineapple, with décor and souvenirs of pineapple motif. What a beautiful place. Spacious. Breathtaking. And that was the lobby. Could the room be as magnificent? We would soon find out.

After getting our parking pass to park in their garage and finding that it was an additional fee, we carried our luggage to our room.

At first, it seemed like any other hotel room. Yes, higher quality furnishing, bigger bathroom. Then we opened the drapes to look at our view.

We both smiled and put our arms around each other. They could not have given us a better room if we had asked for it. Our view? The Space Needle! A clear view of it. I could stand and look at it all day. I wouldn't, of course, because we had places to go and things to see.

Jay had looked ahead at the weather for the next couple of days that we would be there. We decided to go to the Space Needle that afternoon because there was a chance of rain the next day.

Space Needle it was. We were close enough and added that we liked to walk. So with a backpack containing cameras, water bottles on my back, and cell phones in our pockets, we ventured into the port side of Seattle.

We reached the bottom of the Space Needle and looked up. We both shook our heads and laughed. Yeah, right. We were going to go to the top. Both of us had a healthy fear of heights. What were we thinking?

Adventure. That was what we were doing this entire trip. It was an adventure that we would never get to do again. One that would live in our memories forever, we hoped. One that would be a part of us. No matter what we became.

So, we climbed the steps to the Space Needle's front door and walked into our next travel experience. We paid the fee and entered the elevator. The next stop was the top. The elevator door opened, and we walked out with everyone who had joined us. A few feet in front of us was the outside edge of the top of the Space Needle. I clung to the inside wall. Literally, my hand was on the wall to ensure I never left it.

Slowly, as we watched others move to the outer edge, and I watched Jay internally laugh at me while he was fighting his own fears, we eased our way to the edge. We touched the outer glass. We stood on the revolving floor and took the trip around the outside. We viewed the city from high above the crowds. The people and buildings below looked so tiny.

We became comfortable gazing out and down at the world below. I was amazed at myself for overcoming my fear. Once we became accustomed to being there, we reluctantly boarded the elevator and made the return trip to the ground floor. We had gotten over our fear of heights for the time we were up there. Knowing we would probably never be back, we hated to leave but knew the visit would always bring us smiles.

Of course, we shopped in the gift shop for gifts for friends and family and ourselves.

We ventured around the area before weaving our way back to our hotel. We got hungry, so we went downstairs to the lobby and asked about good places to eat dinner. They offered several within walking distance. As we left, instead *of turning in the direction each of them had suggested, we turned to the right. Always rebels!*

McMinna's was a quaint restaurant and bar. We had no idea what to expect when we walked inside. We decided to at least give it a try.

Wine and a burger. Beer and a burger.

One bite of our burgers, and we were in love! With the burger! We both agreed that it was the best burger we had ever eaten. And we had eaten a lot of burgers over the years. And made our own. This one topped them all, and McMinna's quickly became our favorite place to eat in Seattle. Okay. It became about the only place we ate while we were in Seattle... it was that good.

After eating, we returned to the hotel and settled into our room for the evening. It had been a long day.

We opened the drapes and watched as nightfall changed the day's beauty into the breathtaking night skyline. The lights of the Space Needle lit up, and the beauty of the Seattle night captured our hearts. We both took photos of the Space Needle and the city's lights visible through the window.

That night we slept well.

The next morning we got up and walked down to the port area. Pikes is a famous place that everyone visits. Locals and visitors alike. We were no different. We wanted to see what all the hype was about. Interesting, that was for sure. Believe it or not, neither one of us bought a thing.

Jay wanted to find the original Starbucks. We finally did, but the line to get in was so long that he decided it was not worth waiting. Sorry, Starbucks.

The next thing that caught our attention was the aquarium. We paid our fee and walked through, taking a lot of photos. Somehow, neither one of us was impressed that much. We had been to others; this one just didn't do it for us for some reason.

We walked along the boardwalk and stopped in several other shops along the way. We bought coffee at one shop and then found benches to sit on while we watched the people and the water. We watched the ferries come and go and the variety of boats. We imagined what people were doing and made up stories about them. Two police officers rode to us on bicycles and commented that we had the right idea. Sit and enjoy the day.

We walked on to an antique store. A lot of interesting items inside, including a few shelves full of old typewrites. I was fascinated. But again, we didn't buy anything. Then we decided to keep walking around.

That afternoon we returned to the hotel and stopped at McMinna's for a small lunch. Again a good meal. We were getting to know the bartender. All the staff was friendly. While the place was not busy when we were there, we imagined it was a popular spot at night, especially at the bar.

Jay and I walked some more between lunch and dinner. It was our last night there before one more hotel stay and our flight home. I don't think either one of us wanted to go home yet. But we started packing to leave the next morning.

At dinner time, we debated finding a new place to eat. We had walked down to the pier earlier and saw what was there. We had found a place to have a nice breakfast. And we thought about walking back down to that area. Then we agreed – we both wanted another burger!

So we walked across the street and entered our favorite place. Our favorite bartender met us. We ordered our favorite burger. I ordered wine. Jay ordered a beer. Then he ordered a Sangria.

I could end it here and say the rest is history. Which it is. But I will surely want to recall this night's details later in my life. So I will include it. Although, for the rest of my life, I know I will remember the events of this night.

FOREVER it will haunt me. Forever it will be embedded in me. Tonight – changed my world.

~~~~~~

Terri set her journal down again, then stood and walked to her window. It didn't matter what her view was from there. What she was seeing was in her mind's eye. Her journal was correct. What she wrote had been the truth. It was a night she still recalled. There was no need to read the details. Although she would, she always did.
She smiled a sad smile. Memories. Feelings. Emotions. Still strong. Still vivid. Still clear. And yet, she wondered as she purposefully returned to her seat and picked up her journal. She would always wonder. It was time to read the details once again.

~~~~~~

Jay and I enjoyed the best burgers in the country again. There may have been other items on the menu, but we didn't care.

Jay lifted his almost empty glass of Sangria as we finished our food. He looked at me and smiled. I asked why the smile.

He handed me his glass and told me it was really good. I took a sip and agreed. It was very good. I wished I had ordered one.

Then he said, "I think when we finish eating, we should move over to the bar and order one for each of us."

I smiled and said that was a good idea. So we finished eating our burger and told our bartender that we would move to the bar and would like two more Sangrias. He informed us that he did not have much of the main liquor, but if we didn't mind, he would make our drinks as close as he could to them, maybe even better. We told him that was fine.

And so, we sat. We drank. We talked. We ordered another drink. We sat. We drank. We talked. We reminisced about the trip so far. We drank another Sangria.

Then we decided we better get back to the hotel before neither of us could walk the half block to the hotel.

On our way through the hotel lobby, we decided to use the free money the hotel had given us and buy a bottle of wine.

Yes, I know... more drinking. That is not our normal way of living. I think it may have been needed for what took place next.

I was sitting on the ottoman in the room. Jay sat in the armchair. He said he had something to tell me.

I knew we both were drunk because we had already drunk most of the wine we had bought in the hotel lobby, plus all we had already drunk at the bar.

The words Jay said next will stay with me for the rest of my life. I do not remember the entire conversation, but the five words that hit and hurt the most rang loud and clear.

"I do not love you."

I know how we met and began; all we had done together in such a short time was not your normal relationship. I know that Jay had issues to work through. I know I was ready for more of us than he was. But.. "I do not love you."? That hit deep into my soul.

We spent the next hour talking. Jay explained his words to me. I cried. He felt sorry that he had to tell me the truth but felt he owed me. He said he just was not ready. He told me I was more ready for a serious relationship than he was. He was still dealing with some of the things in his past. He didn't want to hold me back. He told me that he was not in love with me as much as he liked me and being with me, traveling together, and everything else.

I told him I loved him no matter what. We continued to talk until we agreed that we could remain friends no matter what. Close friends.

Then we fell silent. There were no more words to say. No hugs to exchange. No apology to say or expected.

The truth was hard to swallow. But when I thought about it, maybe we were better off as friends. At least for the time being. Maybe things would work out in the future, and he would love me. I was not going to give up on him. Even though at that moment in time, he broke my heart.

We went to bed. Neither of us slept very well. Jay knew he had hurt me. I felt heartbroken. I wished that he would realize he had misspoken when morning came.

~~~~~~

Terri let her journal fall open against her stomach. Yes. That was what she remembered about that night—her heart being broken. She felt choked up as she read it, but there were no tears this time. It was part of her past. And things had changed after that day.

Those changes made her smile. She read further.

~~~~~~

I didn't sleep well last night. I know Jay didn't either. Considering the amount of alcohol we each drank, we should have slept for two days. Instead, we were up early, ready to leave to arrive at our last destination before our flight home the next day.

When I woke up this morning, I was sad. I instantly remembered the conversation Jay and I had last night. It had taken away a lot of the joy of the entire trip. I have to get over that and remember how amazing the rest of the trip has been. Jay may have crushed my heart with his words, but I think it is just his wall raised again. I still believe he has more feelings than he allows himself to admit. That is my hope.

In the meantime, I am quiet. I don't know what to say to him. I want to keep crying. I want to tell him he was lying to himself and to me. I want to run away and cut all ties with him. I wanted to wake up and realize last night was a nightmare and did not happen.

Instead, I look at Jay and know that it all happened. His words were his truth. I also see that he has a lot on his mind today and is not talking much. While we may need this quiet day between us, it should have been our last day of fun before returning home to our full reality of life. Between all the alcohol we drank, the after-effects of that, and our conversation, today was not what either of us had planned.

The silence. Only the necessary words are spoken between us. Our smiles are gone.

We went out to breakfast at Denny's, drove around a little for one last time, and then drove to the rental location to return the car. We then took the transport bus to the last hotel we were staying in. This one was close to the airport. We called for a pizza to be delivered to our room later but spent most of the day packing, thinking, and silent. Lost in our personal thoughts. I will always wonder what was on his mind. I doubt I will ever ask him. It may be better if I don't know. After all, I was not willing to share my feelings.

Chapter Nine

High in the Sky

The last early morning of our trip had arrived. The silence of the day before was broken. More out of necessity than our willingness to talk to each other. I looked at Jay as we carried our bags to the first floor and waited for the hotel's transport bus to take us to the correct door at the Seattle Airport.

The dynamics of our trip had changed in the last twenty-four hours, yet I did not want our trip to end. I wanted to back it up and start over. I wanted the ending to go the way I had hoped. I wanted Jay.

We waited for our boarding time and talked about everything we had seen on our trip. We began discussing things we wished we had stopped to see and places we should have visited longer. We even talked of coming back one day.

I didn't understand how Jay could talk about our future together when he told me he did not love me. The only way I saw us traveling together again was if we had grown closer into a loving couple, not simply as friends. Maybe he sees things differently than I do. Maybe there is more that he feels than he is willing to admit.

When they called for our time to board the plane, I looked around the airport one last time. I gazed outside the large windows one last time. It was a place I had never been to before. A place I most likely would never visit again.

We found our seats on the plane. A stranger occupied the window seat. I had the middle, and Jay had the aisle seat in the plane's last row. I could only see a little outside the window. I was not happy, and I could do nothing about it.

The plane lifted off the ground. We were silently saying goodbye to what had been our dream. A bucket list dream adventure for Jay, much more than my dream had ever been.

We landed at Dallas/Fort Worth Airport with several hours to wait until our next flight. We walked around looking for places to eat. By this time, we were talking as good friends again, as our relationship was defined – good friends. We could move on together and enjoy what was left of our adventure.

We chose to eat at Friday's Restaurant. Each of us had a glass of wine. A final toast to us.

Dallas/Fort Worth to Tri-Cities – our last jaunt.

It was dark and very late when we arrived. I was glad Jay remembered where he had parked his car. I had totally forgotten.

The drive home was quiet. More because we were so tired than anything else. Jay was driving me all the way to my home. That way, we could each sleep later the next day and relax. While planning our trip, I had envisioned not only spending the night before our trip together but the night we arrived home together. I am glad he had other ideas. I needed, we needed, the time apart.

Apart. That is what I was afraid we would be. Jay had declared no love for me. I was heartbroken, but when reality came, I knew it was best.

Time will tell what and if we will become anything later on.

~~~~~~

Terri swallowed hard as she recalled those last couple of days of the trip of her lifetime. And her time with Jay. She had hoped for a lifetime with him. She had fallen in love with him. Or thought she had.

Terri remembered the days following their trip and smiled. She had almost forgotten Jay's final words before leaving her place when they got home. Jay told her he did not want to see or talk to her for four days. She recalled being shocked, on top of already being heartbroken. She also remembered when they did speak to each other again, Jay asked her why she had not contacted him for four days.

It had given them both time to get things done and to think.

In their first conversation after the trip, they agreed to be friends and continue to hang out, as they called it. It was never referred to as dating. They were just friends. Terri had resigned herself to the fact that Jay would never love her. And she, in reality, was not deeply in love with him either.

Chapter Ten

Traveling Again

Terri and Jay had continued seeing each other after their West Coast trip. They went on hikes together in the mountains around them. They went out to eat. They talked every night on the phone. They went on road trips. And found places to shop for antiques together.

As fall began, they even planned another trip together. This time a long weekend to a beach on the East coast. Terri was excited that she would have put her feet into oceans on both sides of the country within a couple of months of each other. She wondered how many people got to experience that in their lifetime.

Terri decided to give her and Jay one last chance at love while on this last trip they had planned. She knew she still loved him. Even though Terri did her best to deny it, she knew in her heart that the feelings were there. She hoped Jay would realize or admit that he had feelings for her while they were on this last trip of the year.

She thought back to a short day trip the two had gone on a few weeks after returning home from Seattle. After their hike, they stopped at a Wendy's fast food eatery for a bite. They rarely stopped for fast food, but this day it was the only place they found, and they were hungry. They got their food and sat in a corner booth. Their normal conversation turned serious.

Jay looked at Terri and said he had something he wanted to share. Although Wendy's was not exactly where she would have picked, Terri's hopes grew.

Then her hopes faded. Her wish was not what was on Jay's mind. While he spoke, she held back her emotions. It was better to agree with him and be understanding than to burden him with how she felt inside.

So they agreed on that day, in a corner booth, in a Wendy's, in the middle of nowhere, that they would always be friends. They would always be there for each other. If nothing more grew between them, they would have absolutely no regrets for any of their time together. No regrets. No anger. No hard feelings. No tears.

Terri held in her tears. Being Jay's friend was going to be good enough. They would be there for each other. They also agreed that if or when either of them found someone else in their lives to fall in love with, then that partner would need to accept their friendship. Terri told Jay that whoever he found to love and make a life with would need to meet her approval. She told him that if he called her one day and told her he had fallen in love with someone he had just met, she would give him a talking to because she knew he did not work that way. He did not give his heart to anyone that easily. He took his time. How well she knew that.

They agreed.

Then came the trip to the beach—one last mini-vacation before the end of summer. One last effort in Terri's mind for Jay to fall in love with her. After all, he had taken the time to get to know her. She had taken the time to get to know him. Yes, they each had their quirks. They each had things that were not perfect in the eyes of the other. But what couple did not have that? No person was perfect. Besides, what was perfect?

Terri put her journal down on the coffee table and stood up. She walked to her kitchen and made a single cup of coffee. Strong and black. Her head was spinning, and she needed it to stop. Too many memories were flooding her mind. She didn't need to read more of her journal. She didn't need to relive any more of her life with Jay.

Yet, here she was, over two years later, wondering. Could Jay have changed his mind?

Terri sat back down after drinking a portion of her coffee. She knew she had to read about their last trip together that year.

October was finally here. The leaves had changed. The temperatures were falling at night. The days continued to be warm, with sunshine touching the earth.

Jay and I left early on a Wednesday morning. Destination, Cape Hatteras, NC. I had driven to his place early to park my car while we were away. I felt bad leaving Silvia outside as my car was used to a warm garage, but she was under his carport, and a neighbor said they would keep an eye on her.

We left Jay's house by seven and headed for our nine-hour trip. I continued to hope for things to change. I was giving this trip a final chance.

Yes, I had agreed to always be friends if things didn't grow between us. I held on to the hope that this trip to the beach, a romantic walk at sunset, holding hands, gazing out to the sea, and then to each other. A girl can dream. Or maybe I was being a hopeless romantic.

It was a long trip, but we finally arrived at our hotel. It was going to be home for the next several days. I was happy with the hotel's location—a short walk to the beach. We didn't have an ocean view, but I could walk out of our room and see it from the balcony.

Jay had places he wanted to see while we were at the beach. Lighthouses were one. After unpacking, we got together and planned our next few days full of side trips, walks on the beach, eating, and just relaxing and enjoying the end of summer.

Our first stop was a walk on the beach. As we walked, we talked. We watched the birds. We watched the other people. We watched the waves crash onto the shore. I could get used to this life if I could only afford it. Barefoot, sand between my toes. Salty mist in the air. Ok. Maybe I would rather not have the salty air. Nor all that sand all the time. But it was nice for a few days, with no care in the world. Being with Jay was nice.

We got a good night's sleep after our long drive. The fresh air of the ocean helped.

Day one, and I'm already counting the days until we have to go home because I already do not want to go back. So much to see. And I love being on the beach again.

We visited the Kitty Hawk Museum and walked around the grounds while watching a few airplanes take off.

We went to the sand dunes and climbed to the top, watching the younger people learn to hand glide short distances.

We went to Currituck Beach Lighthouse and found we could climb over two hundred steps to the top. It took a while to reach the top, and I was thankful for the landings along the climb so we could rest. Once at the highest point we could go, I knew it was worth the effort. We could see for miles.

We stopped at a historic mansion and took a tour. We were not allowed to take any photographs while inside. But in the kitchen area, I saw a recipe for Boston Brown Bread like my Grandmother used to make. Jay offered to sneak a photo. I told him not to. He said what are they going to do to him? I shrugged my shoulders. As we left, the lady in charge asked us what we had taken a photo of. We mentioned something which was not what Jay had taken a picture of. The ladies looked at us like children about to be scolded and sent to our rooms for a week. We may not be allowed back in there, as if we would go back. It was fun to break a run.

We stopped at a juice bar and met Julie. She had moved there when she married her husband and started her own juice bar. It was interesting to hear her tell us about the area and other things to see while we were there.

Our tip for anyone traveling is to get to know the locals. They are the ones who know the best places to visit, eat good food, and experience.

All too soon, it is nearing the time to go home. I was having too much fun enjoying the sun and warmth. I did not want to return home.

Plus, I was still waiting for Jay to change his mind about me. About us.

Chapter Eleven

Ocean Views

Two nights were left before our nine-hour drive home. I knew driving home would be an ending of sorts. We had no plans after this trip. I was uncertain of our future. Uncertain of my future.

The sun was setting, and the beach was calling us to go for a walk. I have always loved to walk the beaches: Sunrise, sunset, any time of the day. I could walk for miles and get lost in thought. Looking out over the water and imagining what was below. The photos she had seen and stories she had heard created a picture of brilliant beauty.

Jay and I climbed the steps onto the platform leading to the beach. I looked out at the young people walking. The kids were running and playing. A few older people in their beach chairs relaxed as the evening cast shadows.

I walked ahead of Jay looking for shells. When I stopped, I felt Jay touch my arm. I turned to see what he may be directing me to see. Jay was looking at me. I didn't understand. I had never seen him have that look in his eyes. I had no words.

Jay gently tugged at my arm and directed me to sit on a rock on the shore. He never said a word until I sat down. Then his words changed my world.

Jay told me that what he had told me in Seattle was him holding up the wall he had built around himself to protect his heart from being hurt again. He said he told me those words so I would not keep loving him. He said he regretted saying the first word that hurt me that night.

I could feel the tears building up, and he was not finished speaking.

He held my hands and continued speaking as he sat next to me. Night had fallen, and I never noticed. All I saw was him. All I heard was his voice. Even the ocean had stopped crashing on the shore. The entire world was just Jay and me.

He told me his heart had won and realized he loved me. He said he wanted us to be a couple like couples should be. Two people who tell the world their story. Two people who cannot get enough of each other. Two people who share their lives.

He asked me if I was ready for a true relationship with him. And only him.

I knew we had talked about marriage in the past and ways we could make that work for us. This was not a proposal. This was finally the love connection I had wanted for several months. This was perfect.

I looked at him and smiled. I told him I knew he had built a wall to protect his heart. I knew he had put up defenses to stop me from loving him. I told him I would love to have a real relationship with him. We kissed and held each other for a while. Then Jay took my hand, holding it as we walked along the beach in the darkness, daring the tide waters to capture our feet.

We spent the night in each other's arms. Our smiles were still there the next day when we woke up. I wanted to pinch him to make sure he was real. He sensed that and, looking at me, told me it was real, and he was in love with me.

I didn't want my dream to end.

On our final day at the beach, we seldom let go of each other's hands. I never wanted him to leave my side.

We went to a good restaurant, ordered their best bottle of wine with our dinner, and lifted a toast to us.

Chapter Twelve

Reality

Terri lifted her eyes from reading. She stared into space without noticing anything. Her mind drifted to that last day on the beach with Jay. She had finally gotten what she had hoped for during their dating months. She had loved him long before he admitted he loved her.

What had happened to them? What had changed when they returned home? She let out a sigh. She tried to remember. Her journal had ended with the ending of their trip. She had not written another word on the remaining pages. She smiled when she remembered why her journal had ended. They had gotten too busy. Life had been amazing.

And then it wasn't.

Terri looked at the journal and the last word she had read. "us." The couple they had become had since dissolved. She flipped her journal closed and shook her head. Somehow she felt the whole time she had spent with Jay had been a waste. Not a waste of all they saw and did while together. But a waste of love and desire to be loved. She had learned a lot through it all, including their breakup.

She picked up her journal and carried it into her bedroom, where she placed it inside a dresser drawer. It was time to move forward with the love of her life that she was about to marry. She needed to put the past behind her.

As she turned to leave the room, she noticed a photo of her and Jay still on display. How she had not noticed it over the last two years made her wonder. Although it was partially hidden, why had she left it out? She picked it up and looked at it. She noticed their smiles, the sun reflecting in their eyes. The way her head tilted ever so slightly toward his. She remembered taking that selfie of the two of them. She also remembered the events of that day.

She held the framed photo in her hands as she sat on the edge of her bed. Her mind drifted back.

Jay had taken her on an adventure that day. All he warned her about was to dress for a hike and pack snacks and extra water because it would be a long day. He was going to bring a picnic lunch. She always knew to listen to him about hiking. So she had packed everything she could think of, including the first aid kit she had recently purchased.

Jay picked her up early that morning and headed to the Blue Ridge Parkway. They stopped at several of the overlooks and took photos of the mountains. They listened to the birds. They had a picnic at the one overlook with food Jay had packed for them. After they had finished eating, they went for a short hike. That was when she asked to take a selfie. He had normally been reluctant to have a picture of the two of them together, so she was glad when he said yes. They posed with the mountains in the background. When they reviewed the photo, they agreed it was a good shot.

Terri smiled. She remembered Jay's arm around her and that he reached over and kissed her after the photo was taken. She wished she had captured that as well. It would have been proof that Jay loved her at least a little.

She brushed her fingers over the glass protecting the print. Then quickly set the framed photo down on the dresser face down. Why was she so deep into thinking about Jay at this time in her life? Why had her recent dream been about him instead of Adam? Why the urge to find out where Jay was at the moment and see how he was doing?

She left her room and closed the door she normally left open. Maybe if she kept the door closed, the ghost of her past would not seep back into her mind.

She decided it was time to go for a walk to clear her mind. Time to call Adam to hear his voice, or maybe stop by to see him.

Instead, she picked up her phone and searched for Jay's number. Pulling it up, she stared at the phone icon and hesitated. She glanced at the thought icon and pushed the button to write him a text message. She did not even hesitate when she typed the last question mark. She automatically pressed the send button—and held her breath.

It took mere seconds until she heard the distinguished sound from her phone. It was a special beep she had set up for only Jay's incoming messages. She almost dropped her phone. She had not expected such a fast response. Truthfully she had not expected a reply at all. She had hurt him when they broke up. He said he understood at the time. She wondered if he did. She had lost touch with him after that and assumed he had moved on in his life. So when she saw a reply so fast, she was curious.

Hey, you. How are you? I am surprised but glad to hear from you. Would you like to get together for lunch sometime? We can talk and catch up on our lives. I hope you are doing well.

Terri read the message a few times. The struggle was real. She wanted to see him. To tell him she had met her soulmate and was about to get married. She wanted to thank him for letting her go. For some reason, she could not resist. She typed her response. *Sure, when?* And again, automatically hit send.

The next thing Terri knew was she had agreed to meet with her ex-fiancé. Nothing serious. Coffee with an old friend. Jay had moved on with his life. Hadn't he?

Two days later, she parked her car at the new coffee shop outside town. No one knew where she was. No one knew she had contacted Jay. No one needed to know.

She watched Jay park his car and noticed it was a newer model. She was happy for him. She met him at the front door of the coffee shop. He reached out and hugged her gently before opening the door for her. They were escorted to a booth in the back, and Terri wondered if Jay had requested it. The lady at the door seemed to know him.

Their idle chit-chat changed after they ordered, and Jay asked her how she was and what she had been doing recently. Jay listened with an open mind as Terri told him about the café, Steven, Adam, and the upcoming wedding. She observed Jay's reaction against his responses. Something more was going on with him.

"I am glad you have found your soulmate. Your eyes sparkle that I've not seen in a long time."

"I didn't know they ever sparkled. Thanks."

"I noticed it a few times when we were dating. Before I ruined us."

"You didn't ruin us. We ruined ourselves. I wanted something you were not ready or able to give. Something I was not willing to wait on you to show. I needed or wanted more. And then, when you were ready, I was thrilled. Or so I thought. We didn't have what was needed to survive and be happy. There were too many differences between us."

"Have you found it? Does this Adam person make you happy?"

Terri smiled. "Yes, he does. Thanks."

"I did not do anything. Unless you want to thank me for letting you go?"

"Funny. Letting me go? For the longest time, you were pushing me. I was not happy at the time. You broke my heart. And it took me a while to see beyond what I wanted for us. I gave up when we broke up. Then I met Adam."

"I will say you are looking good. Happiness does wonders for a person's look."

"That it does. Are you happy?" Terri searched his face and his eyes.

Jay smiled. He had purposefully not shown his emotion when they first met for lunch. "I am doing amazing."

"I am so happy for you. Did you find somebody to love?"

"I did. I have changed a lot this past year. Do you remember when we talked about not having any regrets even if we went our separate ways?"

"Yes, and I have none."

"That's just it. I did. I realized I screwed up."

"What do you mean?" Terri was cautious yet hoped he was not about to tell her what she feared the most.

"I never should have let you go. I told you I loved you on the beach in North Carolina. I hoped life would be simple and our love would grow. Then our vacation time ended, and we returned to being the way we had been before our trip. We got busy with our lives and did not nurture the love we proclaimed. I fell back into myself when we returned home and to reality. And that was unfair to you."

Terri didn't say a word while he spoke. The words he was saying were the truth, but it was what she was not prepared to hear.

"You never pushed me to love you, and I appreciate that. You also never questioned why I let things fail between us. Looking back, I think you should have pushed me. Instead, I was the one pushing you away. I am so sorry."

There it was—the words Terri had wanted to hear almost two years ago. She wanted to hear them from the moment she had walked away when their relationship ended. She caught herself playing with thoughts she didn't expect. She looked down. Her heart was pounding. She looked up at Jay, who was watching her.

Their eyes met. The world around them drifted away.

Chapter Thirteen

Easy Decisions

Two days after meeting Jay for coffee, Terri knew where her future was. She had known the moment she saw Jay at the coffee shop, but she fought with herself to be sure. Weighing all her concerns about Adam and about marriage in general. She had to make sure she was ready. It was more about how ready she was for such a commitment than questioning her love for Adam. Adam had her heart.

Adam listened as Terri told him about her conversation with Jay. He already knew about her past and that Jay was a part of it. Adam repeatedly reached for and held her hand as they sat across from each other at her café. She had closed it down for the night, and they enjoyed glasses of wine as they talked. The café had become their place to have private conversations.

She was the love of his life. Her time with Jay did not matter to him. Her past was in the past. Even if she recently revisited it briefly, he trusted her. He knew it was difficult for her to tell him about seeing Jay recently. He also knew that as close as Jay lived to them, he had never seen him at the café or town. He did not feel threatened by him, even if he were to be around more.

Terri ended their conversation by telling Adam that she loved him with all her heart. She added that she felt their bond was meant to be, and she could not wait to spend the rest of her life with him.

Adam looked at her when she stopped talking and smiled.

"So, when are we getting married? You said yes, but we have no date set."

Terri kept her smile and kissed him. She was blessed to have such an understanding man in her life. "I'm ready right now. What date would you like to call ours?"

"Every day. But if you mean for our wedding, how about May?"

"Why the month of May?"

"No particular reason. Most people get married in June. I thought we'd beat the rush. It may make it easier to hire the vendors we will need. Caterer, photographer, cake decorator, you know all the people it takes to make a perfect wedding day."

"You are quite knowledgeable about this? Have you been married before and didn't tell me?"

Adam laughed at Terri, "No, never married. But I have been asked to sing at several."

"Interesting. Are you going to sing at our wedding?"

"You never know. I might." He bent over and kissed her forehead. There wasn't much he would not do for the love of his life. He had waited too long to find the person that made him complete.

"I hope you don't expect me to sing. You know I can't sing."

"I know that. And I do not expect you to."

"I'm unsure how to take that, even if it is true." Terri laughed.

"You know I mean it most positively. I love you no matter what. You are my girl." He reached over and kissed her.

After they went their separate ways for the night, Terri daydreamed about the perfect wedding. She had not been like most little girls who dreamed of and planned their wedding even before having a serious boyfriend. She had been too busy with other things going on in her life. She decided it was time to write down some ideas so she would not forget them.

When she finally turned off her light and closed her eyes to sleep, she had three pages of notes written out with ideas, people for her wedding party, people to contact to help with the catering, photography, cake, and more. For her, this planning was going to be easy.

Her phone rang early the next morning. She was enjoying her second cup of coffee when she picked up her phone and saw that it was Jay. She let it go to voicemail.

A few minutes later, her phone rang again. This time she answered it. "Good morning, my love. How are you?"

"I am feeling on top of the world," Adam replied. She could hear his smile. She had been smiling since she saw it was him calling her.

"I am feeling the same even if I didn't sleep well. I was too busy writing notes for our wedding."

"I anticipated as much. You are the one who does the planning and organizing. We can discuss those at dinner tonight. Are you free for dinner out?"

"I can hand over the reins to my staff and have dinner with the man I love."

"Good. I will make reservations."

"Reservations? Does that mean I need to dress up?"

"No, no need to dress fancy. It is just a place that fills up quickly, and I want to ensure we have a table."

"Ok. Because if it was fancy, I would need more time to get ready."

"You are beautiful no matter what you wear or look like. I love you no matter what."

"I love you too," Terri said and meant it. She smiled. She knew that she had made the right decision in her heart and mind.

Later that evening, they sat facing each other at the Greek restaurant, sharing a bottle of wine and enjoying their meal. Their conversation revolved around their wedding plans. Terri said she would contact Heather to help plan the big day since that was part of her expertise.

73

Adam said that was a good idea. Just as long as Heather gave them the final say in everything. At the end of their main course, the waiter brought a large piece of cake with a note. Terri opened the folded piece of paper. What could be on the note, and who had sent it to them? She looked at Adam but could tell he knew nothing about it.

Adam listened and watched Terri's face as she read it out loud. It was not signed by anyone. The message was clearly good wishes for them. They looked around the room to see if they could find who had sent it. When they could not, they shrugged their shoulders and picked up their forks to sample the cake.

Terri could not wait to get home and make a phone call. She knew who the cake was from. And although she smiled as she read the note and did enjoy the cake, she hoped it would be the last of such things.

Jay answered his phone on the first ring. He knew who it was. He had set a distinct ringtone for Terri when they were together and never changed it.

"WHY? Why did you have to send that cake over to us? And why did you send that note with it? And even more, how did you know where we would be?"

"I wanted you to know that I am happy for you and to wish the two of you many years of love and happiness. That is all. What did you think I was trying to do?"

"Trying to do? Oh, I don't know, ruin my relationship with the man I will marry?"

"I sincerely wish you happiness. That is all I want for you. If you are happy with him, then all the best for you two." Jay hoped she could not read further into his words. He was glad she had called and that he did not have to see her and have a possible altercation.

Jay realized he loved Terri when they had met for coffee. He also knew it was too late for it to work between the two of them. Jay was sincere in simply wanting her to be happy. If he saw that she was, he would leave her alone.

Until then, he would stay in her life as much or as little as she would have him. He would not pursue her. But he would be there for her, as her friend. He was no longer able to be more to her than a friend.

Chapter Fourteen

Wedding Plans

Adam and Terri spent every waking spare moment planning their wedding. Angela came into town to help her sister in any way she could. Angela was an easy choice to be the photographer at the wedding and all the photos leading up to it. How many couples have photo documents of the planning, the details, and the people associated with the big day? How many have a photo journal made of their special moments? Angela would ensure that her sister's wedding was one others only dream of having.

Work continued for them both. And Terri often found herself at Bella Rose to talk with Heather about the details. They had hired her to help with the many things they knew they would forget. The nightmares Terri had heard about and even witnessed in other weddings were enough to know she did not want to do it all independently.

Heather recommended the use of the reception hall at Bella Rose. She also suggested having the wedding outside on the mountain top. If the weather did not cooperate, they could have the ceremony in the pavilion. It was covered and still had a perfect view of the distant mountains.

Andy was the obvious choice to cook the food for the reception, and Karen was honored to be making the cake for them.

Terri and Adam wanted a simple wedding. It had quickly grown to need the use of the hall at Bella Rose. They did not want it any larger. Their wedding party was going to remain close. Terri chose Sara to be her matron of honor. Adam chose Steven as his best man.

With plans falling into place as quickly as needed, Terri and Adam had time to focus on the honeymoon and their future. Life was going to be awesome for them.

Heather had been busy making plans for Terri and Adam's wedding. She had been honored to accept the job when they called her. She began collaborating with them immediately. A late spring wedding, helping to choose the colors, flowers, music, photographer, and Karen making the wedding cake.

Terri was about to call Heather when her phone rang. Adam was calling her.

"Good afternoon, my love. What's on your mind?"

"I just wanted to hear your voice."

"How sweet. But I know there must be something else."

"There is. You know me too well. I just got a call from the travel agency about our honeymoon trip."

"Yes, and what did he have to say?"

"He wants to know if you want to go on a cruise instead of just flying to the island and only visiting one location. He found a great deal on it."

"I never gave a cruise a thought. What do you think?"

"I think it would be amazing. It would allow us to see several places and decide where we want to go on our first anniversary."

"You have given this some thought! I'm with you. You can tell me all about it tonight when I get home."

Chapter Fifteen

Escape

Andy was busy placing orders for the food he needed to prepare the special dishes Adam and Terri wanted for their reception. He also needed to make a phone call to McMinna's Lounge in Seattle. One of the feature foods they requested was the hamburgers from their favorite place in that city. While they had never been there as a couple, they both had memories of being there and agreed the best burgers in the world were there. They did not want burgers at the reception, but they wanted to have meatballs made with the same ingredients.

McMinna's refused to give their secret recipe to anyone. Andy spent days trying to find a way to get it from them. He talked with Karen about his dilemma. It was her idea that encouraged him to travel again. He had not been anywhere since moving to the estate per his mother's request nearly six years prior. When Karen suggested he go to Seattle and have one of the burgers and do his best to duplicate it, he was polite and asked her if she wanted to go with him. She had declined the invitation because of their three little ones. They did not want to leave them with just anyone, and with all of them under five years old, they did not want to burden anyone with that responsibility. Karen told Andy to feel free to go on his own.

As he slept the night before his flight, he dreamed of being on the road again. He dreamed of being free and just going wherever the road took him. He woke up in a sweat. Karen was still asleep when Andy woke up, so she did not see him until after he was gone. She did not have a chance to see the change in him.

Andy drove to the airport and parked his car in the long-term parking lot. He wheeled his carry-on bag to the check-in point inside the airport. He only needed a few things with him and planned on only being there a day or two. He waited for his flight number to show on the board. His phone rang just as the announcement to board came overhead. He quickly answered it.

"Good morning, my love. I tried not to wake you this morning."

"I slept right through it all. I was hoping to at least give you a hug and kiss before you left."

"That's ok. I won't be gone for long. When I get back, you can give me double."

"You have a deal. Have a good time, but not too good of one. Get what you need and come home."

"I should be there no longer than two days. I don't want to be obvious at McMinna's, but it may take a couple of samples to figure out their secret that Adam and Terri like."

"From what I remember, it is Steven's favorite too."

"Oh, great. I will have true testers when I get home."

"I am sure they will be gentle on you."

"I hope so. I have learned a lot during my years as a chef, but I'm not sure about this."

"Have fun while you are there. Don't make it all like a business trip."

"I hope to see a few of the sights while I'm here. Don't worry." Andy heard the second call for boarding. "Karen, I need to board the plane. I will call you when I get to the hotel. Love you."

"I love you too. Be safe, love." Karen waited to hear more from Andy, but he disconnected their call.

Andy boarded the plane. He placed his carry-on overhead and sat at the window seat he had requested. The joy of flying was about to make his day. He had not flown much in his life, but he had always enjoyed the view from the window seat.

When his plane arrived in Seattle, he walked to where a car was waiting to take him to the hotel where he was staying. The room was inviting. But it was also very quiet.

Andy was accustomed to being surrounded by people. At home, he had his wife and three children. At the manor, he had his siblings, more family, and the continued rotation of guests. He turned on the TV for some noise before calling Karen to tell her he was safe and sound in his room.

"I have made it to Seattle," Andy said when Karen answered the phone. He could hear the baby crying in her arms.

"I am glad you made it. I think Rayvn misses you more than I do." Karen said as she did her best to comfort their youngest child.

"I can hear her. She has not been that way since I left, has she?"

"Oh, no, she is just hungry. She will be alright. Your call came just as I was getting ready to feed her."

"Okay. I won't keep you long. I am going to go walk around the area for a while."

"But it's. Oh, wait, you are three hours behind me. I thought it was late and dark out like it is here."

"No, it is still fairly light here. I am tired and will probably get to bed early to avoid the jet lag."

"Good idea, love. Call me in the morning when you get up. Sleep well, dear." Karen said.

"You too. Take care of the kids and tell them I love and miss them. I will be home in a few days."

"I will. I love you."

"Love you too."

They disconnected from their conversation. Andy looked at his cell phone for a moment longer. The love of his life felt so far away. Her voice made him long to be home. Rayvn's crying made him remember the chaos at home.

Andy sat on the edge of the one queen bed in the room. He had opened the curtains when he had arrived, and now he glanced outside. The beauty of the city took his breath away. It was so different from the mountains he looked at every day at home. He stood up and walked to the window. The city lights began to shine as dusk reached out to take over the day. He smiled as he looked down at how small things seemed from his viewpoint. He noticed a few things he wanted to get a closer look at, so he put his shoes back on and left his room. It was time for a walk around the area.

It had been a long time since he had taken the time to walk alone. He shook his head. Come to think of it, when was the last time he was even alone? He entered the elevator and rode it to the lobby.

When the door opened, he heard laughter. Turning to look where it was coming from, he noticed a large group of people standing around the piano near the bar. He started to walk over to them. The voices in his head told him to turn around and walk outside. He knew he should obey the voices, but a young lady had begun to play the piano, and several were singing. He walked over to the bar and leaned against the open corner.

"What can I get you to drink?" a female voice asked.

"Oh, nothing, thank you. I am just listening to that lady sing. She's a beautiful singer."

"That she is. She doesn't stay here very often, but she serenades us when she is here." The bartender walked away.

Andy left the bar soon after the lady finished that one song. The last place he needed to be was a bar. Over five years sober, he didn't need to fall because of a beautiful woman singing.

He walked downtown for a little while. When darkness overtook any natural light, he walked back to the hotel. The lady who had sung at the lounge was standing by the elevator doors. He walked over to her and thanked her for

82

singing. He also told her that she was beautiful. He had meant to say she had a beautiful singing voice. She smiled at him as they both entered the elevator and the doors closed.

The elevator doors opened, and they both walked out. Andy was surprised that she was staying on the same floor as him. He figured celebrities would have better accommodations. The lady smiled as she turned to go to her room, then she looked back and asked Andy if he wanted to join her for a drink. She lifted a bottle of wine that Andy had not noticed before.

He smiled at her and just shook his head. He was not going down that road again. He walked to his room and closed the door.

A few minutes later, he could hear her beautiful voice through his door as she sang in her room. He smiled and opened his door.

Chapter Sixteen

Suspicion

Karen called Andy's cell phone early the next day. She had forgotten about the time difference until Andy did not answer. Karen realized he must still be asleep and made a mental note to call him later. She had three young children to tend to before she could call again. She was thankful that the twins could entertain themselves a little but missed Andy being there to help. She had not taken time for a shower since Andy left.

She picked up the phone and called Grace.

"Good morning, Karen. How are you?" Grace answered as soon as she saw who it was. It was earlier than usual, so she thought something may be wrong.

"Good morning, Grace. I am a little overwhelmed this morning. Andy went on a trip to Seattle yesterday, and I forgot how much I rely on him to be here helping with the kids. Is there any way you can come over to give me a hand?"

Grace heard the twins in the background. "Of course. I would be glad to help. Let me finish getting dressed, and I'll be over. By the way, why did Andy go to Seattle?"

"I will explain that when you get here," Karen said as Rayvn screamed.

"I will be right over. Sounds like you have your hands full."

"Thank you." Karen hung up her phone. She did have her hands full. What were she and Andy thinking, having another child while the twins were so young? She heated the bottle of formula and sat down in her rocking chair to feed the baby. She smiled as soon as Rayvn quieted down.

Now she knew why they had another child. There was no way she would have wanted her life to be any other way.

Karen leaned her head on the back of the rocker while Rayvn finished her bottle and dozed off to sleep. Karen was busy thinking of Andy and how much she loved him. Thinking of all that she had done over the last six years. Meeting Andy, moving, and settling down had been the best decision of her life. She could not have asked for a better family life.

Karen woke up when she heard the doorbell. She glanced at Rayvn, still sleeping soundly in her arms, and slowly moved to answer the door.

Grace walked in with a fresh cup of coffee in her hands. Karen smiled. Grace knew her so well. She took the disposable cup from her as Grace took Rayvn from her arms. The baby stirred slightly, then settled back, cuddled in her grandmother's arms. Step-grandmother, but the family had long since dropped the step connotation of her title.

"So why is Andy in Seattle? Business trip or pleasure?" Grace asked as they sat down in the living room.

"Business. I know it sounds odd for it to be business when Andy works as the chef at the manor, but this trip is for Terri and Adam's wedding."

"For the wedding? I don't understand."

"Terri and Adam have a connection at a lounge in Seattle. One of the things they loved was the burgers at this one bar or restaurant they both visited. They were never there together but found they had the place in common. Anyway, Andy called to get the recipe, and, true to great cooks, they would not share it. So Adam and Terri sent Andy there to try one and see if he could figure out what was so great about them."

"Wow. They must be amazing burgers! But, wait, they are serving burgers at their wedding reception? That is different."

"Yes, it is different. Terri wants Andy to use the recipe to make meatballs to serve along with the other choices."

"Interesting." Grace looked down at Rayvn, who was waking up. "Do you want me to lay her down in her crib?" Grace whispered.

"No, she's good. She slept long enough in our arms." Karen smiled for the first time in the last twenty-four hours.

Grace and Karen continued talking and playing with the children who had come over with their toys. Karen's phone rang Andy's special ring.

"Hello, sleepyhead. How are you?" Karen answered.

"I'm not a sleepyhead. It is only eight AM here. Andy replied as he took a sip of the coffee he had made in his hotel room.

"I know. I just wanted to give you a hard time. It's almost lunchtime here. How was your night?" Karen asked. She did not want him to know about her rough morning. She wanted Andy to enjoy his time there.

"It was good. I walked around the area until night fell, and all the lights in the city came on. This city is beautiful even at night. You need to come out here with me next time."

"Next time?"

"Karen, you would not believe how beautiful it is here."

"I know Steven has talked about it in the past. He used to live there."

"I remember him talking about it, but being here has made his stories come to life in ways I could not imagine."

"We will note it and plan a trip after the kids are a little older."

"Perfect."

"How long are you planning to stay there?"

"I have tonight booked, so I should head home tomorrow. My plane is scheduled to leave late in the afternoon, though. So I may not be home until late."

"Sounds good to me. I miss you."

"I miss you too. I enjoyed being here last night, but it would be better if you were here."

Karen heard a knock on the door. "What was that sound?"

"Must be the cleaning crew wanting to clean my room already. Hang on." Andy went to the door and opened it, expecting to see a maid. Instead, the lady he had met at the lounge the night before stood in the doorway.

"Good morning, are you ready to go for breakfast?" the female voice asked.

Andy held up his fingers to his lips to his guest. "Hey, Karen, I need to go. They want me out of the room while they clean. Good thing I am up and dressed."

"Andy?"

"I will call you later. I'll send pictures as I travel around today. Love you." Andy spoke while glaring at the lady now in his room.

"Okay. Love you too." Karen hung up her phone.

"Are you alright?" Grace asked as she noticed Karen's confused look.

"Yes, sure." She shook the thoughts out of her head. "That was Andy. He just was leaving for breakfast. Just wanted to say good morning and let me know he would call later."

Grace looked at Karen. She sensed something else was going on. She had learned many years ago to stay quiet and keep suspicions to herself unless asked for help. Karen had not asked for help or volunteered any information to warrant Grace's thoughts.

Andy hung up his phone and glared at the lady in his room.

"Why are you here? I told you last night I was not interested in sharing a drink with you."

"That was last night and a drink. I thought we could go together if you were going out for breakfast. What harm is there in that?"

Andy tilted his head. She was right. What was the harm in the two of them going to breakfast together? After all, they probably would have eaten breakfast at the same time if they had eaten at the hotel. "No harm, I assume." He walked to his bed to pick up his jacket.

Together they walked downtown to an eatery the hotel staff recommended. Andy felt uncomfortable the entire time they walked. All he wanted to do was complete his mission of being there and go home. Home to his wife.

Andy enjoyed the balance of his time in Seattle. He had what he thought would be the secrets to the perfect meatballs for Terri and Adam. He had noted places he wanted to take time to visit when he and Karen could return together.

On his trip home, he debated telling Karen the whole truth about his visit.

Chapter Seventeen

Samples

Andy met with Terri and Adam a week after returning from Seattle for a taste test of the foods they had selected for their wedding reception. This included the meatballs. He had attempted three times to make it in different ways to find the closest one to the flavor and texture of the burger he had at McMinna's. In his opinion, the one he had for their tasting was the one that won.

When Terri and Adam arrived at the manor, they were directed to the dining room. As they walked in, they smiled. Not only did Andy have the food samples ready for them, but Heather had taken the time to decorate the table the way they wanted the tables to be for the wedding. Everything was beautiful.

Heather directed them to their seats. She put a small headpiece on Terri's head.

"There, we can proceed to the wedding reception food tasting." Heather walked to the kitchen to help Andy carry the sample plates to Terri and Adam.

"These are samples of the food you suggested for the reception. I did the best I could on them. Taste them and let me know what you think." He placed the plates in front of his friends.

Terri and Adam slowly tasted each food. They liked them all, and choosing a few was not easy. After a few more tastes before making their final mutual agreement, they focused on the cake samples that Karen brought to them.

Half an hour later, they had chosen all the food, cake flavors, and design for their reception. Andy was pleased with their choices and said all he needed was the number of guests so he could adjust the recipes to have enough food made.

"I would like to know how many will be there too." Terri laughed. "Every day, more people find out we are getting married and want to come. I have told them we can only have so many there, but I hate excluding them."

"Maybe we can have a party at the Lounge after returning from our honeymoon," Adam suggested.

"That would be a good idea," Terri said. She turned to Adam, and the two started discussing party plans.

Andy and Karen watched the two of them working together and smiled. They were reminded of themselves. Working together from the very beginning of their relationship.

Karen sighed. As she watched and remembered, she realized that she and Andy had lost much of their closeness since the kids were born. She reached over to hold Andy's hand, but he had turned away to clean up the dishes in the kitchen. She walked over to help him while Terri and Adam continued to talk and laugh while making plans.

Thirty minutes later, they were ready to leave the manor and go home. Heather returned to her home soon after Andy and Karen served the food. She and Terri had talked earlier about the wedding and reception décor.

Andy was the last one to leave the manor. He made sure the doors were locked. He caught up with Karen quickly and walked beside her. Karen reached for her husband's hand, but it was in his pocket. Karen went to the kids' room to check on them when they arrived home. Andy said he would drive the sitter home and be back in a few minutes.

Terri and Adam walked to Adam's car and waved as they drove away. They talked as Adam drove Terri home.

"What did you think of all the food Andy made for us to sample?" Adam asked.

"He is an accomplished chef. And the meatballs were delicious. Not quite what the hamburgers were, but maybe it is because it is meatballs in the sauce instead of a burger."

"Very true. It is good, though. I am glad we chose that to go with the chicken choice for our guests."

"I am too. It will be different from most weddings." Terri turned to face Adam as he drove. "Do you think we are inviting too many people?"

"I think we are doing just fine with the ones we have. Any more who want to come and celebrate with us can come to the lounge party after our honeymoon. We will have a full week of parties if we want." Adam laughed.

"We do have a lot of people who want to be a part of our celebration."

"And that is not counting the people we have met in our past who would want to come if they knew we were together."

"Do you think there would be many more who would want to come?"

"Maybe just a few more. But we can't invite everyone we have ever known."

"That is for sure. That would be more than any venue could hold around here."

"We do know a lot of people. I am glad we do. Makes me feel loved, I guess. For most of my life, I did not have that. I spent most of my years growing up on my own. Friends were few and far between. I had a best friend growing up, but she and I have lost touch over the years. The only time we connect is by a Christmas card each year."

"Have we added her to our invitations?"

"No. I figured she would not come anyway, so why should we invite her?"

"Because she was important to you at one point in your life. And since you still stay in touch even once a year, I think you need to invite her."

"Okay. I guess we could send her and her husband an invitation. I was at her wedding. I guess I owe her."

"It isn't a matter of owing her anything. At one time, you were best friends. What is stopping you from making that connection again?"

"Distance more than anything, I think."

"That should not make it an issue. Friends are friends for life. Or they should be."

"I only wish they would be. She and I had a close connection for many years. She told me secrets that she never shared with anyone else."

"See, we need to invite her. Promise me we will add her and her husband to the list."

"I promise." Terri looked at Adam. He was becoming more wonderful the more she got to know him.

Adam turned onto Terri's driveway and stopped the car near her garage.

"Well, Babe, we have made it. Let me walk you to the door and ensure you are safely inside. Then I will head home."

"Babe, why don't you come inside for a while? We have so much to talk about."

"Are you sure?"

Terri looked at the man she was going to marry. What was wrong with him coming inside for a while? It wasn't like he had never been inside her place before. She did have different feelings at the moment, though. Maybe he was right and should go home. She smiled. If her friends knew her and Adam's restraint, they would laugh at her. It was the twenty-first century! People didn't wait for things anymore. She was proud that she and Adam were not like the modern world. They were still waiting.

"I am sure. It isn't that late."

"Okay." Adam turned the engine off and walked to open Terri's door.

Together they walked inside her house. They still had a lot to talk about, including what they planned for the rest of their lives together.

Chapter Eighteen

Wandering Mind

Andy drove the babysitter home, ensuring she was inside her house before he left for home. On his way home, he stopped at a red light. When it turned green, he turned left.

He found himself on an unknown road, in the dark, with nothing but woods around him an hour later.

He pulled off the road and stopped the car. Leaning his head back, he realized what he had done. He closed his eyes. This was not the time for what his subconscious was raising inside.

He opened his eyes and reached for his cell phone. Then he remembered he had left it at home, thinking he would only be gone a few minutes.

He sat up and put the car in gear. Making a U-turn in the middle of the road, he headed home. He hated that Karen would be worried. He had never left without her knowing where he was.

Andy had shared his past with Karen, and despite all the negativity in his life, she loved him. He could not disappoint her now. He needed to return home—to her and his three little children. He had people depending on him.

He pulled into his driveway in time to see his siblings on the porch with Karen. They waited for him to get out of the car and join them.

"Where have you been?" Karen asked as she wrapped her arms around him. "I was so worried. I thought you had been in a car accident!" She loosened her hold on him and glared into his eyes.

Andy reached for Karen's hand. He knew he had messed up. No excuse for what he had done. It may take him a while to make it up to the love of his life.

Sara and Heather continued to stand by on the porch. They suspected the real reason Andy had been gone for over an hour. It was not up to them to bring it up. It was up to Andy. If he shared the reason with Karen, with them, or kept it all inside was something they had no control over. Andy was their brother but not their responsibility. He had responsibilities of his own. And a new one – the upcoming wedding he had agreed to cater.

Andy turned to his sisters. He hung his head as he walked away from Karen to talk with Sara and Heather.

"I am so sorry for making you all worry about me. I have no idea what I was thinking. I took the babysitter home and was headed right back here. I had even left my cell phone in our kitchen. The next thing I knew, I was in the middle of the woods on a side road."

"Andy." Sara started as she put her hand on his shoulder. "I think we all know what you were thinking or doing."

"Yes, little brother. I think we all know. Karen may not know unless you admit it to her."

"What are you talking about? I have no idea what I was thinking."

"Andy, think about it. It will come to you." Sara gave her brother a hug. She hoped it was the last time he pulled a stunt like that. He had stayed in one place longer than they thought he would, and they were convinced that having a family had taken that desire away. Maybe it was back.

Heather joined in the hug. "We love you, Andy. We are here for you if you want to talk."

"What is there to talk about? I just disappeared for a…" Andy stepped back from the trio's embrace. He suddenly knew what they were thinking.

"I was not running away if that is what you are thinking. I would not do that to my family." Ironically he looked down at his feet.

"Andy, what is wrong?" Karen walked over to him after he had stepped away from his sisters.

"Nothing, Baby. I'm ok. They just reminded me of something."

"Okay. I think it is time we all go home and get some rest. Thank you both for coming to my rescue. I was so scared something had happened to him."

"Karen, any time you need us, call. We are here for you." Sara said, then looked at her brother. "That goes for you too."

She and Heather turned and walked down the steps and went to their homes.

Andy followed Karen into their home. Andy locked the door behind him. He watched Karen as she kept walking down the hallway towards their bedroom. Should he admit the truth to her? No. He knew he could control himself. After all, he had a family and obligations.

The next morning Andy got a call from Terri. She wanted to meet with him about the menu and set everything in the final stages for the wedding. If he was having any issues getting everything they wanted, she wanted to know as far in advance as possible so she could make adjustments.

Andy assured her everything was going as planned and that the reception would be perfect.

After talking with Terri, Andy made some phone calls about the reception. He wanted to verify the delivery of the special treat for the bride and groom.

Once that was confirmed, he went to the manor to work making snacks for the guest. It had become routine to get up early to prepare breakfast for the guests, clean the kitchen and dining room area and then make snacks for the guests for later in the day when they returned from their adventures.

He went through the motions, making the brownies, realizing how much of a routine it was. He had lost his enthusiasm to search for new things to make. After six years of doing the same thing, what else was there? Everyone loved what he made. But he had not created anything new for them to try in years.

After placing the brownies in the oven to bake, he sat at the island and let his mind wander. He envisioned the open road before him. The freedom of going nowhere but with purpose. His purpose—running away.

Since he met Karen, Andy had not thought about his younger days when he began running away from home. His whole life had changed when she came into his life. His reason for staying was that his mother required her children to stay at Bella Rose for five years to claim their full inheritance.

His reason for staying now was his wife and three little children that he was responsible for. He had promised, if not verbally to Karen but silently to himself, that he would not leave.

He shook his head and thought. Why did he have these desires to run away? Had the quick trip to Seattle triggered his blood flowing with the idea to hit the open road again? Was it that he was stressed trying to juggle family and work? The fact that his three children were at such a young age and were a lot to handle?

The oven timer sounded and broke Andy from his deep self-conversation. He stood up to get the brownies out of the oven and let them cool before placing them on the serving plate. He sat back down and immediately had thoughts of the open road running through his mind. Followed quickly by the thought that Karen would kill him if he even mentioned the matter to her.

But, who could he talk to? He didn't want to talk to Joe again. The man already knew too much about the family, in his opinion. True, he had a doctor/patient confidentiality agreement to abide by, but what could Joe tell him that he didn't already realize but did not want to admit?

The truth was, Andy just wanted to run away again. Get away from everything. Not that his life was so bad. It was not bad in any shape or form to an outsider. All people saw was how blessed he was. He had a great job, a wonderful loving family, and an extended family. He had managed to accept and love his biological father. He had also managed to forgive his mother for what she did—for everything she had done to him and his siblings.

Common sense kept him controlled. He had obligations to deal with. The big wedding was coming up, and the bride and groom counted on him. Karen was counting on him. His children were counting on him.

That was the problem.

Chapter Nineteen

The Dream

Andy knew he had no right to feel the way he did. He pushed the feelings of longing behind him. That night he told Karen he wanted to put the babies to bed on his own. She never expected that but took him up on it. She welcomed the few extra minutes to relax and unwind.

Andy first spent time putting Rayvn to bed. She was still so tiny. His little baby girl. The one not planned but loved so much from the moment she was discovered. He and Karen had worried about having another child so close to their twins, but they knew she was a blessing from birth.

He went to the living room to get the twins when Rayvn was asleep. They were a little older and had more energy. It took Andy several minutes to calm them down to lie in their beds while reading bedtime stories. About halfway through the second story, both children were fast asleep. He closed the book and placed it on the nightstand by their beds. He tucked them in a little better and kissed their foreheads. As he left the room, he looked at his family, sleeping soundly. They had not a care in the world. He could only wish his life to be that peaceful.

Karen was waiting for him in the living room. She had changed into comfortable loungewear and was enjoying a sip of wine. Andy looked at his wife and smiled. It had been several years since Andy had stopped drinking. Recently he had the urge to drink again and agreed with Karen to limit his drinking and how often. Together they found that a single drink once a week was something they could handle.

Andy had done well, avoiding drinking more, even knowing there was a bottle or two of wine easily available in his home. They had not told anyone else about his drinking again. They did not want him to fall completely off the wagon. He could control it at home and avoided it completely when he was anywhere else.

Andy poured himself a small drink of wine and joined Karen on the sofa. They turned the television on and kept the volume low to not wake the kids. They didn't even watch much of that anymore together. Life was too busy for them.

Karen snuggled against Andy.

"I miss this," Karen said.

"Miss what?" Andy's mind had begun to wander, and he did not know what was on her mind.

"I miss our alone time. We are both so busy we don't take the time just for us. Plus, your trip West had us apart for the first time since we married."

"You are correct. I've not been away from family since my mother's death."

"I am glad you are over your days of running away. I can only imagine what your family went through during those years when you were gone so often. Can you imagine not knowing where your child is?"

Andy thought about that for a moment. Karen was right. How could he have done that to his parents all those years ago? "I would be searching every day and laying heavy on the police to do their job to find my child."

"Life would stop until they were found."

"I would be too. If only my parents were still alive to apologize to."

"Your father is still alive."

"Yes, Larry is still alive, but he was not the father missing me. He was the one I ran to the last time I ran. I have no idea why I ran to him."

"There was a higher power guiding you. We never would have met if you had not run to him and the lake."

"Somehow, I think we would have met." Karen tilted her head back. Andy reached down and gave her a kiss. The thoughts he had floating around just an hour earlier were gone. He was not ready to run away again. At least not too far from home. For now, he had more important responsibilities that came first.

Karen and Andy finished their wine and walked hand in hand to their bedroom. Karen smiled at her husband. In her eyes, he was perfect.

Andy closed his eyes soon after laying down. Karen was cuddled in his arms the way he liked to sleep. They were both smiling as they fell asleep.

Andy woke with a start while it was still dark out. He opened his eyes to make sure where he was. He closed his eyes and again visualized his dream. Again with the open road in front of him. Wind in his hair. He had no idea where he was nor where he was going, but he seemed to be in a hurry to get there. He opened his eyes and eased himself out from under Karen's arm across his chest.

He walked to the kitchen, then gazed out the window facing the driveway. He poured himself a glass of cold water. After wiping the dream from his mind, he returned to bed to try to sleep. What was the reason for the dream? And why had it been repeated?

Karen stirred when Andy pulled the covers up to cover his chest when he returned to bed. He hoped he had not disturbed her sleep. He did not want her asking him anything. He had no answers, and it was not something he was ready to talk about between the dream and his conscious thoughts.

Chapter Twenty

Release

Since Randall had found Barbara for Ben, word had spread about his success in bringing the two together. His law office took a turn in a new direction. He still had a few cases to oversee that were considered normal everyday family law cases, but now he was beginning to grow his business by finding lost family members. This work took him away from home more often than he liked.

Sara and Randall seemed to be drifting apart because of all his traveling. Sara was consumed with the responsibility of the manor's operations. It was difficult for her to hand over the reins to anyone else with her type-A personality. She knew she could count on Rachelle to run it because she had for a while. She also had Heather, Ben, Andy, and Karen there full time, plus Rachelle's husband Bob, who assisted with details of the family business from time to time. Even Barbara and Steven offered to help when they could. Yet, Sara felt compelled to be the one in charge.

Randall returned home from one trip and found Sara gone. Gayle was also gone. He found a note on the kitchen counter telling him they had gone to the mountain vacation home for a few days. He tried to call Sara, but there was no answer. He went to the manor to see if any family had heard from her.

Heather was the only one at the manor when Randall walked into the kitchen.

"Hi, Randall. Welcome home," Heather said as she continued to clean.

"Hi, Heather. Have you talked to Sara in the last day or so? I'm worried about her. She isn't home. She left me this note but isn't answering her cell phone." Randall held up the note so Heather could read it.

Heather glanced at the note. "All I know is what the note says. She asked Rachelle and me to keep an eye on the manor and that she and Gayle were taking a few days to rest. That's all I know." She stopped cleaning long enough to face her brother-in-law.

"I am just worried. Sara always answers her cell phone. And she just up and left! She never mentioned she was leaving when we spoke the night before. Not even this morning when I called her. Why would she do that?"

"I don't know, Randall. Maybe she just needed to get away for a couple of days and didn't want you to worry about her or talk her out of going."

"Why would I talk her out of it? She knows she can use the vacation home any time she wants. I think something else is going on."

Randall sat down at the island. He felt defeated. Sara had never done anything like this before. He tried to think if Sara had said anything in their last conversation that would have indicated her leaving. Nothing was coming to mind.

"I am going to the vacation home." Randall stood and walked to the door.

"You may just want to give her some space. I don't know what was happening, but she didn't go alone. She took Gayle, right? She didn't leave Gayle alone in the house, did she?"

"No, they are both gone. I will try to call her one more time. If she does not answer, I am going up there. Maybe something happened, and they need help."

Heather started to protest him going but thought better of it. He loved her sister and had every right to know if she was alright. Heather would keep her opinion and what she knew to herself. It was up to Sara and Randall to discuss.

There was no answer when Randall called Sara one more time. He left Sara a voice message that he was on his way to the vacation home and that if she got the message before he arrived, to please call him back.

He asked Heather one last time if she knew anything. He walked out when Heather shook her head and closed the door behind him. Twenty minutes later, he was in his car on the roads Sara should have taken. He would find her if anything had happened to her or their daughter along the way to the house. His mind was going in all sorts of directions about what could be happening with her. He loved her, didn't she know that?

Sara opened the door when she heard a knock. The only person she expected to see was a pizza delivery person. She had packed enough food for the two of them for a week, but she and Gayle wanted a pizza from their favorite place. When she saw it was Randall, she reacted with surprise.

"Hi. What are you doing here?" He asked as Sara opened the door wide and let him inside.

"I needed to get away for a while. That's all. I didn't expect you home so soon. How did the search go? Did you locate the missing person? Connect them together yet?" She had turned away from him and walked back into the house.

"I did locate them and connected them to their lost loved one. This one was an easy one to solve." He realized she had not hugged or kissed him when he entered the house. "I got home and found your note. Since you did not answer your cell phone, I got worried. Are you okay?" He reached for Sara's arm. She pulled away ever so gently.

"Yes, we are fine. Gayle had some issues at school, so we decided some R and R would be good for both of us.

"Are you sure it is nothing else? And what issues is Gayle having?" he looked around for his daughter.

Sara invited Randall to join her in the living room. They sat next to each other on the sofa. Sara continued to answer the inquiries from Randall.

"Gayle got in trouble at school."

"What??? Why??" Randal was ready to fight someone if they had caused trouble for Gayle.

"It's nothing. We needed to discuss her reasons and options without family around to complicate things."

"What makes being around your family complicated?"

"They all have opinions, I get that. I don't get that they feel different from me. I sometimes feel like I don't belong here."

"What do you mean by that? Here at the vacation house or here in our relationship?"

"Here in this family," Sara lowered her eyes.

Randall was shocked. "Of course, you belong with this family. You are always talking with one of your siblings." He stopped talking before adding. "This is you overthinking things as you do."

"What are you saying? I should not think about them anymore?"

"No, I am saying you need to hand over the reins more often. Enjoy life. You have been in control since before your parent's died. After your mother died and left that very odd will, you have been the family leader. You have taken charge. I get why you feel this way. You need to take a break."

"Do you? Do you really see it? I am not overreacting? I'm not having a mental breakdown?" Sara asked. She felt her body relax. Her deep emotions were beginning to release.

"You are not having a mental breakdown. You were wise enough to know you needed to get away for a while. You were smart to delegate some of the responsibility of the manor to those who can run it without you while you are gone. Yes, I said that. You do not need to constantly be there."

Sara began to cry. Randall put his arms around her and held her close. She began to rock as a small child would. Tears flowing freely. The weight of the world was lifted from her.

Gayle walked inside from her hike. She had noticed Randall's car parked out front and smiled when she saw him and Sara together, holding each other. Gayle could not have asked for better adoptive parents. She walked over to them and wrapped her arms around the two of them. She didn't say a word. Her sense of silent understanding often came in handy with friends and family.

The three of them sat there for several more minutes. Sara continued to weep. She could not stop the tears from flowing. The sense of relief Sara felt was powerful. Knowing her husband and daughter were there supporting her was more than she expected. The love she felt was precious.

Gayle released her hold on them and walked to the kitchen. She poured them a drink of the sweet tea she had made earlier that day and carried the filled glasses to her family.

Randall and Sara separated from each other and accepted the drinks eagerly. The three sat quietly together, enjoying the sweet taste of the brew.

Sara broke the silence. "I am so very blessed." She looked at Randall and then at Gayle. "I was so afraid you would not understand. I didn't even understand it. I've never been the one to step back and let someone else take over."

"I know that about you. I have watched you work and take charge for many years. I suspected this day would come."

"What day?" Gayle asked. She may still be a child, but she was smart and observant.

"The day when your mother realizes she needs to take a break. I am glad she knows we are behind her, and she does not want to take a break from us."

"Why would she want to take a break from us? We are perfect."

Randall and Sara laughed. Gayle shrugged her shoulders. "Okay, maybe perfect is not the correct word. I do know we could be a lot worse, though." Gayle said with a smile. She had heard horror stories from some of her classmates about how their family lives were. She felt blessed to be in the one she was.

"Very true that we could be worse." Sara took the last sip of her sweet tea and stood up. She took a deep breath before speaking again. Randall knew she had something important to tell them.

"Okay, my loving family. I am going to take your advice. I am stepping away from Bella Rose Estate's responsibilities. When we go home, I will call my last family meeting."

Randall smiled and stood to hug her. "Whatever you decide to do, we will be by your side. Right, Gayle?"

"Right, Dad. Mom, I will do my best to behave more for you." Gayle said as she hugged her mother again.

"Oh, child, I could not ask for a better daughter. You have never been a problem. Well, ok, maybe a little. The bit about school with your getting into trouble needs to be worked out, but we will manage that." Sara smiled. Her tears were gone, as was the sweet tea.

"Let's go home," Randall said.

"Not yet. I want one more day here. I'd like you to stay if you can." She looked at her husband.

"Of course, I can stay. I will call my office and have them reschedule my appointments for tomorrow. He reached into his pocket and pulled out his cell phone, never letting go of his wife's hand.

112

Chapter Twenty-One

A New Start

Randall followed Sara and Gayle home the next day. As soon as Sara got settled and unpacked, she called her siblings and requested an urgent family meeting for that evening. Heather and Ben said they would be there and asked if the spouses needed to come.

"Truthfully, everyone needs to be there. Rachelle and Bob, Barbara and Steven, Larry and Grace might as well come here too." Sara said.

Yes, what Sara had decided needed to be told to everyone. Maybe even Terri and Adam. But they could hear it later. They were not family. Even though they had become so close in such a short time, it felt as if they were.

After the guests had gone on their evening jaunts, the family gathered in the kitchen around the island. It was crowded, and some had to stand, but Sara wanted this meeting to feel like the original meetings. The island was the only family meeting place in her mind. Everyone wanted to hear what Sara had to say.

"Hi, everyone. I know you wonder what happened to me the other day when I took Gayle and drove away for a few days. Heather, thank you for keeping it quiet and telling Randall when he came home. It was him finding us that helped me make a decision."

Everyone looked at each other. What was Sara talking about?

"I made a decision and have Randall's and Gayles' support. I hope I will have all of yours. It will require more from each of you. More time, more energy, more work."

Andy looked at his oldest sister. He wondered how this would affect what had been on his mind. He did not want her blowing it for him. He listened.

Sara looked around. She felt for each one and knew the burden she was putting on their shoulders. Maybe she didn't have to do it. She shook her head. No, this was something she had to do. There was no easy way to say it. She took a deep breath.

"I have decided to step away from my responsibilities at Bella Rose Estate. I will spend the next few days reviewing my work responsibilities and talking with you about overseeing them while I take some much-needed time off."

There was silence.

Heather spoke. "I will do whatever I can. Just let me know."

"I will do my share, too," Rachelle said. "You know Bob, and I support you in anything you want. You have been a blessing to both of us. If not for you and Randall, who knows where I would be? I would not be happy, that is for sure."

"And she never would have met me," Bob added. He reached for his wife's hand.

Everyone laughed. It was true. So much would have been changed if it had not been for Sara and Randall.

Sara noticed that Andy was quiet. She looked at him. There was something in his eyes. She gave him a look that only he would understand. His reply was silent. She read his look. She knew he needed to be the first person she spoke with.

Everyone else voiced their understanding and willingness to do their part. Karen noticed how quiet Andy was. She also noticed the looks between Sara and her husband. Something was going on between those two. Something she knew better than to get involved with until later.

With family business taken care of for the night, everyone finished their drinks and said goodnight. Sara and Randall were the last to leave.

"Are you positive that is what you want to do?" Randall asked. He wanted to be sure Sara was ready for the change in her life.

"I am more than positive. I felt immediate relief after I made the announcement. There was a release I'd never known through my body. I feel at peace."

"That makes me happy." Randall put his arm around Sara's waist. "Let's go home."

"Yes, let's go home." She smiled. Even her smile felt different. Then her smile faded. Andy. What was on his mind? She had a fear of what she read in his eyes. After all these years at Bella Rose, could it be that he had something on his mind that no one would understand? Was his life about to change? If his life changed, it would change so many other lives. She was unsure the family could handle more than what she was doing to them.

Randall shook her arm. "Are you okay? Your smile left."

"I'm fine. Just had a few thoughts about what is to happen in a short amount of time. That's all." She lied—again, to her husband.

116

Chapter Twenty-Two

Realization

Sara woke up with a lot on her mind the morning of meeting with her baby brother. So much had happened in the six years they had shared their lives at Bella Rose. She thought Andy was happy. He did so much around the manor, with his family, and just for people in general. She could not imagine he would have other things on his mind. Yet, the night of the family meeting, she noticed something. Something she knew no one else saw or suspected.

Andy and Sara agreed to meet at the gazebo. They wanted to talk in private, and even though most people were not at the manor during the day, there was always a chance someone would walk in on them. What they had to say was not anyone else's business. The two had formed a special bond over the years. One that Heather was not included in.

Sara walked to the gazebo and spotted Andy already there waiting. He was usually late, so she was thrilled that he was early. She quietly walked up to him and sat down. He was gazing out into the distant mountain range and seemed to be in his own world. She did not want to interrupt his train of thought, so she sat without saying a word. She knew how that affected people. It was best to leave people alone while they were in that state of mind.

"Hi, Sis," Andy said when he sensed her presence.

"Hello, little brother. How are you?"

"I am fine. Or at least I will be."

"Okay, what is going on with you? I could tell something is on your mind by the look you gave me the other night."

"You noticed that, did you?"

"No one else did, but you and I share a special bond and memories. I can read you, even after all these years."

"I may have given you those looks on purpose. I don't have anyone else I feel I can talk to about what has been on my mind. Then you threw into the realm of change when you said that you were stepping away and putting more responsibility on all of us."

"Yes, I am. I decided it was time to have some R and R time. The Estate will be well taken care of between all of you."

"Are you moving away?"

"No, Randall and I are staying here. I am just taking a break. Enough about me for the moment, though. What is going on with you?"

"It started with my trip to Seattle for the research for Terri and Adam's wedding."

Sara looked at Andy. She had her suspicions of what he was going to say next.

"I got the desire to have the freedom of the road ahead of me again. I even dream about it."

"What is in your dream?"

"I am riding on the highway with the wind in my hair and not a care in the world. I can feel all the worries of my life freed in the dream. When I wake up, I know I cannot have that freedom. I have too many things I am responsible for. I have a loving wife and three perfect children. They need me to be with them. I also have my job here at the manor. And the wedding coming up soon."

"You have a lot going on, I agree. But you have managed it all so well over the years. What do you think triggered this urge to return now?"

"All I can say is I enjoyed my trip. The sad thing is I enjoyed it because I was out there alone. It brought back memories of my past life. All those years when I just ran away and was in hiding."

"Do you have the urge to just run away again?"

Andy looked at his sister briefly. He turned away and looked down at his feet. The urge to run was so strong. "I do, Sis. Before anyone else wakes up, I want to wake up one morning, hop in the car, and go. I know that is something I cannot do. Not now. I can't do that to Karen, my children, or all my family at Bella Rose."

"You are right. You cannot do that. Not now."

"What do I do about it?"

"You face your desire. You talk to Karen about it."

"Wait, you think I need to talk to my wife about it?"

"Yes. She will eventually know something is wrong and want to know what it is. She deserves to know before she suspects anything. She knows about your running away days, but she may not think that is going on. If this started with your trip out West, how have things changed between you and Karen since you returned?"

Andy thought for a moment. "I feel a distance between us."

"If you feel it, then she may feel it too. If she sensed something while you were gone or just returned, she might suspect other things are going on with you."

"What other things could there be?"

"One that comes to my mind is that you are having an affair."

"An affair! I would never do that to Karen." Andy protested.

"I know that. But she may not."

"Oh, wow. You are right. I need to talk to Karen about it. Will you come with me when we talk?"

119

"No. You need to do this on your own. I will offer to watch the kids while you go out somewhere and talk. Have a date night. When was the last time you had one of those?"

"It has been a while. With three little kids, we are exhausted when evening rolls around."

"Ok. Tomorrow night. I will come to your house to watch the kids and ensure they get into bed on time. You are taking your lovely bride out on a well overdue date."

"Thank you, Sis." Andy reached over and gave her a hug. Then he changed the subject. "So why are you stepping away? You are not running away, are you?"

"No, I am not running away. I simply realized that I have taken on too much these last six years. I have capable people who can run this place without me for a while."

"Yes, you do. I admire you for finally taking time off." He shook his head. "I know how ironic that sounds. Just listen, let's make a deal. I promise not to run away. You promise to take time off, get away, relax, and when you are ready, come back, and we will all work together to make the most of our place."

"Thank you, Andy. You are the best. You understand me more than most people."

"Does Randall not understand you?"

"Oh, no, he understands me very well. It was his idea that I needed time away."

"Good. Now, let's go back to the manor and start taking care of the things we need to change in our lives. We can do this." Andy stood up and reached for Sara's hand to help her stand up. As she did, they wrapped their arms around each other and hugged.

Life was changing. For the better for both of them.

Chapter Twenty-Three

Countdown

Terri and Adam were in the final stages of planning their wedding. Heather had been the best help, assuring even the smallest detail was handled.

Terri was getting nervous. One late afternoon she called her sister, Angela, while working at the café.

"Hey, sis. How are you?" Terri asked as cheerfully as she could. She was anxious but did not want Angela to pick up on it immediately.

"Hey, Sis. I am fine. How are you doing? Are you getting excited?"

"More anxious and nervous, I think, than excited."

"What are you nervous about?"

"I'm worried a certain someone will show up at the wedding uninvited. I'm not sure how I will feel if I see him."

"You don't have a thing to worry about."

"I don't? Are you sure?"

"I have been keeping tabs on him since he went out on his own in the business. You know the saying, 'keep your friends close, and your enemies closer?"

"He's not actually an enemy. We ended on friendly terms. Although we are not constantly in touch, we have spoken. She didn't reveal that they had seen each other. He knows I'm getting married. Come to think of it, I have not seen him around here at all in a few months. Sometimes I think he has moved away and didn't bother to tell me." Terri laughed. That would not be like Jay. He always seemed to tell her where he was after they reconnected and caught up with each other's lives.

"Sis, I will make sure he is far away from your wedding day. Besides, the last I heard, he had gotten married and moved away."

"What? Jay got married?" Where did you hear that?" Terri was taken aback by that news. Her initial reaction surprised her. She should be happy for him. Instead, she felt betrayed. She thought they had become close enough friends after they met that he would have told her. She had told him about the wedding. And come to think of it, he had told her he had met someone. He had not continued talking about her or any details, and she had forgotten about it. Now she realized that maybe their coffee meeting had been his closure too, and he had since gotten married.

"I read about it in the paper here. They met while he was on one of his photography assignments, and they fell hook, line, and sinker for each other. They were married a few months after they first met."

"Really?" Terri was happy for him. She still felt betrayed. He certainly had not acted as if he had someone that serious in his life when they had met for coffee that one time. Or maybe it was that she didn't want to see it.

"I can contact him to be sure."

"No. On second thought, can you just ensure he does not show up at the wedding?"

"What are you so afraid of?"

"I don't know. Nothing really. Jay and I ended up as friends. We stayed in touch for a while after we met for coffee." Terri stopped talking.

"And, wait, what?"

"And, come to think of it, we stopped communicating shortly after. Maybe that was when he got married. Did you say he had moved?"

"I did. Let me call him to make sure. And I will devise something to ensure he is far away from here. But, now tell me, when did you meet for coffee?"

"Thank you, Angela. You are the best."

"I know." Angela laughed. She hung up the phone and immediately called Jay. She shook her head, realizing Terri had not answered her question about the coffee with Jay.

Terri hung up her phone, put her sister's question out of her mind, and opened her wedding book. Inside were all the arrangements made with checkmarks indicating their completion. She smiled as she closed the book. Everything was going as planned. In just a couple of weeks, she would walk down the aisle and marry Adam, the man of her dreams.

She smiled. Adam was more than the man of her dreams. She had not been dreaming about a man when he walked into her life. Now her life was about to change as it never had changed before.

She had been an independent woman all her life. She had told herself she did not need someone to complete her. When she met Adam, he knew what she was like and had no intention of changing her. He loved that she was a strong and independent lady. He did not have to take care of her. He wanted to take care of her.

Terri started a countdown on her phone. She smiled for a moment and then let the smile fade. She was happy to be getting married. At the same time, thoughts of losing herself crossed her mind. Adam would never do that to her. He admired her too much. She knew that.

She stood up and walked out the door. Life would be perfect for the two of them.

Chapter Twenty-Four

Assurance

The birds were singing, the cows were mooing, and the sun was cresting over the horizon. It was another perfect day to sit on the back deck sipping morning coffee. The rain from the day before had nourished the lawn, and the lightning strikes helped turn the grass a brilliant shade of green. The long drought was over, and nature was coming to life again.

Jay took a deep breath. He inhaled the fresh air he had expected over the last few years. He had almost forgotten the smog he had grown up with. The quietness of his life now drowned out the noise of his past. His brow no longer creased with frown lines of worry. His tan had replaced the pale skin that had others wondering if he was ill most of the time.

This was living. It had taken Jay a while to adjust to his new life and career. Had he known when he was younger what he knew now, he would not have waited for the large corporate organization to go belly up and force him into a life he now called his calling. Yes, this was living.

His cell phone rang. He pulled it out of his pocket to see who it was. Angela was on the other end. He had not heard from her in over a year. Ever since, well, it didn't matter what had happened. What mattered was what did she want now? He started his own business after their falling out. He smiled anyway as he answered it. He held no animosity. He had learned most of the business from her and a lot about country living, for which he was grateful.

"Hey, Jay, this is Angela. I know you never expected to hear from me again."

"That is putting it mildly. What is on your mind?"

"Well, I have a photoshoot that I would like you to work for me."

"You do remember I own a profitable photography business?"

"Yes, Jay. I know. I think you will like this one, though. It will take you back a few years to where you started."

"Why, in God's name, would I want to return to the city?"

"No, not the city. Back to that first assignment I gave you."

"That hole in the wall?"

"That would be the place."

"Why would I want to go there, either? There is nothing there."

"Years ago, there was nothing there. That has all changed."

"How? Did some celebrity buy it? Is some political giant living there or having a second life there?"

"Funny you should mention those. Yes, a political giant is hiding out there with a celebrity."

"Since when did you become part of the paparazzi?"

"I'm not."

"Then I don't understand."

"The truth is the area there has grown so much since you had been there. I want to do an anniversary edition of "Unknown America." And you are the only one who knows the details of the area. I know you did more than snap a lot of photos while you were there. You got to know the people. I would love for you to reconnect with some of them and write the story. You would have your by-line in my magazine?

"Do I need to have my name associated with your magazine? Didn't we do enough damage to each other?

"We did, I agree. But I need you to do this one last assignment for me."

"Is this an attempt to ensure I am away from Terri for her wedding?"

Angela was speechless for a moment. How did he know her motive? "I would not put it that way. It does happen to fall during the time she is getting married. But that is beside the point."

"I am not living anywhere near Terri anyway. I got married a while ago, and Carrie and I moved to North Carolina on the beach."

"I had heard you got married. I didn't know you had moved so far away."

I have always wanted to live at the beach. When I met Carrie and found out she was from there, it was an easy decision."

"You married her because she lived on the beach?"

"No comment."

"I cannot believe you would do that; oh wait, I can believe that. You found out Terri was getting married, and you jumped the only way you knew how to give her space and let her know you were over her and would not get in her way."

"That is not how it was. I love Carrie."

Angela thought for a moment. She believed in love at first sight. She also remembered Terri and Jay's relationship and how slow they had taken it. In the end, it did not work out for them that way. So maybe the sudden change in Jay's methods would work for him and this Carrie person.

"Ok. I will tell Terri that you are happily married and she has nothing to worry about. I still need you to do this photoshoot for me."

"Okay. When do I need to be there?"

"The twelfth of May for a couple of weeks until you complete the interviews and photo shoots you need for a good size article."

"I can be there. Thank you for the recommendation and confidence in my work. I never dreamed we would be working together again."

"Neither did I, Jay. Neither did I. I will send you all the details you will need. Thanks, Jay. You are the best."

"I don't think I am the best, but I'll take it. I wasn't the best for your sister, obviously."

"Jay, Terri is happy. Leave her alone now."

"Oh, I am. I had already put my foot in my mouth since their engagement. Lucky for me, she forgave me."

Angela did not need to know what happened or the details of anything between him and her sister. "Goodbye, Jay. We will be in touch."

They hung up their phones. Jay still wondered why he was being sent to the middle of nowhere again. It had taken him forever to get away from that place and even longer to ignore the memories.

After Angela hung up from Jay, she called her sister.

"Hey, Angela, what's going on?"

"Hi. I just got off the phone from Jay."

"Oh. Okay. What did he have to say?"

"Don't you sound positive?"

"Sorry. I was thinking of other things and not expecting you to have talked with Jay so soon."

"I decided to get it over with as soon as possible."

"So, what did he have to say?"

"You will be happy with what I learned."

"Oh? I hope you are correct."

"First, he accepted my assignment to return to the first place he photographed to capture the area's advancements. Second, he wanted to let you know that not only has he moved away, which is why you have not seen him in a while, but I verified that he got married."

"So he did get married?" Terri sat down. She didn't know why, but that news being fact shocked her.

"You and he were no longer together. You and Adam were serious and then got engaged. Jay realized he had lost his chance for good at that point."

"It certainly did not take him long to walk away from me and find someone new."

"Terri, you told him to walk away."

Terri knew her little sister was right. She had found her soulmate in Adam. Why was she having these feelings? Nope, she needed to let him go. "You are right. I told him to leave and to leave me alone. I told him I had a new life, which did not include him. Now I know why he was so calm when I told him I was with someone else, and it was time for him to move on."

So why was she having a hard time hearing that Jay was married? Angela had told her earlier, but it was just now sinking in for some reason.

"Sis, why are you struggling with this?"

"I think because he did it so quickly. He and I took our relationship slow, and it ended. Now he just finds someone and gets married?" Terri took a deep breath. He had every right to do what made him happy. Terri smiled and tilted her head. Yes, Jay deserved his happiness. She had found hers.

"I asked him how he could have done it so fast. He told me that she had a house on the beach."

"And that was enough for him to get married and move there? I am glad he has moved away. I would have to knock some sense into him if he still lived here."

"Well, he has married, moved to the East Coast, and is happy. So now it is your turn to let him be. Get him out of your mind."

"You are right. Time to concentrate on the man who makes me smile all the time. Adam may have a few faults, but who doesn't?"

"Good way to think. You have my assurance that Jay will be nowhere near here on your wedding day. Now let's get busy making the final wedding arrangements."

"I agree. Time to focus on Adam and me. Forever the duo."

The sisters hung up, but Terri kept thinking about Jay. She was happy for him. He deserved that. Her heart would always love him. And secretly, she hoped they could reconnect and be friends again.

Chapter Twenty-Five

The Move

Everything was coming together for the wedding. Adam had arranged all the details for the honeymoon. With the help of Heather, Angela, and many others, Terri had all the wedding details complete. The couple found themselves with an evening free. They sat in Terri's home, enjoying a glass of red wine and discussing their coming wedding.

"Can you believe we only have a week before we are married?" Adam asked as he took a sip from the stemless wine glass that had been an early wedding gift from Steven and Barbara.

"I have not slept a full night in over a week. I know everything is taken care of, but I still fear we have forgotten something or that something will go wrong."

"What could possibly go wrong? We have worked hard to cover everything. We have Heather, Andy, Karen, and your sister handling everything."

"I am so thankful for all of them. To have my sister come to share our day makes it even better. When her career and the magazine took off and grew, we saw less and less of her. I used to see her often," Terri said and immediately regretted bringing the subject to the light. Maybe Adam would ignore the indication from her past.

Adam took the last drink of his wine. He knew what Terri was referring to when she mentioned how often she spent time with Angela. He knew all about her past. He also trusted her that her past was behind her.

Terri stood up and took his glass from him to refill. She had emptied hers as well. Neither of them had to work the next day, so another glass of wine would not be a problem. She owed a lounge but did not drink very often. Adam used to drink a lot, maybe too much, for many years but had cut back to only a few drinks a week. Terri had voiced her concerns about his drinking soon after they met. He realized his drinking would be a deal-breaker if he did not stop the route his drinking was taking him. He had stopped for a while before moving to the area and landing his job in construction. It was easy to drink. He preferred to drink when he sang karaoke. He had told her it helped him relax and face all those people. Terri stood by him without nagging him to stop. The love that grew quickly and easily led him to do what was best for them. He could not remember the last time he was drunk. Sober was a much better way to live.

Terri walked back into the living room, where Adam was waiting for her. He smiled when he saw her, and it lit up the room. It always had. Terri smiled back. From the bottom of her heart, she knew that her life was now perfect. Adam was her soulmate.

Adam took the wine glass from Terri and waited for her to sit by his side. He put his arm around her shoulders, and she leaned back, resting her head on his shoulder. It was a common position for them. She hoped that part of their relationship would not end. She loved being by his side and in his arms.

As they sipped their wine, they talked about the plans for the next day. They were getting up early, picking up the rental truck, and moving Adam's things into her house with the help of movers and several friends. She had moved things around to make room for his and make her house their home. They were putting some of his things and some of her things into storage until after their honeymoon. Then they had plans to decide what items to keep or sell in a yard sale. It would not be an easy task.

"I think it is time for me to head home," Adam said when he looked at the clock on the wall. He could still drive and knew it was best to leave before they decided to drink one more.

Terri walked him to his car. They kissed goodbye, and he drove away from her house. He was looking forward to the move the next day.

On his way home, he thought of how his life was about to change as it never had before. He had vowed to himself that he was never going to get married. So far in his life, he had been able to keep that vow to himself. Another woman had tried to win his love. No one had even come close to holding his heart the way Terri did.

He pulled into his parking spot of the apartment. The inside lights were on. He had forgotten to turn them off in the morning when he left for work. He laughed at himself. That behavior would need to stop because he was sure Terri would prefer everything to be perfect in her, soon to be their home.

He often thought Terri was a class above him and would question her about why she loved him. He agreed with her reply that there was no explanation for why she loved him. He felt the same way. He had no idea why he loved her. They agreed to spend their entire married life accepting their love without the need to explain it to anyone, even each other. They had yet been unable to explain their connection.

Terri cleared up the kitchen and washed the wine glasses. She looked around at the empty spaces she had made for Adam's things. It made her smile.

The next morning Adam called Terri and asked if she was on her way to help with the move. The movers were loading up the large furniture to take to the storage unit were finishing, and their friends were on their way to help. She told him her keys were in her hands and she would be there soon.

It took them less than three hours to get everything loaded into the vehicles to transport to Terri's home. With all their friends helping, it did not take long. The last item was loaded into Terri's car.

Adam walked into his apartment one last time to assure everything was removed. He opened his closet door and stood on his toes to check the top shelf. Then he reached into the corner and pulled down a tiny box.

As he turned, he saw Terri standing in the doorway, looking down the hallway. He quickly put the box into his jeans pocket and closed the closet door. His shirt covered the pockets on his jeans, and he walked to the doorway to join his love.

Chapter Twenty-Six

Sisters

Terri and Adam were exhausted by the end of the day. They had worked long into the night unpacking his things and placing them where they belonged in their home. They laughed when they finally sat down with a glass of red wine.

"What a day!" Adam said as he took a sip of wine and looked around the room. The day before, there were a lot of empty places in the room. His collections and favorite photos now occupied shelves of the bookcases or held prominent places on the walls. He looked around the room and felt a sense of belonging. He smiled and raised his glass to Terri.

"Yes, what a day. I did not expect to get so much accomplished today. I would have been happy to get your boxes over here. But with all your help and our energy, look at it all." Terri raised her glass to his.

"I didn't think you would like a disheveled house, so I pushed to make it as organized as possible for you as quickly as possible."

"You know me well. The trick will be to help me keep it this way."

"I will do my best. You know how I am, though."

"I do, which scares me," she laughed. She had decided to give in a little to his way of living. She did not want something so trivial to cause issues for them.

When they had finished their wine, Adam stood up and reached for Terri's hand. He pulled her off the sofa and into his arms. The feeling he had when she was in his arms was one he never wanted to lose. They kissed each other just as Terri's phone rang.

Adam pulled away and laughed. "So much for romance."

"We can start over where we left off," Terri said as she answered her phone before letting it go to voicemail.

"Angela? What is wrong?" Terri's stepped away from Adam and listened as her sister spoke.

"Nothing. Why?"

"Angela, do you know what time it is here?"

"Oh, I am so sorry. Aren't you usually still up at this hour anyway?"

"Angela, what day is this?"

Angela did not immediately speak. "OH! Sis! I am so sorry. Did I interrupt anything?"

"As a matter of fact, almost." Terri laughed as she replied and walked back to Adam. "So why are you calling?"

"I wanted to let you know that my plane has been delayed, and I won't be in until late tomorrow afternoon. The earliest flight I could get doesn't leave until first thing in the morning tomorrow, instead of tonight and the red eye I was hoping for."

"Alright. That still is okay. We have plenty of time to get things done once you arrive. I am glad you called to let me know. You know how I am. I would have been worried if you were not here when I first expected it. And with the delay, you can get some sleep."

"I know you would have been. Now, go back to what you and Adam were doing. I will call you when I am at the airport or close to it, if I can, so you can pick me up."

"Okay. Sounds good. We will pick you up tomorrow afternoon. Get some sleep, Sis."

"I will do my best." Angela hung up her phone. She looked around for a comfortable place to sit and take a nap. Even the floor looked good at the moment.

Thirty minutes later, Adam and Terri were settled in and almost asleep in each other's arms. It was the beginning of their lives together in this house. They had less than a week until the wedding.

~~~~~~

The sun was shining through the window when Adam awoke. He smiled when he felt Terri still cuddled next to him with his arm around her. He doubted if either one of them had moved in hours. It was a wonderful feeling.

Terri blinked. Adam's movements had woken her. She looked up into Adam's face and smiled.

"Good morning, beautiful," Adam whispered and kissed her forehead.

"Good morning, Babe." She said and raised her head to kiss his face.

"I could get used to this."

"You had better get used to this." She moved to sit up. He pulled her back down. They both laughed. Life and living together would be fun.

After showers and getting dressed, they had to go their separate ways to work. Terri still had the Café to operate and her sister to pick up from the airport later in the day. Adam had construction work to complete before the wedding.

At noon Terri got a call from Angela. She was at the airport and ready to be picked up. Terri told her she would be there as soon as she could.

"That's okay. Take your time."

"What do you mean, take my time? I would imagine you are ready to get away from an airport."

"Maybe not," Angela replied in a teasing voice.

"Sis, what is his name?"

"What makes you say it's a man?"

"I know you, little sis. I will take my time driving to the airport."

"Thank you. Wait until you meet him!"

"Angela! This is my wedding, not your meet-my-new-boyfriend week."

"Oh, I know. I am just teasing you. Keeping you on your toes and relaxed."

"Funny. I will see you in about an hour." Terri hung up her phone. She sure hoped her sister would leave the man at the airport. This was her wedding and not her sister's time to shine with a new boyfriend to show off.

Terri parked her car in the short-term parking lot. She knew if her sister had met someone, she would be at the airport longer than a simple passenger pick-up at baggage claim. The moment Terri walked into the small airport, she spotted her sister. She waved as she walked toward her and the man she was with. She stopped and took her cell phone out of her pocket as she got closer. She pushed the shortcut button to call her sister.

"Hey. Why are you calling me? I know you see me."

"Sis, who is that man you are with?"

"Why? I will introduce you when you get close enough."

"Angela, walk away from him and come here. Tell him you will be right back. Tell him anything you want to tell him but walk away without him knowing I told you to."

Angela looked at her phone. Then at the man waiting for her just a few feet away. She told him she would be right back, and quickly but without raising suspicion, she walked away.

"Sis, what is wrong with you?" Angela whispered when she caught up with her sister. Terri had moved, so she was out of the sight range of the man her sister seemed so into.

"That man? Do you have any idea who that man is?"

"Obviously not like you do. Who is he?"

"That man is Jeff."

"Okay. Yes, his name is Jeff. But who is Jeff? And why are you bothered by him?"

"He is Jay's brother!"

"What is he doing here?" Angela turned to look at the man she had been talking with.

"I would say he is here to gather all the information he can find on me and my wedding."

Angela fell quiet.

"Why are you not saying anything?"

"Well, I had no idea who he was. I am so sorry, Terri."

"Why are you sorry? You obviously did not know."

" I am sorry because he and I had so much time to talk."

Terri looked at her sister. As much as she loved her, she knew Angela had a way of opening up and sharing things when she shouldn't. "I am afraid to ask. What did you tell him?"

"Everything." Angela hung her head. She would never learn to keep her mouth shut. Now she may have just ruined her sister's perfect day.

"Oh, Angela. How could you?" Terri walked away from her for a moment. Her sister was the only family she had left, but she sometimes wanted to strangle her for things she did.

"I didn't know. He kept asking me questions about myself and what I was doing in the area. I told him everything, Sis. I am so sorry. What should we do?"

"We will walk back to him and act like nothing is wrong."

"What exactly is wrong? Everything I told him is things his brother already knows. Plus, Jay is married and has moved on. What difference does it make what he knows about you and your life now?"

"I guess nothing. I did not want to be reminded about that part of my life anymore. Jeff was always an issue with Jay and me. Jay rarely spoke with him when we were together; he said Jeff was bad news."

"Well, let's go talk with him. He did not seem like a man who was bad news. He was telling me about his life and his ex-wife."

"Wait, what? His ex-wife? I never thought he would get divorced."

"Oh, you want me away from him because you thought he was married?"

"You got me. I knew what kind of a man he was a few years ago. He was always cheating on his wife. I am not surprised he is now divorced. But, I am telling you, you do not want to get involved with him. He Is bad news."

"Okay. I won't get involved with Jeff. I do want to say goodbye to him, though. He does not need to know what I know about him."

"Believe me, when he sees me, he will know you know. He will be the one to walk away."

Angela and Terri walked to where Jeff was standing. He was facing away from them, talking with another woman with his hand on her shoulder. Angela tapped Terri on the shoulder and motioned for her to follow her. Together they walked away, picked up Angela's luggage, and went to Terri's car. Angela had seen what Terri was talking about.

"Thank you for saving me, Sis." That was all Angela had to say. They did not talk about him on the way home. Instead, they talked about the wedding coming in less than a week.

Chapter Twenty-Seven

Anticipation

Terri awoke alone in her home. Adam had spent the night at Steven and Barbara's to keep with the tradition of not seeing the bride on the wedding day before her walk down the aisle.

Terri looked around her room before rising from her bed. This was the last night she was going to be alone. This was the last morning she would wake up with just memories of her dreams. Her dreams were hours away from becoming a reality.

In the few days Adam had spent with her, she had grown accustomed to having him by her side as she fell asleep and then awoke.

She rolled over to face where he would be and smiled. It was the beginning of the rest of her life.

Adam shook his head when he sat up in the spare bedroom of his friend's house. He had come a long way in the last several years. His past life had been such that he never thought he would find someone to love, much less someone who would love him. Terri loved him despite all he had been through. Despite his record. Despite his past. She loved him as he loved her –unconditionally.

He stood up and walked over to the window and gazed out. His life was about to become as beautiful as the day was outside. Both were perfect.

Bella Rose was buzzing early. Heather had accepted all the help she was offered to get the decorations up in the reception hall. Andy had hired a few of the staff from the café to help him. Terri had closed the café for the day to allow her staff to attend her wedding. Karen put the final touches on the wedding cake before taking it over to the hall. Some assembly needed to be done there. Sara was busy ensuring the manor guests had everything they needed. All of them were there for the wedding. Rachelle arrived and took over so Sara could prepare for her wedding role. Ben and Randall were getting ready to escort the guests to their seats when the time came.

Angela arrived at Terri's early to help her get ready. Hair, makeup, gown, shoes, jewelry, the works. Her older sister was getting married, and Angela was determined to make Terri's beauty stand out.

Angela's phone rang while Terri was taking her shower. She pulled it out of her purse and saw who it was. Pushing the indicator to ignore, she returned her phone to her purse. She would turn it off, except she needed it if Terri or someone else in the family needed her.

Terri walked from the bathroom with a towel wrapped around her head and her light bathroom wrapped around her shoulders. Angela looked at her and laughed.

"Why are you laughing?" Terri asked. She walked past the mirror in her living room and understood. She looked about as far away from beautiful as anyone could get.

"Okay, little Sis. I am in your hands now." Terri said as she sat down on the chair in her kitchen. On the table in front of her, Angela had placed the hairdryer, curling irons, hair accessories, makeup, and a cup of fresh coffee.

"Ah, you know what I needed most," Terri said as she lifted the cup of black coffee to her lips.

"Be careful not to drink too much of that. You want to be awake but not jittery as you walk down the aisle. Today is your big day. You don't want to do anything to ruin it."

"I don't plan to. Now, do your magic on this head of hair."

Angela dried her sister's hair. It reminded her of when they were kids and would fix each other's hair and put makeup on each other. "I promise to do a better job than I did when we were kids." She picked up the heated curling iron and put controlled curls in place. Then she started applying the makeup, paying close attention to accentuating her beautiful eyes.

An hour later, Angela held a hand mirror in front of Terri. Terri almost cried. Looking back at her was a picture of someone she did not recognize. "Who is this person?" Terri asked while laughing.

"That person is the most loving, caring, and wonderful person I know. You are the most beautiful bride, and Adam will be blown away when he sees you. Now, it is time to get you dressed in the gown."

"Just one more cup of coffee?" Terri lifted her twice-emptied cup.

"No, you have had enough. It's time now for water."

"Okay, if you say so." Terri stood and walked to her bedroom, where her wedding dress awaited her. She closed the door behind her. Terri knew she would need Angela's help to put the dress on and not mess up her hair and make-up, but she needed a few minutes alone first.

Making sure her hands were clean, Terri took the dress off the hanger and laid it on the bed. She stepped back to admire the one she and Angela had selected. Terri did not want the normal elegant white wedding gown. That was not her style. At least, that was what she thought.

When she shopped at the bridal store, she tried on several styles. The one that came home with her was perfect. White, floor-length, lace-covered bodice, heart neckline, with a short removable train. And form-fitting.

Sara's gown was the same style, in light blue teal and without a train. Adam and Steven were going to be dressed in black tuxes. Adam would be wearing a white shirt, and Steven would have a light blue teal shirt to match the matron of honor.

Angela knocked on her sister's bedroom door but did not wait for Terri to tell her to enter. She never had waited. That was the relationship they shared.

Terri carefully dabbed at a tear as Angela entered the room. She hoped her sister did not notice and that she had not ruined her makeup.

"So, what are the tears all about, Sis? This is the day you have waited for all your life."

"No, this is the day I never thought would happen. I had already given up on finding a soulmate when I moved to this area. It is a small town, and I certainly never dreamed Mr. Right would live here."

"If I remember correctly, he didn't live here; he moved here."

"Very true. I am so glad he did."

"I know you are. Now, let's get you dressed and the rest of your makeup on. Time is moving on, and we need to do the same."

"Have you checked on all the other arrangements? Are the guys ready? Have the flowers arrived?"

"Terri. Calm down. Everything is being taken care of. I made a few phone calls after you walked in here. Sara is busy getting ready. She took care of a few other things this morning. Heather, Andy, and Karen have made sure everything else is as it should be"

Terri took a deep breath. "Okay. I am not used to having so many other people in charge. I trust you. It will be a perfect day."

The sisters took their time getting Terri dressed and the final touches into her upswept hair and the jewelry just right. Angela had the wedding ring to give Steven once everyone was at the chapel. She knew enough not to trust a man with them ahead of time.

As the clock ticked the minutes off until the time of the ceremony, everything fell into place. An hour before the ceremony, Angela and Terri got into Terri's SUV and headed from one side of town to the other. Bella Rose was about to become famous. More than anyone, except one person, knew.

Terri looked at all the vehicles already parked in the parking lot of the Bella Rose chapel. She did not realize they had invited so many people.

"Are all those people for our wedding?" She asked Angela.

"Yes, my dear Sister. They are all here for your big day." Under her breath, as quiet as she could, she added, "At least, most of them are people you invited."

"What did you say?" Terri knew she had heard something, but she did not comprehend it.

"Nothing. I just agreed that you had invited all these people."

"I don't believe you, but I will not argue with the lady who made sure I am ready for this event."

" You better not argue with me. We both know how that would end."

"Yes, I would win, and you would run away."

"I only did that once when we were little kids," Angela responded. She truly had not behaved that way since.

"I know. And you know how I don't forget anything."

"Oh, I remember. All the time, you bring up things about our past." She changed the subject before Terri mentioned anything else about their childhood. "Today is your day, Sis. Chin up, a smile on; let's get inside the chapel before Adam and Steven show up and see you."

"Okay. Help me out of the SUV. I don't need to fall or get my gown dirty.

Angela parked the SUV as close to the chapel's side door as possible. They needed to sneak into the designated bridal room and hide until it was time to walk down the aisle. She helped Terri into the room for the bridal party. Sara was already inside, waiting for them.

"You are beautiful! Sara said to Terri when they entered. She walked over to help carry some of the emergency supplies Angela had brought.

"What is all this?" Sara asked.

"I have been involved with enough weddings to now have a supply of things that may be needed at weddings." She reached into one of the cases and pulled out the hairdryer, curling iron, hairspray, and other hair essentials.

"I must ask, do you know who all those people wandering around taking photos of everyone and everything are doing here?" Sara asked Angela. She would have asked Terri, but since Angela dealt more with photography for her magazine, she assumed Angela had something to do with the camera team.

Terri looked at her sister. "Yes, why so many extra people? I know Adam, and I did not invite all of them." She was glad Sara had asked her question for her.

"Well, ladies, it was supposed to be a surprise, but since the camera team obviously doesn't know how to be discreet, I hired them to do a feature on the wedding or weddings in general, and we are featuring Bella Rose in that upcoming edition." She waited for their response.

"You are using my wedding to feature Bella Rose in "Unknown America?" Terri asked with a sense of anger.

"Now, Sis, it isn't like that. I just wanted a great photographer to capture your big day. The idea to feature it in my magazine was not the original purpose."

"But it is the purpose now?" Sara asked. "I wish you had run it past me before assuming we wanted to be in your publication."

"Why would you not want to be in a magazine? It will bring you more business."

"Ever think that we are fine the way we are?"

"I'm with Sara. Maybe we like our small town the way it is. We don't need all that attention."

"Don't cast the idea aside. It will bring you so much in the months and years ahead." Angela responded. She knew she would need to sell the idea to them but hoped it would be after the wedding, not before. If they requested that she stop, it would ruin her ideas.

Sara and Terri looked at each other. They each were used to running major decisions through their spouses or at least the other people involved in the businesses. They did not say a word, just shrugged their shoulders. Maybe Angela did have a good idea.

"Okay. You have my permission. However, if I feel the team or any of the cameramen or women are getting in the way of my wedding day celebrations, they will have to go." Terri gave in. She knew how her sister was fighting to hold on to her magazine.

Sara nodded her head. "I am in agreement with Terri. You have my permission. However, before you put any photo or written piece to print, you will need our written permission and approval of what you put into it."

"Agreed." Angela put her hand out for a handshake agreement between both ladies.

"Now, let us get this wedding started."

There was a knock on the door. The florist entered when Angela opened the door for her. She had the bridal bouquet and the one to toss at the reception. She also had the bouquet for Sara and a corsage for Angela. The florist told them that with the help of Ben, all the floral decorations were done. Her next stop was the boutonniere to Adam and Steven.

Terri held her bouquet and felt a tear form in her throat. She turned away from Sara and Angela. Holding the flowers made her wedding more real than putting on her gown.

Another knock on the door came when Rachelle came to let them know it was time. The wedding was about to start.

147

She assured them that Adam and Steven were ready, the guests were seated, and the music had begun.

Terri took one last look in the full-length mirror. The anticipation of the day, so long in waiting and planning, had arrived. She was about to get married.

Chapter Twenty Eight

I Do

Adam stood in front of the chapel with Steven by his side. What a long journey they had shared. Who would have imagined all those years ago that the two criminals would be best friends, with one standing with the other on his wedding day, in a little town on the other side of the country from where they met?

Adam looked out at the guests waiting for his bride and for when Terri and he would say their I do's. To commit their lives to each other. To promise to love, honor, and cherish each other until death. He looked at Steven, then the minister. He felt nervous and excited.

The music changed, and Adam turned to face the back of the church. This was the beginning of the rest of his life.

The doors dividing the chapel and the foyer opened. Sara stood at the opening in her blue teal gown. Her bouquet of teal and white flowers mixed with simple greenery and teal and white ribbons cascaded down in front of her. The guests turned to watch the processional.

Sara focused on the front of the church. She smiled when she saw Adam and Steven standing there. She glanced to the front pew and saw Randall. Her smile grew as memories of her wedding filled her thoughts. Her wedding had been beautiful, but this one seemed even more so. She was not sure why.

Again the music changed. The guests rose from their seats and watched as Terri began her slow walk to her future.

Adam was mesmerized by his bride's beauty as she reached him. He did all he could to hold back a tear.

Happiness was not a powerful enough word for what he felt. His future stood beside him.

The minister began to speak after the music stopped. Then he turned it over to Adam and Terri, who had written their personal vows to each other.

Adam spoke first. He faced Terri and took her hands in his after she gave her bouquet to Sara.

"My dear sweet Terri. When I moved to this little town after the roughest time in my life was over, I never imagined it would lead to the best day and time in my life. I was not looking for anyone when you walked into my life. One look at you, and I was smitten, but I knew I had better take my time. I slowly won you over. Despite all the setbacks in my past, you accepted me for who I am. You don't try to change me, yet I have changed. You don't ask a lot of me, but I give you all I am. You are my rock. You are my love. I am honored to stand before you, all of our guests, and God to vow that you will always be my number one. I will always be there for you. I will protect you as I stand by your side. Together we will walk through the rest of our lives. I love you, Terri." He ended it with those words of love.

"Adam, my love. When you walked into my life, into my café, I knew you would be a part of my life forever. I did not realize how, but I knew that my life was more complete just by knowing you. Then my heart felt love like I'd never felt it before. We both tried to hide our true feelings, but love won out. You are my love, my rock, and my all. My life was complete on my own, but you have added a new dimension of growth. I am honored to stand before you, our guests, and God to vow my love for you. I will spend the rest of my life walking by your side. Lifting you up when you need it. Loving and respecting you, enjoying each day, knowing that our days are limited. I love you, Adam."

The minister took his cue, finished the ceremony with the ring exchange, and announced them as Mr. and Mrs.

Adam and Terri kissed a gentle, lasting kiss before facing their guests. Sara gave Terri her bouquet back just before the newly announced husband and wife hurried down the aisle. Sara and Steven followed behind them, then rushed outside to meet with Angela's team for wedding photos.

Terri was amazed at all the photos the team wanted to take. It was more than she remembered being taken at any wedding she had attended. She wondered why so many were being taken but didn't say anything. Soon they were called to the reception hall for the reception. Hand in hand, Terri and Adam walked to the hall. Then stopped and kissed before they opened the doors. Their eyes sparkling, their smiles never-ending; this was their beginning.

The guests had gathered inside, waiting for the newlyweds. A few members of the camera team were set up in the back corner, ready to take portraits of couples who wanted a professional photo taken. It was rare for couples to dress up like they do for a wedding. This was an opportunity for many at a beautiful portrait.

Andy had the food set out in the buffet warmers. Karen had set up the wedding cake on its own table near the food. Guests had taken their gifts and cards to the designated gift table, then admired the cake Karen had made. Many took photos of her work. A few even asked for her business card.

When Adam and Terri walked in, everyone rose and cheered. They went to the bridal table and sat down for a few moments. Steven clanged his champagne glass with a knife to get everyone's attention. He stood at the bridal table to make a toast to his friends.

"May I have everyone's attention?" Steven then waited for the room to be quiet. "I want to make a toast to this lovely couple. Adam and I go back several years. It was not the best start to a friendship. In fact, it ended rather badly for many years." Steven looked at Adam but smiled. "The powers that be led both of us here from across the country, where we reconnected and met Terri. I have watched the two of them from the moment they saw each other. I knew before they did that there was love in the air. I am honored to have stood up with them today as they declared their love for one another and witnessed the beginning of the rest of their lives. To Adam and Terri, cherish every day together and let your love grow with each new sunrise."

Everyone cheered and took a drink. Terri and Adam kissed each other. Terri looked around in amazement. She looked at Adam and caught him smiling at her. His eyes sparkled. Life could not get any better.

The rest of the evening was spent eating the amazing food Andy had prepared. Dancing to the music provided by the DJ that Adam had hired.

Adam had written a special love song for their first dance. He had recorded himself singing it for the DJ to play for them. It was his declaration of eternal love to her.

When the time came for the cake cutting, Karen brought the bride and groom to the cake table. Her masterpiece cake was the best she had made. Each layer had a different flavor. The white icing was then decorated with icing roses in two shades of teal to match the wedding colors. Cascading down in a spiral, rested the ribbons with tiny roses on them. The cake topper was a bride and groom specially designed to look like Terri and Adam.

Terri and Adam picked up the cake knife and made the first cuts into the cake. They each lifted a small piece, and true to tradition, they fed each other the first piece. The flavor of that bottom layer was peach. Not a typical wedding cake. The bottom layer was for everyone. The top layer, the one they would seal and keep for their first anniversary, was raspberry infused with dark rum. That would be an amazing treat for them in a year.

As the reception ended, it was time to toss the bouquet. Instead of tossing it, Terri walked over to Angela and handed the bouquet to her. "Thank you, Sis. You have helped make this day the best it could be. I am so thankful for you being here. Now, it is your turn to find your true love."

"It will be a long time until I do that. I have too much going on to get involved with anyone."

"That is what I thought too. Then Adam walked into my life."

"I am so glad he did. I have never seen you so happy. I pray the two of you never lose that feeling."

154

Chapter Twenty-Nine

Contentment

The wedding was over. Terri and Adam were away on their honeymoon enjoying a cruise. It was the first time on a cruise for each of them.

Sara, Heather, Andy, and their spouses returned to the reception hall to complete the cleaning the day after the wedding. There was not a lot left to be done. After the wedding and reception, they only wanted to go home and relax, so they only did what they had to. The wedding day had been draining.

"Were our weddings so exhausting?" Karen asked. "I hope not. If ours was, I apologize. I certainly did not plan on that. It was supposed to be a simple celebration."

"Your wedding was a simple affair. Our weddings were simple, compared to what Terri and Adam had."

"Oh, I don't think theirs was as elaborate as some of the weddings I have heard about."

"I agree. Some cakes I have been asked to make have been over the top!" Karen added. "I have had to turn some away because I am not that good or because they would have taken so long to make that the price would have been outrageous."

"Have you made any of the over-the-top ones?"

"Only one. And that was so nerve-racking I vowed never to do another one that I was not sure I could do."

"But, you are so good at it. Where did you go to school to learn how to decorate cakes?"

"I taught myself. I did take a few online courses and watched internet videos, but it's mostly self-taught."

"You are amazing. That's all I can say." Heather concluded.

After cleaning up the reception hall and chapel, the ladies retired into the kitchen area of the manor and continued talking. Ben, Randall, and Andy soon joined them.

The conversation changed from the manor's business to what was to come next for all of them.

Heather added details about Barbara and Steven into the conversation. They may not be a part of the immediate family, but they all agreed that she was a family member since Barbara was Ben's sister.

They each had goals they aimed to reach. Sara seemed to think she had reached her goal. Randall felt he had reached his as well. Even more than they had planned was that they were parents to Grace. They adored her and wanted the best for her. She had been a blessing to them and to the entire family. She never had a cross word for any of them.

Heather told the group that she was just beginning to reach her goal. She acquired new clients as word spread of her home interior talents and her party and event planning. She loved her work.

Ben was content with his work at the manor. His life felt complete since he had found his sister. They were still getting to know each other, but many people mentioned how much they were alike.

Andy commented that his life was more than he had ever hoped for. In his earlier years, he never dreamed of being able to settle down in one place for very long. To see him married with three children would have shocked most people who knew him in his rebellious years. He told everyone that he was very content and happy.

Karen and Andy left the manor and went home. They talked a while about the joy in their lives since the time they first met at Lake Wallenpaupack.

"I am so glad I found you when I was running away. You, my love, changed my life."

"You were the one who changed my life. I was going nowhere and did not even know it. How Larry and Grace could own the Marina for all those years is beyond me. Now I know there is more to life than staying in one place all the time."

"Moving around all the time is not the way to live. At least not the way I did."

"I realize that, but you got to see more of the country than I hope to."

"Maybe not. Maybe once the kids are older, we can travel more. Take them all on vacation. Explore the area around here on day trips. There is a lot to do out there. A lot to see. I would love to take the kids to different places, so they don't think being here is the only life to have."

"That would be nice. I can start planning."

"I think planning now is a little early. The kids are too little to remember being places. I would prefer to wait until they are older for some of the places I want to go."

"Where do you want to go?"

"I would love to travel West. The stories from Adam and Steven and even Terri make it sound exciting."

"I agree. And we can still plan. Dreams are a great way to expand on reality. With places to go and people to see and get to know."

"You are right. Right now, we need to get some sleep. You can begin planning and dreaming tomorrow."

Later that night, Andy lay wide awake. Why had he lied to all of his family? Why had he not admitted that he was feeling restless again? Why had he not opened up for help? He rolled away from Karen and fell asleep into a dream.

Chapter Thirty

Dreamworld of Reality

Andy was driving down the highway alone. The forest was on either side of him. The sun was high in the sky, with the sunbeams touching the ground through the branches of the trees. It was a beautiful scene. He caught himself smiling at the beauty. He turned off the main road and followed the signs to a cabin. Once there, he parked his car and unloaded his things into the rustic cabin that faced the river flowing below. After putting his things away, he stood out on the deck overlooking the river and the neighboring cabins in the distance.

This was heaven. That was what he thought as the sun set and the temperatures dropped. Still warm enough to stay outside, Andy returned to the inside. He poured himself a drink and sat facing the large flat-screen television. Picking up the remote, he turned it on and just left it on the first channel that came to light. Once he took the time to pay attention to the show, he realized it was a breaking story on the news about a runaway little boy.

He listened to the rest of the story, knowing that he was in the area of the boy they were calling a runaway. He paid attention to the boy's looks in case he ran across him in the morning. He hoped they found the boy before that, then heard the newscaster say they were stopping the search for the night due to the darkness and the thick forest.

He felt himself drifting to sleep. He swallowed the last of his drink and got up to go to bed. He turned the television off, so the room was quiet for a good night's sleep.

There was a faint knock on his door. Andy barely heard it and did not respond immediately. Again there was a knock on the door. When the knocking continued, he listened, hoping it would eventually stop. Instead, it faintly continued. He rose to open the door. Not knowing who to expect, he was still shocked at who he saw. A little boy stood at the door. His head hung low even as Andy bent down to his level. Andy stepped outside to look for an adult who should have been with this child. There was no one else around. No sounds from the woods that surrounded the cabin.

Andy reached for the little boy's hand and gently led him into the room, closing the door behind them. Andy asked what his name was, but the boy did not answer.

The boy looked around the cabin, walked into the bedroom, climbed onto the bed, and curled up. He was immediately asleep.

Andy watched his actions and shook his head. He had no idea what was going on with this child. Then he looked at the boy's face that he could finally see. It was the missing child. There was something about this child that made him smile. He gently placed a blanket on the boy up to his shoulders and kissed his forehead. Andy would wait a while before making the call that he had been found. Something was telling him to wait and let the child rest. Andy closed the bedroom door and retreated to the couch in the living area. He lay down and pulled the throw blanket over himself, but sleep would not come.

His mind drifted. There was something about the child in the other room. He felt a connection. He got up, walked to the bedroom, opened the door, and watched the boy sleep.

The little boy stirred from his sleep and opened his eyes. He sat up in bed and saw Andy watching him. He was afraid and tried to run out past Andy. Andy reached over and caught him in midstride.

Andy sat him down in the living room and tried to talk with him. The boy refused to speak. In the silence, Andy heard all the answers and understood. He would make a phone call when the day dawned.

Chapter Thirty-One

Running

Andy rolled over and faced Karen. His mind was foggy from his dream. Her peaceful face while she slept made him smile. How had he deserved such a wonderful person in his life? She was the answer to prayers he never prayed. She was his life.

He rolled over and got out of bed. Looking out the window, he remembered his dream. That little boy spoke no words but told Andy more than words could have. And Andy knew what he had to do.

He glanced at Karen, still sleeping soundly, and walked out of the room. He kept walking. To his car and drove away.

Karen woke up when she heard Ryan calling her name from their room. She looked over to Andy, but he was already up and gone. She smiled. It was just like him to be up and out early. He had breakfast to make in the manor and liked to get there early to prepare it. She loved that her husband was such a loving man and father who cared so much about his family and everyone he met.

Twenty minutes later, the phone rang. Karen carried Rayvn in her arms while she answered it.

"Karen, is Andy still there?"

"No, he left early this morning to go to the manor to make breakfast. Why? Is he not there?"

"No, and he never made it here. I made breakfast for our guests from things he had ready to cook, but he has not been seen by anyone here."

"That is not like him. Let me make a few phone calls to see where he may have gone. Thank you for letting me know."

Karen lay Rayvn in the playpen with River and Ryan. The older babies loved when their baby sister joined them. They treated her with gentleness.

Karen made a phone call to Larry. He picked up after the third ring that Karen heard.

"Good morning. How are you?" Larry asked.

"Hi, Larry. I am good, I think. Andy is missing."

"What do you mean missing?"

"I mean, he left early this morning, and I thought he went to the manor to make breakfast for the guests, but Sara just called to ask if he was here."

"Did he have an appointment this morning?"

"No. Not that I know of." Karen tried to think of something she may have forgotten about. She looked at the calendar on the refrigerator to see if anything was written on it for Andy. Nothing.

"He has not called me in several days, so I don't know of any place he may have gone. Sorry. I will ask Grace in a minute and see if she knows anything. I will call you back."

"Okay. Thank you. Since we married, I have never known Andy to take off like this. I know he used to run away but never gave it a thought that he may do it again."

"What makes you think he may have run away?"

"I don't know. It was the first thing I thought of, though, for some reason."

"It will all work out, Karen. Keep me updated, and I will let you know if we hear from him."

"Thank you." Karen hung up the phone and called Sara.

"Hi, Have you heard anything?"

"No. I called Larry to see if he or Grace knew anything, but they have not talked to him in a few days and had no suggestions about where he may have gone."

"I keep trying his cell phone, but it only goes to his voicemail. I have left a few messages."

"You don't think he ran away again for long, do you?"

"I hope not. I thought Andy was over all that when he met you. You saved him from all that. He had settled down after Mama died."

"I thought so. But maybe he had a wild hair. Maybe something, and he just had to get away for a while."

"Let's hope it is a short while if that is the case."

"I agree. Karen, do you need any help with the kids today? I can come over, or why don't you come over to the manor?"

"I'll be fine. I want to stay here for when he comes home."

"Okay. Call me if you need anything or if you hear from him."

"I will. You too."

Karen set her phone down and went to check on her kids.

~~~~~~

Andy turned the corner and found what he was looking for. Solitude, beauty, and memories. He pulled into a parking spot and turned the engine off. Then he just sat inside his car. Windows rolled up, music still playing through his phone. Loud music. Rock music. Old music. Old memories. A few minutes later, when the song was finished, he opened his car door and stepped out. He put the ear bud in his ear to hear the music but not disturb anyone. Plus, people would maybe leave him alone more with the earbuds in. He had discovered that trick a few years ago.

He looked around and debated which direction to go. He needed to climb. The higher, the better. The farther away, the better.

He glanced at his phone and saw that voicemail messages were waiting. He saw that there were text messages as well. He shoved the phone into his jeans pocket. He could not deal with that right now. He hoped when it was all over, that his family would understand. Karen would. Larry would. At least, he hoped they would.

He turned to the right, secured his backpack with the needed supplies on his back, and started climbing the mountain. He had a few locations on the mountain that he wanted to visit and experience the views and the memories. No one knew of his memories of the mountain. He had never told his family, and there was no need to tell Karen.

At the top of the first peak he wanted to reach, he found the large rock to sit on while looking out over the view of the vast countryside below. He looked around and smiled. He had fond memories of this location.

His memories returned to his childhood and the first time he had run away from home. Soon after he left the house, he started hitchhiking. The first car to stop and pick him up was a man in a pickup truck who said he was headed to the mountains to hike. He said he would drop Andy off anywhere he wanted, or he could join him on the hike. Andy had chosen to go for a hike. He had never been hiking much, so he thought it was a great opportunity to try something new. While he was there on the mountain, he had time to think.

As he sat on the same rock he had when he was a young child, he smiled, remembering how easy it was to run from home. He hung his head when he realized that was exactly what he was doing again. He did not plan to stay long but needed to take this trip alone to have closure.

Andy picked up a small stone from the ground and tossed it over the edge. He watched as it descended until he could no longer see it. Then, he turned and walked back along the same path he had used to hike up the mountain.

He drove the quarter of a mile to the next parking lot. He parked his car in the shade, then got out and walked to the beginning of the path. The beginning was paved to make it accessible to wheelchairs and easy for all ages to hike.

After the pavement ended, he turned to the left. He knew what was at the end of the path he chose. For him, it was another chance for closure. This time it would take him longer to reach that point mentally. It was something he had put out of his mind for most of his life.

At the end of the trail, Andy spotted the tree he remembered. He walked over to it and looked up. He was unsure how he felt when he saw what he was looking for. He hesitated. He did not see anyone else around nor hear anyone approaching from the trail.

He took off the backpack, removed the pocket knife from its side pocket, and walked over to the tree. Standing next to it, he felt an odd sensation run through him. Memories, this time from his teen years. After that time, he began to run farther away from home. It always amazed him that his family never found him when he hid so close to home.

Andy took his pocket knife and started to carve into the tree. He carefully cut around the carved-out letters that were shoulder height now. When he had put them there, they were at his waist level.

Carving the piece of bark away from the tree took him longer than he thought it would. He held it in his hand when it was removed. He wondered how many people had seen it over the years and what they thought it meant. He assumed no one knew the emotions behind it and even doubted anyone tried to guess.

He placed it inside his backpack and put his knife away. Then he sat on the bench placed there in recent years. Looking over his shoulder, he noticed a rainbow in the distant sky. Then he noticed the rain cloud approaching. He stood up, grabbed his backpack, and started down the trail to his car.

Chapter Thirty-Two

Confession

Karen put her three children down for their naps. It had been a long day with still no word from Andy. Sara had come to visit for a while, and then Larry and Grace had stopped in. Between all of them, they had no idea where Andy might be. He was still not answering his cell phone. He had not called or texted any of them. Larry called the police, and Sara called the hospital. No one had him on their records. No car accidents were reported, and no admittance to hospitals. There was no sign of him. And they could not report him missing until he was gone for twenty-four hours.

All Karen wanted to do was cry. How could the man of her dreams do this to her and their children? Did he really run away? How long would he be gone this time? She had heard all the stories from him and his family. The ones about his childhood and history of running. She understood why he ran when he was younger. As an adult and a husband and father to three young children, he now had all the reasons in the world to stay home. He was loved by everyone he knew. Everyone he knew cared for him.

Karen sat down in the rocking chair to rest while Ryan, River, and Rayvn all napped. She, too, was fast asleep.

She awoke when she heard a car door slam shut. Rushing to the front door, she hoped it was Andy. Instead, it was a police officer. Karen burst into tears.

The officer stepped inside and reached for Karen to hold her up as her knees buckled. He walked her to the nearest chair.

"Ma'am, are you okay? I'm Officer Richards. I stopped by on our routine stops to invite you and your family to a local charity event to raise money for the people affected by the floods a month ago. I did not mean to make you cry just seeing me. What's going on?"

Karen shook her head and wiped a tear. "I am so sorry, she sobbed. My husband disappeared this morning, and we have been searching for him. They won't let us report him missing yet, but we have contacted the police. We were told they had no reports of any accidents, then you knock on my door."

"I do apologize, Ma'am. Is there anything I can do for you?"

"Find my husband."

"I wish I could do something, but like you said, you cannot report him as missing until he is gone for twenty-four hours unless he has a serious medical condition."

"Believe me, when he does come home, he will have a medical condition." Karen managed to laugh slightly as she wiped the last of her tears.

"Let me call the station and see if there is any further news. Let me have his name." Officer Richards called the main office as soon as Karen gave him Andy's full name. When he was off the phone, he told Karen there was no word about him or any accidents.

Karen thanked him and walked him out the front door.

Two hours after the officer left, another car pulled up to their house. This time it was Andy. Karen did not know whether to laugh, cry, be mad, or act like nothing had happened. She simply wrapped her arms around his neck as she met him on the front porch. She was so glad to see him, she could not be upset with him. At least not immediately.

"Where have you been all day?" Karen demanded after she had pulled away from him, and they walked inside.

"It's a long story."

"I have a lifetime to listen," Karen said as she sat back down.

"Honestly, I want to talk to the whole family about my actions today. They all deserve to know what is going on."

"Okay, let's call them and have them come over."

"Well, we normally have the family meetings at the manor, but since the kids are napping, maybe this once we can have it here."

Karen kissed Andy, and they both got on their cell phones to call the family together.

Thirty minutes later, everyone was gathered in their living room. The kids had woken up, but Andy put them in the playpen to play.

Andy stood before his family, with Karen standing by his side.

"First, let me apologize for running away today. I know it is not something any of you expected from me after these years of staying in one location. I woke up with the urge to run in the middle of the night. I could not control it. I knew what I had to do, and no one would understand if I had mentioned it first. So I took off. I am sorry."

"It's okay little brother," Heather said. "We will always love you."

"I hope so. I also don't understand why you love me." He turned toward Karen. "Especially you. Why do you love me? We are two different people from two different walks of life. You are smarter than I am. You are more in control of life than I am. You always have been. There are so many days that I just watch you and wonder how we, as two unlikely souls, found each other and have made it work."

Karen leaned her head on Andy's shoulder. "You, my love, are the answer to so many of my childhood prayers. You are the one I wanted and needed without knowing what or who I needed. I was determined to live a life on my own. Then you came along and were my other half. You will always be my other half. I don't want you to ever doubt my love for you or question why."

"Thank you for that," Andy said, kissing Karen on her forehead. Now, let me explain my actions today."

The family listened as Andy told his story.

"When I was a kid and ran away for the first time, I ran to Roan Mountain. I remember Mama taking us there when we were small. I remember seeing all the places I could hide. So when I had my first urge to run, that was the only place I thought of. At that time, I didn't stay long, and when Mama and Daddy found me, I was not there but closer to home. They never asked me where I had been." He took a breath and waited for any response. No one said a word. They knew there was more to his story.

"When I was a teenager and ran away again, I ran to the same mountain. This time I found a different trail to hike and hide in. I found a shallow cave and hid from any potential searchers. The problem was, there were none. No one came close to looking for me up there. I had run away, but not that far. It hurt when no one came looking for me, or other hikers did not even question me." He took a drink of water and continued.

"One day, I climbed out to the edge of the mountain. A fence is built around the edge to prevent people from falling off. But I climbed around that so I could stand on the extreme edge. To the left of the cliff was a small tree. I felt so alone; I had one thing in mind. At the same time, I wanted to leave a message to anyone who would find it. I had my pocket knife with me and carved words into the tree. I changed my mind about my original goal, hiked back down the trail, and moved on to an area farther away."

"Are you saying you were going to jump off the mountain?" Ben asked.

"I was," Andy admitted. "Until I looked over the edge and realized that no one would ever find me if I did. I guess I still had hope of my family wanting me."

"What do you mean 'family wanting you?" Sara asked. "Of course, we wanted you."

"I know that now, but at that time, you know how things were between Glen and me."

"I remember," Sara nodded her head.

"Today, I had to get away. I have felt the urge lately to run and did not want to. I wanted to run before the wedding and knew that would not go over very well. Today I knew I had to go, and I knew where. I also knew it would not be the same experience I needed to have if I told anyone."

"Where did you go?" Ben asked.

"I returned to the spot I went to as a teenager, on Roan Mountain. I walked out to the edge and looked down like I did before. I had no desire to jump this time. My only desire was to have closure and remove what I had put there." Andy reached into the backpack that had been sitting beside him. He pulled out the piece of bark he had removed from the tree. He turned it so his family could see.

Carved into the bark were the words: *No One Cares*.

Sara immediately teared up. She got up and put her arms around her little brother. In seconds Heather was right beside her. The three siblings hung on to each other for several moments as tears fell. Everyone else was silent.

Karen watched as her husband melted in the arms of his sisters. She felt a love of family she had not yet experienced. Karen wiped the tears from her face and smiled. Andy may have wondered why she married and loved him and thought they were two unlikely souls to be matched together, but this was what love and family were all about. This is why she loved him and knew they belonged together. Love, pure and simple. Her heart ached for him. She knew that this action was the closure of his past life.

The siblings finally separated without words left to speak. There were no words to say. Sara wanted to say sorry, but it was not her place. It was their parent's place to say it, but they were both gone. She knew that Andy taking down those words of anger and hurt was his own forgiveness to all those he thought did not care.

Andy placed the bark on the coffee table. "I want to frame that somehow. I know I should throw it away because you all care about me and each other. Instead, I want it as a reminder that we need to always care for and love each other. It will remind me of my past and my enriched life now."

Chapter Thirty-Three

Cruisin'

The ship had sailed. Is that the right word to use when a cruise ship leaves port?

Terri and Adam had enjoyed a great flight to Charlotte, where they spent the night before boarding the cruise ship they would call home for the seven-day cruise. Neither had been on a cruise and were a little apprehensive about it. Their friends had suggested it to Adam, and he surprised his bride with the trip as their honeymoon.

As they were boarding the ship, they were met by cameras to capture their moment of arrival. They took time to pose and wondered if the photo showed how unsure they were about being there. Maybe there would be an 'after' photo to compare. Terri hoped it would be a better pose.

They had to wait to get into their room, so they joined the thousands of other cruisers and walked around the deck to one of the bars. A lady was handing out free drinks, so they indulged.

"This could be an interesting trip," Adam said as he lifted his souvenir glass to his wife. They clinked glasses and sipped their drinks.

"Oh, you are so right! This is amazing." Terri took another sip.

An announcement sounded that their rooms were ready, and there was a mandatory safety meeting in forty-five minutes, informing them of where the guests of each section of the ship were to meet.

Adam and Terri followed their maps to their room. The ship was huge, and they realized it may take a while to figure out where everything was. They mainly needed their room, the location of the safety meeting, and where the food was. They would figure out the rest of the ship later.

Adam opened the door to their room, bent down, scooped Terri up in his arms, and carried her into the room. "I know it is not the threshold into our new home, but it is the threshold to our new life together. May these past few days be the perfect beginning of the rest of our lives."

Terri kissed him as he gently laid her on the bed. He returned to the hallway and carried their luggage inside as she lay on the bed smiling. Terri herself to rest on her bent left arm, watched him, and smiled. This life was already more than she had imagined it could be.

The safety meeting was over, and they headed to the lido deck, where they were told all the food was. Amazed by all the choices, they examined each section and chose a simple fruit salad to hold them over until their first formal dinner. Then they walked to a higher deck to watch the ship leave the port. They waved at everyone on the shore, watching their family and friends depart, and watched as the ship slowly moved farther away from land. Terri felt a bit woozy, but she controlled it by holding on to Adam and taking deep breaths. She was determined not to get seasick.

At the dinner that night, which they found out in time was not formal, they met other couples who sat near them. Terri looked around while she ate and wondered who everyone was and what their stories were. Adam watched her and smiled. While they ate, they learned a little about each couple and shared a little about themselves. All they had to say was that this was their honeymoon. Everyone raised a glass to congratulate them.

Later that evening, they talked as they walked around the upper deck to watch the night sky before going to the first night's entertainment.

"Tomorrow, we stay on the ship, but from what I hear, there is a lot to do."

"I heard about a few things. Did you hear about the karaoke contest?"

"I did." Adam looked at Terri and winked.

"Of course you did. I should have known that. That is probably why you booked this particular cruise."

"No, but it did help narrow down which one I wanted to take you on. It was the stops along the way that intrigued me more."

On their way to the entertainment, they stopped by the kiosk where Adam signed up for the next afternoon's karaoke contest.

By the end of the night, they were exhausted. True to their nature, they stayed up as late as possible, enjoying everything around them. They had experienced the ocean view until darkness set in when they could no longer see beyond the ship. The food stood up to its reputation that first night. The entertainment was good. They heard one man comment that the entertainment would get better each night. The first night was just an introduction to events on the ship, the excursions available, where things are located, and then a musical number by a band that would be there for the duration.

Terri and Adam joined many others on the lido deck for breakfast and coffee the next morning. They had slept well and awoke early, which allowed them to watch the dawn take over the night on the ocean. Terri had her camera ready at all times and captured some great scenes. She would show them to everyone when they got home. Especially Angela. Maybe her sister could do a photo write-up about cruising even if it was not all in America.

Adam told Terri he wanted to find out more about the karaoke contest and see if he could practice somewhere. She said she would wander around, take photos, and catch up with him for lunch. Terri had worried about getting lost on the ship, but they explored enough the first night that she knew she could find him later.

Adam located the person to discuss his singing and where he could practice. He also found out more about the prize available to the winner. He was determined to win.

After a great lunch together and walking the ship to watch the ocean, Terri joined her husband at the contest. She stood to the side near the stage to capture him on film. She knew he was good and wanted to save the memories. She was shocked when the emcee announced the prize for the winner and knew Adam would fight to win. This, she thought, was going to be interesting. When it was Adam's turn to sing, Terri stood out of everyone's way to video his performance.

The days that followed were filled with getting off the ship at the various ports to explore and enjoy the exciting areas of a world they had never seen. Terri was amazed at all the beauty.

Each evening on the ship, they were busy meeting new people, enjoying the best meals they had ever had, attending the shows, and Adam continued to compete in the karaoke contest. Each night he was voted on to the next round.

The last day of the cruise was at sea. No more ports with new places to visit. No more unseen beauty. No more unexpected adventures. It was shopping day on the ship, with special entertainment most of the day. A day to pack for their trip home.

And, of course, it was the last night for Adam to sing. He was running low on songs that were good enough to potentially win the contest. There were only two contestants left. The one-hour show would be filled with former contestants, a couple of special guests, and Adam and one other contestant doing their best to win the grand prize.

Terri and Adam had made a few good friends while on the cruise. They almost hated that it would most likely be the last time they saw some of them. Terri had invited them all to their hometown and her café and lounge. One couple said they would try to come to visit soon. Others said it was too far for them to go but invited Terri and Adam to their area. Terri made a note of the addresses and emails she collected.

It was finally time for Adam to sing. The auditorium was full. Everyone had heard about the contest, and since there was not much else to do at that time of the evening, more people attended.

Terri took her regular seat to video her husband singing. She knew he had it in him to win, even though the other contestant was amazing. The judges would have a difficult time selecting the winner.

An hour later, Adam and Terri were standing with the people responsible for the contest and the prize. Adam had won! The prize of ten thousand dollars would be sent to his bank account in two increments. The first would be sent immediately. Adam's balance would be presented at a special awards ceremony in Nashville, Tennessee.

Terri and Adam could not have been happier. Their life together was off to an amazing beginning. She hoped it would continue.

The next morning they awoke to the ship already docked at the home port. Terri and Adam walked down for their last breakfast on the ship. They ate outside to enjoy the final day as long as possible. Neither of them wanted to leave. Their new friends joined them as they were finishing their coffee. They all talked about staying in touch after they got home.

Terri and Adam later joined the others who were leaving the ship when it was their time slot. As they stepped off the ship and onto the sidewalk, they turned to view the ship one last time. They wrapped their arms around each other. Their lives were just beginning, and what a beginning they had.

They had so many stories to share with everyone when they got home. It would take months to tell them all. Luckily, they had years ahead of them to share those and create and share a lifetime of more as they were made.

Life was amazing. Terri smiled, thinking about how Adam had walked into her life when she was not looking. How he had waited for her when she thought she had things to deal with that she thought he would not understand. He never questioned her. He never doubted her. She felt blessed. She shook her head.

"Why are you shaking your head?" Adam asked.

Terri had not noticed him looking and felt caught. "Oh, thinking about how we met and how much we have already been through. You are an amazing person to put up with me."

"You are the amazing one. You know my past and still love me."

"Loving you is easy. Your past helped make you who you are. My past made me who I am. I love you for your strength to overcome what life attempted to place upon you. You stood strong and are a better person because of that."

"You are the strong one."

"Together, we will make a great team. I can't wait to spend the rest of my life with you."

"Ditto," Adam said.

They laughed as they continued walking. Life was beginning for them."

Chapter Thirty-Four

Follow Your Heart

When Terri and Adam returned from their cruise, they had a free day before they each had to return to work. They had arranged to rest, do laundry, and settle into their home. The few days they had lived together before their wedding had not been enough to establish how their house would be.

The morning after they returned, Terri got a call from Angela, who had returned to her condominium after the wedding. While the sisters spent time together preparing for the wedding, they discussed the possibility of Angela moving closer to Terri and Adam. Since her work could be done anywhere, Angela had no reason not to move. She was still single and had no other permanent connection to her current location.

"Hey, Sis! How are you?" Terri said when she answered her cell phone.

"I have made a decision."

"Yes, is it what I think it is? Have you decided to move closer?"

"Yes, I have. Nothing is keeping me here. In the short time I spent with you and those around you, I fell in love with the area. I need to follow my heart. I cannot wait to get out of here and find a place to live there."

Terri looked at Adam. What would her new husband think if she invited her sister to live with them? No, she would not do that to him. "You can stay at the manor at Bella Rose, where the wedding took place. I am sure they would have a room you can rent while looking for an apartment."

"That would be wonderful!" Angela was sipping on coffee as she spoke. "I loved that place. And they are such a loving family. Are you sure they'd have room?"

"Only way to find out is to give them a call. I am sure Sara can find room for you."

"Didn't Sara say she was stepping down for a while? Who else would be in charge?"

"I would just call the main phone. Let them know who you are and that I recommend you stay there. Add that you plan to stay a while until you find an apartment. They may even know of some apartments available."

"Do you know of any available?"

"Not at the moment, but I will ask Adam if he knows of any."

"Knows of any what?" Adam asked as he walked into the living room and heard what his wife had said.

"Of any apartments for rent. Angela is moving here." Terri replied.

"Tell that husband of yours hello. He had better be taking good care of you." Angela laughed.

"I will. And he is." Terri smiled as she spoke. He was taking great care of her. She was happier than she had ever been.

"I will let you two get on with your day. I will call the manor and see what they have available and when. I will also need a storage unit for all my belongings until I find a place." Angela began thinking of everything she would have to do for this move to work. It may be more than she anticipated. Then again, it was not the first time she had moved.

"There are several of those in this area. We will help you as much as possible to make your move easy. Love you, Sis."

"Love you, too, Sis. Bye." Angela disconnected from her conversation with Terri. She turned around and smiled at Jeff.

Terri put her cell phone on the kitchen counter, where she joined Adam for the fresh coffee he had made. He asked about her conversation with her sister.

"Angela is planning to move here. I guess she fell in love with the area during her short visit. Just as we both did." Terri winked.

"Are you sure you want your sister living close to you?"

"Why wouldn't I? She's amazing."

"She also tends to move around a lot. She has connections to your ex-boyfriend and tends to take over wherever she goes. You've told me that much."

"I think she has calmed down from always taking over things. She was fine during our wedding."

"True, she was. But didn't you have to threaten her beforehand?"

Terri laughed as she took another sip of coffee. That was true. She had warned her while they were at the airport. Told her to behave. But that was also directed toward the man she had met on the flight. Terri knew the man. He was trouble.

"Yes, I did. This time she listened. She doesn't always listen. So I think she has changed in recent years."

"Time will tell. I just hope you all get along when she moves here." Adam stood and put his arms around Terri's waist. "I will stand by you no matter what happens between the two of you."

"Thanks, Love. You get better every day."

"Ha. I am not sure about that, but I try to do my best. I need to get busy if we go back to work tomorrow."

"Yes, we need to get a few things done today." Terri placed her empty coffee mug next to the coffee maker. She would have more later. Coffee was her downfall.

Adam gathered the empty suitcases to put them in the spare closet. Terri gathered the dirty clothes and started a load of laundry. She smiled as Adam walked past the room. This was the new beginning of her life. She had a wonderful husband; her sister, who had listened to her, wanted to move closer; her business was going well, and her new life was good.

Angela called the manor soon after talking with Terri. She wanted to get things moving along as soon as she could to move. She was at a break in her work with nothing other than the next edition that featured Bella Rose and her sister's wedding. That was not due out for two months. And what better place to work on it than at Bella Rose? She could gather more information than she had in the short time she was there for the wedding.

Angela was waiting to hear from Jay with his newest photos and write-up about the little town that had grown since the first time he had been there. Since he had started his own photojournalism company, she was not expecting his piece to arrive any time soon. Jay had been busy with his own work. Plus, he had recently gotten married and moved. She had witnessed the slowing of her photo contractors' productivity when they first married. It usually picked up within a few weeks.

While Angela spoke with Rachelle at the manor, reserving her room three weeks later, she asked about a storage unit in the area. Rachelle gave her the information for a couple of them. Angela then made a few phone calls and put a deposit on a unit near the small town she would be living in. From there, she called her local movers. It was time to start packing.

Jeff left Angela's house soon after she had talked with Terri. He had things to take care of. He already lived in the area Angela was moving to, but he had connections to where she currently lived. His ex-wife was living outside of town. He had lived there for the last five years before his divorce. He now wondered how he had never noticed Angela in town when he was there. She was beautiful. How could he not have seen her? But then, she did travel the country with her work. And he had been trying to make his marriage work. When that ended, he started traveling more; that was how they had met on the airplane instead of in town.

Angela was exactly who he felt he needed at this time in his life. His marriage had ended badly. He was thankful that they had never had any children. His ex-wife had left him for someone she met at her job. He had done all he could to hang on to the marriage, but he knew there was no saving it in the end. When he met Angela, he had finally put his past behind him. It had taken a while, but after several months of barely doing more than his job and sleeping, he knew there was more to life and living. He knew if God put someone new into his life, he would seize the opportunity and treat that person with love, compassion, trust, and dignity. A lady deserved that.

Jeff was excited that Angela was moving to be near him. He realized she was moving to be near her sister and not him, but he was still excited. He was hoping their relationship would grow. They had made no promises to each other. They were not even officially dating. He also knew that his brother had dated Angela's sister. That could cause a problem. He remembered the relationship between Jay and Terri. It had not lasted very long, yet they had done so many things together. He never did know the real reason they broke up. He would need to ask Angela sometime.

Two weeks later, Angela was all packed and on her way to Tennessee. She was driving and taking her time. The movers were also on their way to meet Terri and Adam to put things into the storage unit. When Angela got settled into the manor, she planned to spend time at the storage unit, getting out only what she needed. She would not need that much until she found an apartment.

Jeff had flown back to his home the week before. He and Angela had spent little time together with her busy packing and closing her business locally. They discussed getting together once she was moved and settled in. He told her he would help her find a place to live when she was ready.

~~~~~~

Terri and Adam had returned to their jobs after their honeymoon and found a routine they fell into as a married couple. Everything was going well. Terri was looking forward to having her sister so close. They had talked often while Angela prepared for her move. Angela had not told her sister more details about Jeff. That subject needed to be discussed in person. She didn't think Terri knew Jeff lived so close to her and wondered what her sister would think about her and Jeff being together. Only time would tell, and only time would get Terri to accept Jeff in her life.

Terri sensed her sister was keeping something from her but tossed that idea aside, contributing her suspicions to anxiety about moving.

~~~~~~

Jay had sent the photos and write-up to Angela for her next publication. He also sent her a letter saying it was the last assignment he would do for her. He had his own business and needed to focus on it. He wished her the best as she continued her work.

When Angela read the letter Jay had included, she found it interesting that he had not mentioned Terri. Nor had he mentioned Jeff. This meant he was over Terri since he married and did not know about her and Jeff's meeting and their relationship. She wondered what he would think once he found out.

She also wondered what Terri would tell her when she discovered that she and Jeff had stayed in touch after the wedding. She expected to hear more of what she had been told at the airport. And nothing official was going on between her and Jeff, so it did not matter. Not yet, anyway.

Angela spent her first night on the road at a small hotel. She could have pushed herself to make the trip in one day, but it meant no sleep for twenty-four hours or more. She preferred to spend a night along the way in a hotel and arrive rested.

When she settled in for the night, she called Terri to tell her where she was and when she expected to arrive the next day if everything went according to plan.

Terri was glad for the phone call. It was late at night, and she began worrying about her baby sister. Once she spoke with Angela, she relaxed and enjoyed a glass of wine with Adam before they went to bed. It was amazing to have her sister back in her life. She was looking forward to her being close. Life was just beginning the way it should - with family.

Chapter Thirty-Five

Agenda

Angela arrived at Bella Rose early on a Saturday morning. She was exhausted from her trip. Spending the night at the hotel on the way had been a wise choice. Rachelle met her at the front door.

"Welcome back, Angela. It is so good to have you here. And to know that you have decided to move to the area is even better news."

"Thank you. It feels good to have made that choice to be near my sister. I thank you and your family for making room for me."

"Oh, this is not exactly owned by my family. In a roundabout way, I guess it is if you want to stretch the family relations some."

"Well, that sounds interesting. I would love to hear the full story."

"Maybe one day."

"Well, I don't know if Terri or even Sara told you or not, but I am doing a feature story on Bella Rose for my next magazine edition."

"I had heard a little about that. I thought it was mainly about Terri's wedding being here."

"Part of it is, but I know there is history here, and I wanted to write about it."

"How interesting. And Sara said it was all right to do?"

"Yes, she loved the idea."

"In that case, I would be glad to sit down with you and tell you anything you want to know that can help you."

"Thank you. I thought I had everything, but what you just mentioned may add to the story."

Rachelle helped Angela carry her bags to her room. She had rented her the first room on the first floor. It would give her access to the back deck and gardens, with easy access to the kitchen and the family.

Angela had been to the manor during her sister's wedding but only to visit for one day. She had stayed in a hotel in town the rest of her time in the area. When Angela saw her room, she was even more impressed with Bella Rose Estate. Her brief conversation with Rachelle and the beauty of her room made her want to write more than she had planned about Bella Rose.

Angela called her sister when she was settled into her room. They made arrangements to meet at the café lounge after dinner. Angela said she had a meeting in town, so that would be perfect.

Terri didn't ask what her meeting was about. She assumed it was about an apartment or something to do with the magazine.

Angela drove to the next town to meet Jeff for dinner. She had not told Terri any details of her meeting and was glad her sister had not asked. How would she explain about Jeff after Terri had warned her not to get involved with him?

Jeff met Angela at the door of the little Mom and Pop restaurant he had suggested. Moe's had been in business for years and was now operated by the original owner's son. Jeff had gotten to know Moe several years earlier when they met at a local club. Jeff introduced Angela to Moe when Moe came to their table to say hello to Jeff.

"Long time, no see, my friend," Moe began reaching out to shake Jeff's hand but hesitated and looked at the lady with Jeff. "And who is this fine young lady?" Moe looked at Angela and smiled.

"This is my friend, Angela. She is new to the area, but her sister owns the café and lounge near Bella Rose."

"Good to meet you, Angela. I have heard great things about your sister's place. I hope you will like it in this area. You've got a good friend here with you. Jeff is a great guy." He patted Jeff on his shoulder. Deep down, he knew Jeff's life story and knew he was a good guy.

"Good to meet you too, Moe. I think Jeff is a good guy." Angela touched Jeff's arm and smiled. "At least he is so far."

"You two kids, order whatever you want. It's on the house." Then he walked away as the waitress brought their drinks.

"Moe seems like a nice man," Angela said before taking a drink of her sweet tea.

"He is. He and I go back a few years. We've been friends since the day we met." Jeff skimmed over the menu. "What would you like to have to eat?"

"I want the pulled pork platter. I will see how it compares to others I've had."

"We will make that an order for two, then. I know Moe makes good pulled pork."

Jeff told the waitress what they wanted when she returned and handed her both menus.

"So, what did you want to talk to me about?" Angela asked.

"I have found a couple of apartments for us, I mean, for you to look at. A friend owns the one, but you are under no obligation to rent it from her if you don't like it."

"You don't waste time, do you?"

"Not usually. I can only imagine living in a hotel room for a long time. I figured you'd want to move as soon as you could."

"Living at the manor is wonderful. I would like my own place soon, but I'm okay there if it takes me a while to find what I will be comfortable living in. It all depends on the location too. I am sure you have my safety in mind when looking."

"Of course. I know where the bad sections of the cities are around here. Believe me, you do not want to live near them."

"Not if I can help it. Thank you for your help."

Their meals arrived, and they continued talking while they ate. Jeff left the waitress a good tip when they finished and thanked Moe for their meal. Jeff then walked Angela to her car before going to his.

Angela could not get Jeff off her mind as she drove back to the manor. She had plenty of time before meeting her sister. As she drove, she wondered why Jeff was so eager to find an apartment for her. She had also caught his slip of saying for *us* instead of for *you* when talking about it. She wondered if there was a hidden agenda to what he was doing.

She put that out of her mind when she returned to her room. Setting outside her door was some mail that had come for her. A package lay on top of the other mail. She picked it up and looked at the return address. It was from Jay.

She took the package inside, closed her door, and set the package on her dresser while quickly scanning through the other mail. Frustrated but laughing that she was already getting junk mail, she tossed most of it into the small trash can by the door.

She sat down and opened the package. Inside was a thumb drive and a letter. The letter stated that the thumb drive was more photos he had taken and forgot to include with the last ones he sent. He wished her the best with the future of "Unknown America." Nothing more was written. Not even his name. She wondered why he had not even signed it. She set it all aside for the time being. She would look at the photos later. She had other things to do first. Looking at the two apartments came first. She had called about seeing them on her way home.

She drove to the one closest and met the owner. Together they looked at the apartment and discussed the requirements to rent it and what she would be free to do and required not to do while living there. It was a beautiful place, but Angela told her she had one more to look at that afternoon, but she would let her know either way by the end of the day. Even though the lady was a friend of Jeff's, Angela did not have a good feeling about it.

She drove about five miles out of town to the next one. When she drove up the driveway and saw it, she knew she wanted to live there. It was perfect - from the outside. She walked around the property surrounding the building until the owner arrived. He apologized for being late, then opened the front door and let Angela walk in. Angela fell in love the minute she walked inside. This was her place. She felt it. Her heart skipped a beat. She discussed the rules, regulations, and freedoms she would have if renting it. She was comfortable with everything the man said.

An hour later, she had the keys to her new apartment. She smiled from ear to ear. Her sister would be proud of her. And, yes, Jeff would approve too. She could not wait to tell Terri about it. She drove to the café to talk to her sister and show her the photos she had taken of the new place.

Terri saw Angela walk in and walked up to greet her. "Hi, Sis. How are you? I tried to call you earlier, but you never answered. I was starting to worry about you."

Angela pulled her cell phone from her purse. "Sorry, I had it on silent while I was at lunch with Jeff." She said without thinking.

"Jeff?" The Jeff? The one I told you to stay away from before the wedding?"

Angela hung her head, hiding a smile, but her eyes continued to look at Terri. "Yep, *that,* Jeff." She raised her head. "Now, don't go telling me how bad of a person he is.

You don't know him as well as you think. He isn't that man you told me he was."

"No? I will wait and see about that one. How serious are you two?" Terri directed Angela to the lounge area to avoid her afternoon crowd of customers.

"We are just friends, Sis. Nothing more, yet."

"Don't 'yet' me. You know..."

"Sis, Stop. I am old enough to make up my mind and wise enough to do my research. Jeff is a nice man. Trust me."

Terri laughed. "Trust me. Oh, you have a few things to learn about living here. Trust me, and Bless her heart are common sayings in this area. Each of those phrases has an alternative agenda."

"Okay, so I have a lot to learn. You will be happy to know that I will have a lot of time to learn it because I just put a deposit down on an apartment." She pulled up her photos on her phone to show Terri.

Terri looked at the front view and knew exactly where the apartment was. She looked at all the other photos Angela showed her of the place. Then noticed the next photo that her sister tried to hide.

"Wait! What is that photo? Where were you?"

Angela knew she had been caught. "Oops. Maybe Jeff and I are a little more together than I said we were. That is us at the beach while you and Adam were on your honeymoon."

"A little more? Okay, Sis. Spill it. What is going on?"

"Nothing. We are just friends, having a good time."

"Angela. I warned you."

"He is divorced. I told you that before, and I made sure of that detail before going anywhere with him. I was not going to break up a marriage. You should know me better than that."

"I was hoping I did. When was his divorce final?"

"It was finalized not too long ago. They have a mutual, friendly divorce. It is all good, Sis."

"I sure hope so, for your sake. I could care less about Jeff. I don't want him hurting you like his brother hurt me before we agreed to our friendship. Now Jay and I are at least talking to each other again."

"Wait, what? Now it is your turn to do the talking."

Terri laughed. It's all good, as you say. He called right after Adam and I returned from our honeymoon to wish us both well. He said he and his wife were happy. And that they are expecting their first child! We talked for a while. Even Adam spoke with him for a few minutes. We all agreed to keep the past in the past and be happy for each other."

"Wow, and you don't think Jeff can change? I think you are wrong. If Jay can change, and the four of you get along, trust that Jeff can too."

"You are right. People change. It will take me a while to feel that way about Jeff, though. He always seemed to have something up his sleeve."

Chapter Thirty-Six

Home Sweet Home

Terri had swallowed her concerns about Jeff by the time Angela was ready to move into her new apartment. It took her a few times of being with him and her sister to accept that he may have changed. Terri talked to Adam about her concerns. He reminded her that, yes, people change. All she had to do was look at him and his past compared to where he was now. When Adam reminded her of that, she nodded her head. Her husband was right.

The moving day took all day. Instead of hiring movers or a large box truck, they relied on friends with pickup trucks and SUVs. When they were about halfway through, they took a break and enjoyed lunch that Terri had her staff make and Steven deliver. He then stayed for a few hours before returning to open the lounge for the evening.

Angela was grateful for everyone's help. Terri took over putting things away in the kitchen. Adam, Jeff, and Steven moved the furniture into place. The apartment was the perfect size for one person, with enough room to have a small dinner party if she wanted. An open kitchen and dining area, which included the living room, made it look larger.

Angela stepped back for a few minutes and watched her home take shape. She began looking at the walls and imagining what artwork she would display. She had a lot of framed photographs she could hang on the walls if she wanted. Somehow, as she looked around, she was unsure if that was what she wanted. This was a fresh start for her. This might be a time for her to change her home décor aspirations.

Jeff stepped outside after they had eaten. He wanted a break from all the hustle. He had become used to the quiet after his divorce. This family time got to his emotions. He peeked through the kitchen window and watched the sisters work together. It was nice that they got along so well. He was even more impressed that Terri finally accepted him. He remembered when she did not like him much. During the months Terri dated and traveled with his brother, Jeff had not been a nice person to her. He thought he was looking out for his brother. He later realized he had possibly hindered what could have been a beautiful life. He soon changed his mind when he watched Terri and Adam together. And he knew his brother with his new wife were another happy couple. He hoped someday to have what they all had. Someone to love who loved him in return.

Terri helped her sister make the bed in the master bedroom.

"So, sis, how does it feel to have your own place again?"

"It feels great. It will take a little bit to get used to living in this area, but I've lived in a few places, so that process should not take me long. Plus, here I know people. I have moved to other places, not knowing a soul who lived there."

"I have no idea how you ever did that. I did it when I came here, which was difficult for me. I soon made friends and got to know the community, but it was still an adjustment."

"I'm glad you found this area to live in. It is beautiful."

"It is, and I think you will get accustomed to living here quickly. The people are amazing. We will need to take my next day off work to help you explore. There is a lot to do when you look for it. The place can also be a hole in the wall if you let it. I never let that happen."

"Well, we won't let that happen. Between you, Adam and Jeff, I don't have a chance of becoming a hermit in my house."

"Speaking of Jeff. What is the story there, girl? Talk to me. I have watched the two of you all day today. Something is happening. Talk." Terri sat down on her sister's bed. She wanted to hear the whole story.

"What? Nothing is going on."

"Oh, don't tell me that. I saw how he looks at you."

"What do you mean? We're just friends."

"If you think that, you must step back and think again. He likes you, Sis."

"And if he does? How would that make you feel? I mean, you used to date his brother."

"Yes, his brother. Not him. And as I have to admit to myself, he had changed from how he was when I knew him. I don't want you holding back how you may feel about him on my account. Love is love, sister."

Angela smiled big. Terri then saw the gleam in her sister's eyes that she was looking for.

"I was so afraid you would not approve. When you first told me not to get involved with him at the airport before your wedding, I tried to step away before anything happened. Then, when I went home, I ran into him again. His ex-wife lives there, and he was taking care of the last things following their divorce."

"How long have they been divorced? You're not a rebound attraction, are you? I don't want you to get hurt if that is the case."

"The divorce was a year ago. She just recently moved to a new house there and found things that were his or that she needed him to handle for her. They still get along, but the marriage fell apart thanks to her."

"Okay. I don't want you to get hurt if you want this relationship will grow into something stronger."

"I think I do. We get along so well. We agree we don't understand what it is between us, but we want to see where it goes."

Terri wiped her eye. She reached over and hugged her little sister, who had joined her on the bed. "I love you, sis. I hope it develops into something magical."

"Why the tear?"

"You and Jeff not understanding what the connection is? That is exactly how Adam and I feel. We still don't understand it. Looking at us or knowing our stories makes no sense to some people. We are like two unlikely souls who found each other. You and Jeff remind me of that."

Angela smiled and shook her head.

"What?"

"We used to think the same thing about you and Jay. The two of you were so different, but we thought it would work into something lasting for a while."

"Agreed. Unfortunately, or maybe, fortunately, it did not. Now he has found his soulmate, and I have found mine. Maybe you have found yours too."

"Maybe. Time will tell."

The sisters stood and left the room. It was late, and Terri said she needed to get to the lounge. Jeff and Adam had been outside talking while the girls had been inside. The four of them decided to go to the lounge for something more to eat and a few drinks to relax.

When they arrived at the lounge, the music was playing. Steven had started playing the music without Adam and the karaoke. When Steven saw Adam, he motioned for him to come to the bar.

"Hey, what's up? The music sounds good, by the way."

"Thanks. I decided the lounge needed something since you were not here. Are you going to get the karaoke going for the night?"

"I wasn't planning to, but if you have people wanting to sing, we certainly can. Let me tell Terri." Adam turned and walked right into his wife. Her smile was all he needed to see to know that he had her approval to start the karaoke system. He reached over and kissed her.

"You are the best, you know that?"

"I know. Now, go play. I don't think Jeff has heard you sing, and Angela has only heard you once."

"You got it. Any requests?"

"You know I always let you choose the songs. Let me go tell Angela and Jeff you are going to sing. Heck, maybe Jeff sings. I don't know. I know Jay didn't, but I don't remember if his brother does."

"Are you alright with your sister dating your ex-boyfriend's brother?" Adam asked. He was concerned that the connection would be painful for her.

"I am fine with it. When I first learned she was talking to him, I warned her to stay away from him, but then she told me that he had changed and was divorced. That helped. Then in the short time we have gotten to know him, I see that he has changed. Plus, we all have a good relationship with Jay now that he is married. And the fact that he and his wife live a good distance away. I don't have any issues."

"I am glad. You are a remarkable woman." He kissed her again and walked to the stage to set up karaoke for the night. A few minutes later, the music was loud, and Adam was singing. Other people were lining up to sing, including Jeff.

Terri checked on her kitchen crew before returning to sit with Angela. They talked while enjoying a glass of wine and listening to the singers.

"Well, sis. This is your new life. Think you can handle it?"

"This is the best. I think we may spend a lot of time here since Jeff seems to enjoy singing. You may get sick of us being here all the time."

"I don't even stay here all the time. I trust Steven to handle it, so there are nights I go home early. Adam isn't always here, either. He has another guy that does the

201

karaoke system some nights. I am surprised he was not here tonight."

The girls settled back and enjoyed the singing. Some were amazing. Others, Terri at least gave them credit for trying. She was not even brave enough to do that. When Jeff sang, both girls were impressed. He was good. Not as good as Adam, Terri thought. But, still worth listening to.

Chapter Thirty-Seven

Friendship

Angela settled into her apartment quickly. She loved the location and the neighbors she met when she went out for her walks around the property and the pond. On the other side of the pond was a walking trail for the public. She sat on the bench at the pond in the evenings to watch the world slow down. She often saw the Canadian Geese that lived there, the turtles in the pond, and a wide variety of birds. She also walked the trail when she had time.

She met other locals and some visitors as they walked the trail. She became familiar with the regular walkers, slowly making new friends. It was such a relaxing place to be. She was grateful that Jeff suggested it to her.

Angela spent a lot of time downtown and in the surrounding towns promoting her photojournalism business. She discovered a small publishing company and arranged for them to produce her next magazine publication. She was accustomed to sending her articles and photos online to the publisher she had been using. They were quick, but she liked the idea of being more hands-on all through the process to the final publication of her work, as well as being able to support a local business.

She continued seeing Jeff when they could work out time together. Her work took her out of town, and his job kept him busy on call for twelve-hour shifts as a helicopter pilot for the local med-a-vac associated with the local hospital. He had a lot of free time but could not leave the hospital during his shift. He loved his job and being able to help people when they needed it the most. He had some medical training through his military service but preferred the pilot work. He had four days off each week, which helped.

Jay contacted Jeff one day and, during their conversation, found out that his brother was dating Angela. He was unsure how to handle that, knowing there would be family gatherings and they would all be together. He shrugged it off when he realized unless he traveled to see Jeff, the chances of seeing Terri were slim. Besides, he was happily married. He was glad Jeff had found Angela. He liked working with her for the past few years. He and Terri had managed to revive their friendship after she and Adam married. He hoped it would remain. He loved his wife, but there was just something about Terri. She would always have a place in his heart. One he knew would only ever be as a friend. He was grateful for the friendship. He appreciated that Carrie loved him and accepted that friendship.

Jeff told Jay how he had met Angela and that in the beginning, Terri told Angela to stay away from him. He then ran into Angela in the town she lived and where his ex-wife had relocated.

"I am so glad Angela was moving away from there. I liked her when I met her but was not thrilled with the thought of having to see her and risk seeing my ex." Jeff told Jay.

"I would say not. You had a rough divorce. Everything okay with the ex now?"

"Yes. She settled down and is happy to be away from me."

"I am glad. You know Terri and I are friends, right? I even talked to her husband, Adam."

"I know. I think that is great. I like her and Adam together. And I am happy for you and Carrie."

"Thanks. I am happy. First time in a long time for me."

"I remember you were a mess after you and Terri broke it off. I hoped you would find someone new."

"We are a better fit, I think."

"I'm glad. Glad you realized things would not work out before you had to go through a divorce."

"Me too. I called to tell you to look for my latest travel report in Angela's magazine, but I guess you know all about that."

"Yes, she told me about giving you that assignment. You do know why she gave that to you, right?"

"Yes, I know. Angela didn't want me ruining Terri's wedding. She knew she had nothing to worry about when I told her I was married and had moved away. I took the job anyway. I'm glad I did."

"Why?"

"I learned a lot going back there after so many years since the original visit."

"Really? What is to learn about a tiny town?"

"Ha, little brother, you need to read the article and see the pictures to find out."

"Oh, that is cruel. I will have Angela tell me about it first."

"Good luck with that. Angela never shared her articles before they were published."

"I know. I have tried to read a feature article Angela is working on, but she hides it from me."

"That's Angela. I wish you the best of luck with her. She can be a handful. At least when it comes to business. And if she is anything like Terri, you are also in for a treat. Treat her right. She deserves it."

"I am doing my best, brother. Doing my best."

The brothers talked a little longer before hanging up. Jay never did tell him the true reason he called.

Jeff hung up his phone but didn't move. Something about that conversation seemed off. He wondered if Jay had something else on his mind that he didn't tell him. He shook his head and walked outside. If something were going on with Jay, he would have told him. He sat out on his deck and watched the moon rise. It was a beautiful night.

Carrie looked at Jay when he got off his phone.

"You didn't tell him, did you?"

"No," Jay said. "I could not find the words to tell him."

"You will need to tell him eventually."

"I know." Jay walked to their kitchen and poured himself a glass of red wine.

Carrie watched as he took it to the living room and sat down. She poured herself a glass of white wine and joined him. Her husband always poured her one when he had one. She knew things were weighing heavy on him. She took a sip of her wine and leaned her head onto his shoulder.

"We will get through this."

"I know. I am glad you are here for me."

" Forever and always." She raised her head and kissed his cheek.

Jay got up and walked outside their home to the deck. Carrie stayed behind, knowing he wanted to be alone. She had learned this about him early into their relationship. He was a private person. Jay appreciated her understanding. She did not demand to know his every thought. He shared most of what was on his mind with her out of respect and love for her.

Jay sipped more wine as he looked out over the land behind their house. He was so blessed. Now Jay had a life-changing issue to deal with. He was thankful that it was not a health issue. His business was at a breaking point. He had been approached by a major publication to join their team of photojournalists. The money was great. The benefits were also great. The issue was his need to be away from Carrie and all of his family. The initial assignment would take him out of the country for six months without contact with those he knew. His name would be changed, and his appearance would be altered for the time he was away.

Jay stood there as the darkness settled in. He wondered how he had managed to grab the attention of this publication to the point of their request. As he remembered, he shook his head. His documentation and photos of a local crime scene and his follow-up story. His ability to contact the victim's family, talk with the authorities, and do it all and stay safe. That is what now had him questioning his abilities. How did he get that good? He shook his head. It was his need to start his own business after his breakup with Terri and his desire to break the work connection with Angela. He had forced himself to step so far out of his comfort zone that it had led to his current situation. He had two weeks to make a final decision.

Carrie walked outside and stood by Jay.

"Babe, I know the offer is one you never expected. One you never dreamed would be out there, let alone available to you."

Jay put his arm around his wife. The love of his life. How could he walk away from her, even for six months, and not be promised a safe return home? "Babe, how can I go?"

"Babe, how can you not go?" This will be amazing for you and what it could mean to the country."

Jay took a deep breath and blew it out. He swallowed the last of his wine. He turned to Carrie, held her face in his hands, and kissed her. Together they walked back inside. His decision was made up. He had several phone calls to make the next day. The night now belonged to just him and Carrie.

Chapter Thirty-Eight

Getting Away

The weekend arrived with plans to get away for a few days. It was a rare occurrence that the manor had no guests. Sara suspected that Rachelle had done that on purpose. It was something she had never thought of doing. To her, the business had always needed to be open for anyone who wanted to stay with them. Except when they were doing the remodel, it had stayed open from when her grandparents started it many years prior.

"I cannot get over how Rachelle has made this place prosper over the last six months," Sara told Randall before he left to close up his office for a few days.

"I know. Who knew she had it in her?"

Sara laughed. "We both did. Remember?"

"Oh, I remember. Our trip as friends to Florida when we met her and made the connection. How can I ever forget it? That was when I realized I loved you. Rachelle knew it the moment she saw us together."

"You're right. She knew it before we did." Sara reached over and kissed Randall. "How could we not bring her here after that? She has been amazing."

"She has. And now the entire family can get away for a long weekend to just relax. Has that ever happened?"

"Never that I know of. This long weekend should be a lot of fun!" Sara was smiling and drinking her coffee. One of the best things was bringing her to join the family; the other was knowing when to step back and let others run the business. She, well, the whole family, had been blessed.

Sara's phone rang, and she answered it without looking at who the caller was.

"Hello, Sara speaking."

"Sara, hi. How are you?"

"Fine, what's up, Sis? Sara asked Heather.

"Are you ready to go yet?"

"No. And Randall needs to run to the office for a few minutes. Then we will be. Why?"

"Ben just talked with Barbara. She is not sure she and Steven will be able to go. She had an emergency child placement last night, which got complicated."

"Complicated? How?"

"Oh, nothing too bad. There were no fatalities."

"Heather! Now you have me concerned! What happened?"

"The child's family caused trouble, and the police had to be contacted. It is all taken care of now. The parents are both in jail, but Barbara must stay close to deal with the legalities."

"It's the weekend. Can't it wait until Monday or Tuesday?" Sara realized as soon as the words left her mouth that the question had an obvious answer. No. There is no right or wrong time when dealing with children in abusive situations. It was anytime.

"You know that answer."

"I do know the answer. I just wish Barbara was not so good at her job. We have the place rented for three days for all of the family. Who can we take along for that extra room we have if they can't go?"

"Ben suggested the newlyweds, Terri and Adam."

"There's an idea. I wonder if they can get away? Do you want to call them, or should I?"

"I will call them. That would be great to have them join us. I like the two of them."

"I do too. I like Terri's sister too. Too bad we don't have more space. We'd see if Angela wanted to join us."

"That would be amazing. Can we fit one more?"

"Maybe, but she'd have to share a room with Terri and Adam, and I am not sure they would want that early in their marriage." Sara laughed. Newlyweds. She remembers being one.

Two hours later, it was all arranged. Terri and Adam would be joining them. They did invite Angela, but she said she would be on an assignment and unable to join them. She told them she would join them for one of the days if she could.

The morning arrived for the family to head to their vacation. They had rented a large cabin in Pigeon Forge. It would be a chance to enjoy the mountains. They could each do their own thing or go together to the same place if they wanted. They were taking food to cook their own breakfast and a dinner or two. The other meals were whatever they wanted to eat out.

Sara and Randall planned to just lounge at the pool. Adam and Terri talked of driving through Cade's Cove they had heard so much about. Andy and Karen planned to take the little ones to the parks and entertainment places designed for toddlers. Gayle wanted to go with Adam and Terri because they mentioned seeing bears. Heather and Ben were taking their kids to Dollywood. It would be impossible to take a single car since they each had different places they wanted to go, so they formed a caravan and followed each other on the two-hour trip.

The owner met them when they arrived at the cabin and reviewed all the rules and amenities. They were impressed at all there was to do in the little community. These included a pool, tennis court, gift shop, and recreation room full of games. The kids were excited about the ice cream truck coming by every day.

That evening they all spent time at the pool and just relaxing. It had been a while since the entire family had been together. They had not had any family meetings for a while. Plus, they now had the addition of Adam and Terri. They had gotten to know Terri when she bought the Downtown Café and welcomed Adam into their lives easily when he got involved with the café. When he and Terri married, they considered them part of their family. They had no problem discussing family topics with them around.

As the conversation continued, Sara realized Adam was at ease with the family discussion. Her heart filled with pride, and she smiled as she watched her family. She felt a lot older than she was sometimes. It was true that she was the oldest family member, even though Randall was a little older. When she took those thoughts a little deeper, she realized she was the hierarchy of the family. That was a role she had never thought of until she stepped back from working so hard at the manor.

When the thoughts of the manor came to mind, her thoughts drifted over the years she had been there. So much to happen in her lifetime.

Adam had gone for a walk around the grounds while the family talked. He was at ease around them, but something was drawing him away. Several minutes later, he returned with things he found while he walked. Terri saw that he had his hands curled up, holding something.

"What treasures did you find here?" Terri asked, reaching to open his hand.

"What did you find?" Gayle asked. She was always curious about the unknown. To her, life was a mystery waiting to give more clues and be discovered.

"Just a few stones and this." Adam placed his treasures on the coffee table for everyone to see.

Sara gasped.

Adam looked at her, surprised. It was just a few rocks and an old key.

"What? Why the gasp?" Adam asked.

Heather and Andy looked at the small pile on the table. They both looked at Sara. They understood their sister's reaction.

"That style key has a history related to the manor." Andy volunteered the answer to Adam.

"That's interesting. A good connection, I hope."

Sara, Heather, and Andy looked at each other. "It was a good connection," Andy said.

"And yet, therein lies a mystery we have yet to solve," Sara said in a ghostly voice. She then changed her voice back to normal. "And one I was thinking about a few minutes ago while you were out walking." She added.

Heather rubbed her arm. The hairs were standing on edge. "That, my dear sister, is freaky."

"I know. That is why I gasped when I saw it."

"So, what is the mystery yet to be solved?" Terri asked. She had been listening and became curious.

Sara shook her head. "I'm not sure you want to know."

"Sure we do. Unless it is a deep dark family secret."

"We don't know yet. It could be nothing. It could be a lot more. The history of Bella Rose turned out to be a lot more than we expected... with the use of a key like that one." Sara pointed to the key.

"I am up to hear about it if you want to share. Maybe we can help solve the mystery." Terri offered.

"Maybe one day. Not tonight." Sara shook her head. She wanted to think about it first.

"Well, here, if you want to have the key, you are welcome to it." Adam lifted the key from the pile of stones and handed it to Sara.

Sara withdrew her hand. "No. You keep it. I have enough issues with the keys I do have. Believe me, when you hear the story, you will understand."

"Very well. I will keep these under lock and key, no pun intended, until you decide you want them. You are welcome to it at any time."

"Thank you. In reality, that key probably has nothing to do with my keys since it is so far from the estate. So feel free to keep it anywhere you want. I will have no need for it."

The family slowly gathered themselves up and retired to their rooms for the night. Andy told them he would have breakfast and coffee ready early in the morning. Everyone groaned. It was a vacation. Early breakfast time was not needed.

"Just make it simple so we can eat whenever we wake up. I am not pushing myself over the next three days." Randall said as he, Sara, and Gayle left the living room area.

Gayle turned to Adam before she left the room. "Hang on to that key. There is something about it that intrigues me," she whispered.

"I will. Anytime you want to see it let me know." Adam put it and the few stones into a plastic bag he brought for that reason. He was always collecting something.

Chapter Thirty-Nine

Assignment

Jay and Carrie spent the weekend discussing the job offer he had been given by the international magazine. How they had discovered him was beyond Jay. Maybe it was one of his photos or stories he had published. Maybe it had something to do with Angela and her connections, with the added idea that he needed to be as far away from Terri as possible. He doubted it was the latter because the last he knew, all was friendly between him and Terri and their spouses.

Carrie was impressed that her husband had been contacted to do such an assignment for the publication. If he was able to do this, he could become world known. Everyone and every publication would be requesting his services and expertise.

"Jay, I know this will take you away from me for six months, maybe longer if you need more time. It will be a slight hardship on me, but you forget, I had spent years being single taking care of myself before you entered my life."

"That's one of the things that keeps me wanting to do it and makes me want to stay. Fear that you will rediscover the joys of living on your own." Jay laughed. Her finding joy being on her own again was the least of his concerns.

"I know you will be fine while I am gone. You are a strong woman. You have your family and friends nearby to keep you occupied and your work to keep you busy. That is not my worry."

"What are you worried about?"

"Can I stay out of touch with everyone I know for that long?"

"It isn't like you will be alone while you are away. You will have other people with you to help document your journey. Yes?"

"Yes. Some. But they want me to do most of it alone. To document living alone, with little to no human contact. They want my documentary to be of the area as seen by someone on their own. Someone with few friends, no family, and little contact with the rest of the modern world."

"Are you sure you are the right person for that? You are from a corporate world. You had all the latest technology at your fingertips at one time. This assignment is going to be a stretch for you."

"Yes, but a true test of the imagination. The place has nothing modern. Running water, but that is about it. Electricity is limited. Even my write-ups will be done on paper and pen, for the most part, until I can get to power for the computer. There is no internet access. Which helps explain and provide the seclusion from family and friends."

"It is quite a challenge. But I know you can do it. And I don't want you to worry about me being here alone. I will be just fine. You know that."

"Yes, I do. You are self-sufficient. You have people around you who love you and will be there for you if you need them. I am concerned about the baby, but I will be back in time. Plus, if you need me for anything major or an emergency, you can contact the people who can contact me, and the assignment will end."

"So, call them and tell them you are ready, willing, and able to go." She rubbed her belly, which had not even begun to show. "We will be just fine."

Jay put his arms around his wife. He held her close. To think he would be unable to hold her or talk to her for six months bothered him. He had waited most of his life to find her. He had tried to keep Terri in his life at the end of their relationship until he realized it was too late. Now he understood why. He was meant to find Carrie.

Carrie held him close until he was ready to let go. Then she let him walk outside, where he called the publication company to let them know he was ready for the assignment.

Twenty minutes later, he returned to his wife with the date he was to leave and a few other details. They had two weeks to prepare.

Jay needed to call his brother back to tell him he would be away for a while. He would also ask Jeff to let Terri know what was going on.

"Hey, brother. No contact for a while and then twice in the same week? What's going on?" Jeff asked when Jay called.

"Well, little brother. I will be gone for a while. I have accepted a photojournalism assignment for a major publication that requires seclusion for a period of time."

"Seclusion? How much seclusion? And how much time? You will be in touch, won't you?"

"No. No contact at all for the time that I am away. Not even with Carrie. And it is for six months."

"Wait, you are not even going to be with Carrie?"

"No. No one. I cannot tell you where I will be either. Carrie will not even know for sure, although if she needs to reach me, she has the person to contact who can reach me."

"Are you feeling alright? Why would you do such a thing? And for that long!"

"Think about the recognition when it is all over, and my story is published? I will be in high demand for my skills."

"So, you would give up the life you know and love for a little recognition? You are such a selfish person."

"Jeff! I don't look at it that way. I see the study as about the human condition of living without the internet, without a lot of power. About how people cope after being so used to all our luxuries."

"Good for you. I see it as giving up on life."

"No way is that the issue. I will occasionally be around a few other people, mainly those who have lived away from civilization as we know it. And the majority of the time, I will be totally alone. For some, this will be history. For others, it will be a mystery. For all, I hope it will be interesting."

'Oh, it will be interesting for sure. And I cannot wait to see the photos you capture. Good luck, Brother. I will keep tabs on your family for you."

"Thank you, Jeff. I don't think Carrie will need much of that, but it does make me feel better about leaving her."

"Does Terri know you are leaving?"

"Not yet. I was hoping you could tell her and Adam."

"I would, but it will be much better coming from you."

"I don't have the time to contact her and explain everything. I barely have time to tell you. If you have any questions, Carrie is here and can answer some of them. Although she may not have all the answers."

"How can you do this to your family?"

"How could I pass it up? What an opportunity."

"It will get your name out there, that is for sure. Good luck, Brother. You will be in all of our prayers. Tell Carrie if she needs anything to call me. I know we have not become that close in the short amount of time you two have been together, considering what I was going through at the time with my divorce. But life is better now. For all of us. Well, I hope it is better for you during this expedition."

"It will be, brother. Thank you for the prayers. I will get back in touch with you as soon as I can. Love you."

"Love you, too." Jeff closed his phone and just stared at it. His brother would not be in touch with him for six months. He smiled briefly. He remembered when they were little kids and wished his brother would stop talking to him. Now, he was not prepared for this to happen.

Jeff opened his phone and closed it again. This news was better said in person. He went to his car and drove to the Downtown Café and Lounge.

Carrie arranged for a day off work the day she was taking Jay to the airport. She did not know her husband's final destination. She only knew the first leg of this flight was taking him to a connecting flight. Jay was not allowing her even into the airport to get a hint of where he was going. He hated being that way with her. He had never kept anything from her before. She knew his background. Everything. She knew about his relationship with Terri and how he messed things up with her. He was truly blessed that Carrie still loved him despite all that and his history.

Carrie parked her car in front of the airport. She and Jay stood on the sidewalk for as long as they could, saying goodbye. They both had tears as they gradually let go of each other, sliding their hands apart as they stepped out into separate directions. Carrie watched as her husband entered the airport, and the door closed behind him. Collecting herself, she got into her car and drove to the edge of the airport, where she parked facing the airfield. She wanted to watch the planes take off for as long as possible. Maybe Jay would see her parked there as the plane took off.

Jeff took Terri into her office to tell her the news. He knew that even though the relationship between her and his brother did not last long, their friendship would. Terri deserved to know what was going on, as much as he knew and could share. Adam joined them in the office, per Terri's request.

Terri took the news better than Jeff expected. For some reason, he thought more feelings were left between her and his brother. When he saw her reaction, he knew her love for Adam was true love. Adam's love for her was also true because he accepted the friendship Jay and Terri maintained. He only hoped that he and Angela would have that kind of love someday.

A week later, Carrie got a phone call.

Chapter Forty

Refreshed

The family returned to Bella Rose after spending three wonderful days away. They had kept busy most of the time while in the Smoky Mountains, but all agreed it was a much needed and refreshing change of pace. Everyone had new energy.

On the last night of their stay, they joined a few others from neighboring cabins for a large campfire near the pool. The younger people enjoyed a late-night swim before joining everyone for smores and drinks near the fire. Several people shared the experiences they had during their stay. Adam and Terri were thrilled to see a bear and her cups while driving through Cades Cove and showed everyone the photos they had taken on their phone. Terri had also taken several with her Canon Camera that she planned to post on social media. If any were exceptional, she would have the best ones enlarged and framed. She would hang at least one up on the gallery wall in the café.

One young couple from another cabin shared their wedding photos. They had just married in a small chapel in the mountains and were staying there for their honeymoon. Adam looked at Terri and said they should have married in the mountains. She then reminded him that they had. It was just different mountains. He smiled and hugged his wife. Yes, they had, and it was a beautiful wedding. Their honeymoon was even better.

Andy had spent some time at one of the local restaurants while away and was able to learn a few new recipes. It seemed that no matter where he went, he never stopped working. And maybe that was what led to his attempt to run away not long before. He needed to learn to relax more. His life had become filled with work and family but little to no alone time. Maybe Sara had the right idea of stepping away from the manor work for a while.

Ben and Heather had a wonderful time away. Their boys were old enough to play independently and make friends with other children their age. Marc had even made friends with a little girl older than him. Ben laughed at his son's antics to win a girl's heart at such a young age. He would need to keep an eye on him in the future.

Rachelle and Bob returned home with a new sense of living. They both had been so busy, like the others, that they had lost touch with each other the way things were when they first married. When they spoke with the newlyweds and looked at the photos they shared, it reminded them of what they had promised each other at their wedding, to always find time for each other. It was time to get back to that promise.

The doors to Bella Rose Manor opened early the day after everyone returned home. Guests were scheduled to arrive later that day. Andy began making snacks and planning the menu for the week. Rachelle and Heather cleaned all the rooms.

Ben continued his routine of getting fresh flowers for each new guest's room. Over the years, his gardens had produced the flowers they needed in the spring and summer. He no longer needed to rely on the florist shop in town. In winter, he supplied the room with flowers from the florist or dried floral arrangements he and Heather created from his garden flowers. He enjoyed working with his wife and how creative she was. He had been blessed when he found her, and he was glad they had worked things out and stayed together. He could not imagine his life without her.

Sara sat in her living room after Randall returned to work the day after they returned home. Gayle had gone out with a girlfriend from town, leaving Sara alone. She enjoyed the peace and quiet, but as she sipped her coffee, she began to wonder what she should be doing. Stepping away from the duties of the manor felt like such a good idea when she did it. She felt at peace about it. After spending all that time with family on vacation, she realized she missed them more than she thought. Maybe it was time to go back, or maybe it was time to look elsewhere for something to occupy her time. She finished her coffee and stepped outside. Soon she found herself sitting in the gazebo gazing out at the mountains. She smiled. No matter what she did in the future, this was where she belonged for the moment.

Terri was impressed with how her staff had kept the café and lounge going while she was away for a few days. Maybe this indicated that she could take longer breaks and enjoy her time with Adam more. They had talked about doing some traveling. After spending time in the Smoky Mountains, they both wanted to go more places. She knew Adam could take time off at most any time. His contractors could work without him. Steven could run the karaoke without him for a week or two. Terri decided she would talk with Adam about her idea. They were young; why not get away once in a while?

Steven was glad to see Terri back to work. It was not easy to run the place without her. They made a good team. He appreciated her confidence in him to run it all while she was away but preferred to be in charge of the lounge and bar, not the café.

Everything was back to normal by the end of the week. Guests enjoyed the manor and getting to know the family while exploring the neighboring highlights. A few repeat guests asked where Sara was and were surprised to hear she had stepped down. Some questioned if she was okay or had health issues. They were assured that she was in perfect health.

Sara heard about the concerns and decided it was time she got involved again with the manor. She would talk it over with Randall and get his feedback. Randall had always been her supporter and the person she bounced ideas off. He tended to have a different perspective, which helped her see things clearer.

During their conversation about her returning to work at the manor, Randall suggested she do something else. She was intrigued by what he had to say. It certainly would be a change for her. It was something her mother did, as did her grandmother. She had thought about it years ago but never pursued the idea. Life got in the way, forcing her to push it aside. A lot of it she had temporarily forgotten. Maybe Randall was right. It was time to write again. It was time to dig up the past, write the stories, and include the last several years' events.

Sara dreamed that night. She had not had a dream in a long time. She attributed her lack of dreaming to her lack of sleep. When she awoke the next morning, she was not full of energy as she usually was when she first got out of bed. She lay there trying to recall the dream. Searching behind her closed eyes for details she may have missed. Colors that would stand out. People or places that had been included.

She heard Randall enter the room and speak. She raised her hand to stop him, never opening her eyes. Somehow, although he never saw that reaction before, he understood. So much so that instead of turning around and leaving the room, he carefully backed out and quietly closed the door.

He drank his coffee, wrote Sara a note, and left for work.

Chapter Forty-One

Emergency

Jeff answered his phone on the third ring when he noticed it was from Carrie. Jay told him that Carrie would contact him if she needed anything while he was away. He did not expect her to, and certainly not so soon after Jay went on his mission.

"Carrie, It is good to hear from you."

"Thanks. Jay told me I could contact you. I hope it is okay for me to call."

"Of course it is. I did not expect it so soon, but what can I do for you?"

"Have you heard from your brother since he left?"

"No. And I don't expect to since he told me it was a secret mission and he was not to have contact with friends or family members. Why?"

"I got a call last night. I was not near my phone, so I missed it. They did not leave a message, but the number is one I am not familiar with. I was hoping it was Jay, and maybe he called you too."

"No, I have not gotten a call from him. Sorry. I am sure he would have left a message if it was important or if it was him."

"You are right. I just miss him. I know it has only been a week, and I have several months before he returns home. I hope it will get easier as time goes on."

"It will."

"Thanks, Jeff. I will try not to be a nuisance to you while he is away. I was on my own before he came into my life; you would think I would be okay now."

"This time, it is different. You are with the love of your life, and now he is gone. Lucky for you, he will be returning. The six months will go faster than you think."

"Thanks, Jeff. Yes, I know they will. I guess I worry too much."

"You have no need to worry. He may be on his own for the assignment, but I feel he has people watching over him."

"I hope so. Thanks again, Jeff. I will be fine."

"You are welcome. I am here for you."

"I will let you know if he does contact me. Goodbye, Jeff."

"I will let you know if he calls me as well. Goodbye, Carrie."

Jeff disconnected from Carrie's call. He hoped his brother was all right. A strange phone number and no message could mean Jay was in danger. If he had been, Jeff would have hoped that Jay would have a least left a word or two. But, if he had done that, it could have made matters worse for Carrie. She may have worried more; he knew Jay would not want that for his bride.

Jeff went about his day as normal. He never mentioned to anyone the phone call from Carrie. There was no need. While he was at work and had some free time, he logged into his computer and did some research – looking for Jay. An hour later, he still had not found anything that would lead him to know where his brother was. An emergency call came in as he was closing his computer. It was time to fly.

Sara heard the helicopter fly over the manor. It was rare to hear it so close. She walked outside to watch where it may be going. She was shocked when it seemed to land nearby. She listened for a few minutes and could still hear the propellers. She could not hold in her curiosity, so she got in her car and drove down Rose Lane to the bottom of the hill. She hoped she would know which direction to turn when she reached the bottom.

There was no need to know which way to turn. The helicopter had landed in the field across the main road. She parked her car and stepped out. She knew to stay out of the way but could not help but watch the medical team as they worked on the accident. Sara shuddered. It brought back memories of how it must have looked when Ben and Heather had been in their accident. She lifted a prayer for those involved.

It did not take them long, and the helicopter soon took off with the patient to the hospital. An ambulance left soon afterward to go back to the station. The police stayed behind to clean up the debris as the wrecker hauled the car away. It had been a single-vehicle accident, but the car was totaled.

Sara turned her car around and returned home, where she broke down in tears. She said a few more prayers and made a mental note to call Jeff later and ask for any details he had. She was going to watch the evening news to see if it had made the news. Being a single-car accident, it may not have.

Sara's phone rang a few minutes later. It was Randall calling her to make sure she was safe.

"I am fine. Why do you ask?"

"I heard on the scanner about an accident at the bottom of the hill. I was hoping it was not you or someone from the manor."

"No, we are all fine. I drove to the bottom of the hill when I heard the helicopter land, but I did not recognize the car involved."

"Okay. That is good news. I worry anytime I hear of an accident and know that you may be out on the road."

"No need to worry at any time. If I were ever in an accident, you would be about the first to know. You are my emergency contact person."

227

"That is good to know. You are mine as well. I hope there is never a need for someone to use them."

"I agree. Please be careful when you come home. After seeing that accident, it reminds me of how we take driving for granted and don't pay enough attention all the time."

"I will be careful. We may want to check the area tonight and ensure all the debris is off the road. So often, the police don't clean it all up."

"Sounds like you have been around a few accidents?"

"I hear a lot of stories."

"I'm sure you do."

Randall changed the subject and told Sara he needed to return to work. "I love you. See you when I get home later," he ended the conversation.

"I love you too. See you later." Sara then disconnected the call.

Sara poured herself a cold glass of water and entered her spare room. Her desk inside was covered with papers and journals. Everything she had left sitting for the last several months and some for over a couple of years. Life had taken over, and she never returned to what she wanted to work on. Her writing would start up again, but first, she needed to clean.

An hour later, she looked at the desk's cleared top. Clear, that is, except for a blank notebook, her laptop computer, and a key.

Chapter Forty-Two

Words

Sara called Adam and left a message asking if he still had the key he had found while on their vacation. At the time, she did not want anything to do with it. Now, after finding the one on her desk, under all those papers, she wanted to not only see it, she wanted to keep it.

Adam called her an hour later and said he would be glad to drop it off if she wanted. She said she would come to the Café and Lounge the next morning to get it if that was all right. Adam was fine with that agreement. It would save him time and money.

Once she had her answer, Sara could work on her writing plan. The process would take planning, and she didn't start until just before it was time for her to make dinner for Randall. He said he would come home late, so she had extra time to organize the journals. She placed the newer ones at the bottom, and several minutes later, she had the oldest journal on top, with a blank notepad flat on her desk so she could start making notes.

She wrote the latest events about Bella Rose Estate and her family on the first page. She continued to write until she heard Randall walk into the kitchen. She jumped and apologized immediately for not having dinner ready.

"That is perfectly fine, Babe. I do not need to eat the moment I get home. I appreciate you having our meal ready most of the time, but it is not anything I require. We could work on making something together for a change."

"What do you have in mind? I didn't even make it to the store today."

Randall opened the pantry door and pulled out a can of sauce and a pizza crust. "When in doubt, make a pizza. It is easy enough to make. Here, cut up the onion." He handed Sara the onion and a knife. They had not cooked together in a few months. Whoever made it home first was the one who made the dinner.

Sara smiled and gave Randall a kiss on his cheek. She had chosen a great man when she chose him. His patience and understanding had come in handy many times in her and her family's lives.

Together they made the pizza, and Randall placed it in the oven to bake. While they waited, Sara made a salad for the two of them. Their daughter was still spending time with her friend, giving them one more night alone.

Sara told Randall about finding the key at the bottom of her pile of papers and journals. He found it fascinating and asked about the key Adam had found.

"I called Adam, and I will pick that one up tomorrow. I want to compare all of the keys. I know what the ones on that desk from the manor go to. I wonder what the other ones unlock and if they are somehow related. They all seem to be similar."

"I would love to have more time and help you look. You are quite the mystery girl."

"Thanks for at least wanting to hunt for more journals and read through them. I never know what I will find."

"You do have a way of bringing up the past."

"I only bring up what I find."

"True, but it is time for you to bring it to light so others can read about it and not just for the family."

Sara smiled as she took a slice of pizza that Randall had cut a few minutes after pulling it from the oven. "I agree. I did talk with my siblings about it when I stepped away from the manor work. Mainly about reading more in-depth and to see if there are more journals anywhere."

"Did you tell them you wanted to write about it?"

"Not at that time. We had decided before not to make it public. I will talk to them again. Time has passed, and maybe they will change their minds and want to share our history."

"It is worth asking. I would love to see what you write. You have told me about the journals, but I know there must be more to them than what you have shared."

"There is a lot more," Sara said. Her mind drifted back to some of what she had read; in so doing, it had changed their lives.

"I am sure you will find the words to tell a great historic story of Bella Rose."

"Thanks. Even if it doesn't sell many copies, it will be fun to write it and for the family to have it. Not everyone needs to read the entirety of the journals."

"That would be time-consuming. Plus, the wear and tear on what is historic. You don't want everyone handling them."

"True."

"Once you have read through them, you may want to put them inside a shadow box on display in the grand room of the manor."

"That sounds like a wonderful idea."

"That way, all the guests could see just a sampling of your mother and grandmother's words written years ago."

"I will bring that up to my family when I ask about writing the family history. Thanks for the idea."

"Anything I can do to help." He touched his wife's hand. He loved her with all his heart. He always had. Even before she knew he existed. He nearly laughed.

"What was that noise?" Sara asked and laughed.

"I thought about how long I have loved you. I don't think you knew I was alive when I first knew."

"Oh, I knew you were alive. I just was not interested," Sara admitted.

"You need to add that to one of your books."

"I'll be sure to add that in the modern chapters." Sara kissed her husband on the forehead.

The next day she sat in her spare room she referred to as her writing room. She picked up the key and examined it closely. She then walked to the office in the manor and opened the top drawer. In the back of the drawer, she found the keys she wanted. They had been a part of her family from before she was born. She took them home with her to compare them. She heard a vehicle driving up her driveway when she reached the front door. She turned as Adam parked his car and got out.

She met him on her front porch. He wanted to know more about the keys when she showed him the other ones in her hand. And decided to bring the key to her instead of waiting for her to come to the Lounge.

She smiled. She forgot that not everyone knew about the keys. At least not the entire story. She explained it briefly, telling him they were used to open special pieces of furniture. She added that he could read all about it in the book she would write. He was content with those answers. Sara was glad he had not pushed for a deeper story.

Adam returned to his car. He sat inside and watched as Sara went inside her house. He sensed there was more to those keys than she was revealing. He would find out someday. He started his car and drove away.

Sara took the keys to her writing room and laid them side by side. Then, she opened her laptop computer and began to write. Words that would tell the story of the keys. Or at least as much as she knew about them. There was still that mystery about them that no one had been able to explain.

Chapter Forty-Three

Conversations

Adam drove home and met Terri, who had just arrived from the café. Since their wedding, they never wanted to be apart. Adam's construction work was beginning to take him out of town. So far, he had made it home each night, although some nights were a little late. Terri had stopped working at the Café until closing each night. Instead, she had learned Steven and her crew could handle the business without her. She was thankful to have employees she could trust.

Terri did not feel like cooking, so she brought food from the café. Adam was just happy to eat dinner with his wife. While they ate, Adam told her that he had taken the key to Sara.

"What is it about the key?" Terri asked.

"I am not completely sure. Something about unlocking secrets about Bella Rose. Sara is writing a book about it."

"That will be interesting to read. I wonder if she needs help publishing it. I can get her together with Angela and see if my sister has the connections she could use."

"That would be awesome. You may want to call Sara tomorrow or some time and suggest that. Or check with Angela first to see if she knows someone."

Terri and Adam continued to talk about different things. Terri mentioned that one of her employees would have a baby soon, and she needed to find a temporary replacement. That led them to talk about having their own children. Terri said she was almost too old to have any but would love to try. Adam winked at her.

"What you are thinking is not what is specifically on my mind."

"A guy can try," Adam laughed.

"I am thinking more of becoming a foster parent. Have you talked with Barbara for any amount of time? Her work with the foster care system is impressive. There are so many children out there that need a safe place to live and a family that loves them."

"How would we handle them? We both work." Adam voiced his concern.

"I have been wondering about that. Parents do it all the time. Both parents work. They take them to daycare or a babysitter."

"I would prefer they not have that much time on their own. I sometimes work late. Eventually, some of my work will take me out of town overnight. I don't like that, but the bigger jobs are farther away."

"I know. I was thinking about that today. Then I realized that with the people I have on staff now, plus with Steven there, I can leave the Café business to be run by my employees. And maybe I can let them run it without me for a while."

"Gives us something to think about. Have you talked with Barbara about it? I'm sure she would love you to apply to become a foster parent."

"I can call her tomorrow and have her come over to talk with us so we can at least be ready when the time comes. We may need to child-proof the house."

"Child-proofing the house is not what concerns me. I am a contractor, so I think I can handle that task."

"What worries you about it?"

"Not being good enough."

"How can we not be good enough?" Terri then remembered his time in jail. She hoped that would not play a part in the selection process. Adam had come so far beyond those days.

Adam looked at Terri and knew what was on her mind.

"I don't know, but it could be anything." She skirted the thought. "Let me call Barbara tomorrow and have her come out to talk with us."

"That sounds good to me." Adam kissed his wife and wondered how he got to be so lucky in love.

The couple talked for another hour about becoming parents and how it would change their lives. The conclusion was that being there for children who needed a loving family and safe home would be a blessing they could not walk away from. If they could pass all the requirements.

Terri talked to Steven the next day at the lounge to find the best time to talk to Barbara. Steven told her that Barbara was planning to be there that evening and she could talk then. Steven did not ask Terri why she wanted to talk to her.

Barbara walked into the café early that evening. She had gotten off work a little early and had no children to place, so she took advantage of the free time. Terri met her at the door.

"Hi, Barbara. How are you?"

"I'm good. I finally got a break from work. How are you? Did you enjoy the family vacation?"

"Yes, Adam and I had a great time. It is surprising how we forget to take time out for ourselves."

"I know. I tell my families they need to take a break from time to time, but I never seem to do it myself."

"Except for our wedding cruise, I have not gotten away for a while either. The cruise was exciting, by the way. You and Steven need to take one someday."

"We have talked about it. Just never get around to booking one. Is Steven in the lounge?" Barbara changed the subject.

"Yes, he is. Barbara, if you have a few minutes, I want to talk to you about something."

"Sure. What about. Nothing going on regarding Steven, is it?"

"Oh, no. Not at all. Steven is a godsend. No. Adam and I have begun talking about becoming foster parents."

"Oh, that is wonderful! I can set time aside in a couple of days unless you want to discuss a few things tonight. I am free for a change."

"Free, yes. But, do you want to talk business after hours?"

"When it comes to the children, I can talk about helping them any time of the day or night. They need people to love them and show that they care."

"That is what Adam and I want to provide for them. A safe place to live and a loving family."

"I think the two of you would be amazing foster parents," Barbara said.

"Thanks. I do have a few main questions."

"Let me order something to eat first, then we can talk."

"Of course. Order anything you want; it's on the house." Terri said. She took Barbara's order and went to the back to help make it. She called Adam and asked if he wanted to come down and talk to Barbara with her. He said he was on his way.

A few minutes later, Adam arrived, and he and Terri sat with Barbara while she ate.

"What are some of your questions about being a foster parent?"

"You get right to the point," Terri laughed. She liked that about Steven's wife.

"First and foremost is that I have a criminal record. How does that affect the chances of being a foster parent."

"It depends on the charge and how long ago."

"A felony drug charge about seven years ago or more."

"If it was over five years ago, even though it is a felony, you are fine. We will need documentation of the charge and conviction. Also, your release papers with details of any ongoing probation or requirements."

"That surprises me. But I am thrilled. I have no problem getting the required papers to you. I will connect you to my probation officer if you need to talk with her."

"Thanks. You say, 'her,' I assume you are referring to Tessa."

"Yes, how did you know?"

"She is the only female working the felony cases in this area."

"The crime and time were in Washington, but I am here now, so they transferred the case. Now that my time has been paid, I don't stay in touch with her anymore."

"Okay. What other questions do you have?" Barbara asked.

They continued to talk until they could not hear the music of the lounge playing. It was already closing time.

"I will check my schedule and set up an appointment with you to complete the necessary paperwork. I am thrilled you want to join the foster care program as a parent to our needy children." Barbara stood to leave.

"Thank you." Terri stood with Adam, and they reached out to shake her hand.

They each went their separate ways. Barbara went to find Steven and told him she was going home to get some sleep.

The following day Barbara called Terri to set up a time to sit and fill out the forms.

A few days later, they sat in Barbara's office filling out all the paperwork and learned how she had become so involved in the foster care system. They were surprised that a broken system that caused her so much pain and loneliness led to this much-improved program. Her resilience in overcoming hardships as a young child was enough to inspire anyone to become involved.

Terri wanted to know how they could help her more. They knew it was going to take almost six months before they would be able to receive their certification for foster parenting and asked if there was anything they could do before that.

Barbara said one of the things she would love to see was more awareness of the need for foster parents.

Terri suggested posters or even an event at the café to get the word out. Maybe a fundraiser to start a local supply base for foster parents to access everyday things or even special supplies. Terri didn't know what was needed most, but she wanted to help.

Barbara told her she did not know what was needed at the moment but would keep her in mind if she thought of anything more than getting the word out about the need.

Terri said she would gladly hang a poster in her front window if Barbara had one.

Barbara opened her file cabinet and pulled out her latest poster, handing it to Terri. "Thank you so much for this. Not everyone is willing to do that much."

"How can they not promote this? Every child deserves a loving home."

"For so many years, the representation of foster parents and children who needed a different home came with a negative connotation."

"It's not the children's fault they need a better home."

"No, but adults seem to think that a bad parent makes for a bad child, and they are unwilling to risk having a 'bad' child."

"We need to do what we can to change that. Adam and I will talk about what can be done."

"Thank you both so much." She said, aware that Adam had not said anything this time. Barbara was accustomed to Adam doing most of the talking. To see him mostly quiet was a bit unusual.

"Why don't we keep the posters up, talk to everyone we see at the café and lounge, and then schedule a dinner meeting to tell the public about it? Get the word out. Some people may not realize how great the need is"

"You are right. We need to keep the posters up, and even if we don't say anything, it will at least be on their minds for a few minutes if they see the poster."

Chapter Forty-Four

Love at First Sight

Terri and Adam took their time and made their spare bedroom one that would work for an infant or a teenager. The crib could be easily moved out of the room, and the décor changed. The walls were neutral in color and worked for both males and females.

Terri arranged that she could take time off work immediately after receiving their first foster child.

Then, they waited.

The waiting period felt longer than the four to six months it took. All background checks, the interviews, the training, the home inspection, and finally, the approval.

Terri called Barbara one day and asked if there was anything else they could do. Barbara said no. And not to be disappointed that they were not getting a child. By not getting one, it meant there was not a child needing foster care. And that was the ultimate goal. Every child deserved a loving home environment and loving parents.

While they waited, their marriage bond became closer. All the talk and planning for a child led them to see how much they loved each other. They never knew what drew them to each other, and now maybe it was because God knew their love would blossom and be what they and a child or children needed. A couple truly in love.

Terri was at work when Barbara called her. She needed Terri and Adam immediately for an infant female. One that had been exposed to drugs and may have witnessed a crime, although she was far too young to speak about it. They only hoped she was young enough to never remember it.

Terri called Adam, who was working on a construction site out of town. Adam said he would be home as soon as he could. Terri understood. Her husband always had a good project manager on the job, and Adam would take a few moments to leave that job in Donovan's capable hands. They had worked together for a few years and trusted each other. Both men had the same work ethic.

Terri drove to the police station, where the child was being cared for by an officer. Barbara was filling out the paperwork on the laptop when Terri arrived.

"So glad you could make it on such short notice. I had no idea which family to place this innocent child with, and your name came to mind. You will be perfect." Barbara stood and indicated for Terri to follow her to another room.

There Terri saw the infant sleeping in the officer's arms. "Such a peaceful little soul," Terri said. Suddenly she was nervous. What were all those things they had learned in the training sessions? She felt unqualified.

Barbara lifted the child from the officer and gently handed Terri the bundle of receiving blankets that cuddled the tiny baby girl. "Her name is Makenna."

Terri looked down at the sweet baby girl now sleeping in her arms. Terri's heart melted. She knew she was not supposed to feel that way about a foster child. She knew she was to keep her emotional attachment distant. If she did not, her heart would be broken when it came time to return the child to its parents or be adopted.

Adam arrived thirty minutes later and rushed into Barbara's office. He stopped in his tracks when he saw his bride holding a small bundle. He knew, wrapped inside the receiving blankets, was the beginning of a new life for him, his wife, and this child. Their time with the infant was only temporary, but he hoped they would be a good influence on it, even if they never knew what impact they might have when the child grew up.

He kissed Terri and then looked at the being about to change his life. His smile grew bigger when he looked down at the child sleeping in Terri's arms. A tear escaped his eye. This was love.

Terri placed the bundle into Adam's arms. "Say hello to Makenna."

"Hello, Makenna. Welcome to your new world." Adam touched the baby's cheek with his index finger. The whole outside world disappeared from his mind. There was no greater feeling than what he felt at that moment.

Terri touched his arm and brought him back to reality. Barbara was talking.

"I can see the love you instantly have for Makenna. May I remind you this is only temporary? However, due to the circumstances of her parents, temporary could be for a long time. Are you able to commit to that? I know you signed on to be foster parents long-term. I want you to be honest with yourselves and with me. As we had discussed in the beginning, foster care could be having a child for a few days, a few years, or longer."

Terri and Adam looked at each other and the innocent bundle in Adam's arms. "Yes, we are in it for as long as needed," Terri said, and Adam nodded in agreement.

"Good. I knew I had made the right decision in placing her with you. Do you have any questions?"

Terri and Adam shook their heads. Both of them were at a loss of what to ask.

"Alright, then. Let me finish the paperwork, and you can take this little one home."

"Home." Adam looked at Terri. "Yes, now we have a real home."

"And a family," Terri added.

"Yes, you do," Barbara said. "Try to love her so you can give her back when the time comes. That part will not be an easy one."

"I already can't imagine that. But I know if her parents could have taken care of her, they would have. In time maybe they will be those loving parents again."

"In the meantime, we are here for her," Adam added. He handed Makenna back to Terri before signing the papers Barbara had completed.

An hour later, Terri and Adam walked into their home with Makenna in the car carrier. This was the beginning of a whole new life for them.

Life changed immediately for the new foster parents. Terri, who had worked all her adult life, now was a stay-at-home mom most days. After the first two weeks, she felt confident taking Makenna out with her for errands and stopping at the café to check on her crew. Her café crew loved when the two of them stopped in and fell in love with the new addition almost as fast as Terri and Adam had.

Adam continued to work with his construction company but hated being away. His latest projects were out of town and required overnight stays. He felt bad leaving Donovan to do all of them, so the two men made up a work schedule. One would go home for a few days while the other one stayed. Then they would switch times. The project was scheduled to finish in another month. The two men could not wait. They did their best to make the next project closer to home.

When Adam could not be home, he and Terri face-timed, and Terri always ensured that Mackenna was there to listen and for Adam to see her.

When Adam came home the first time after being away a full week, he was surprised at how much their baby seemed to have grown. When he spoke to her, she smiled. The face-timing had worked. He may not have been there, but she had gotten to know his voice.

The days turned into weeks with Makenna. The love they had for her only grew. Yet Terri kept reality in the back of her mind. Someday, she would have to give her up.

Chapter Forty-Five

Home

Six months had gone faster than Jay expected. His time on his own, exploring various places, proved how resilient a person could be when they had to be.

His initial belief was that he would have no contact with his family and friends. He assumed he would be around other people and live a normal life while writing and capturing the photogenic world he was exposed to. The reality was quite different.

Alone. All alone. He could not make his own decisions other than what to write and photograph. His food was delivered while he slept. He had no choice in the food. No choice in how often it was delivered. He could choose when to sleep but found he slept when it was dark and awoke with the sun. He lost track of the days he was gone.

He wrote. Every day he wrote something and captured the world around him. Over time, his thoughts and writings changed. The photos he took changed. In the beginning, he noticed the larger world around him. The landscape. The things in the distance. The beauty of a big wild world.

The ideas he wrote changed. In the beginning, he wrote more general ideas. An overview of the world he sat in. He wrote as if his story was a history of where he was. A look at the big picture of things.

Over time, he began to notice the little things. The birds, the animals he encountered, and the sounds around him. He noticed the world at his feet. The flowers, the weeds, even the bugs at work.

His words to people wavered. He began by speaking of missing his family and friends. He changed to write about himself and how he was coping with the life he was seemingly condemned to live. The anger of having no choice in so many things. The fear that he would never get out of this living.

The nights turned into days with little sleep. He wrote of craving human interaction, human touch, and another human voice.

His long stories became short notes. Then just single words. Adjectives. Adverbs. Nouns. Individual. On a single page.

On the day the six months were up, he heard the plane coming again. He knew it was time for another food delivery and expected the drone to drop it off. Instead, the plane's engine turned to silence. He raised his head from an attempted sleep.

A human! A live person was walking towards him. For a moment, he was thrilled. He stood up. Then wiped his eyes for fear that he had reached the stage of aloneness where he saw mirages. When he opened his eyes again, the man stood before him. Jay reached out and touched him. Then grabbed his arm. The man responded by touching his shoulder and spoke. Jay heard the sweetness of the human voice. It would not have mattered what the man said. Jay would have been thrilled. His words were more than he had come to expect.

"Time to go home, Jay. Your time is over here."

Jay could hardly believe his eyes nor his ears. It had been so long since he had seen another person close to him.

"Has it been six months already?" Jay asked. He was trying to be lighthearted. Inside he was jumping for joy.

"It has been six months, yes. You have been to two island countries, seen some amazing sights and I am sure you have taken the best photos possible. I am looking forward to what you have written."

Jay's smile faded. He knew he had slacked off during the last several days of isolation. His stories had become single words. His photos were what anyone else with a camera would take photos of. Jay did his best work at the beginning of his adventure.

"I am not sure how the ending is going to be. The beginning is when I had my best ideas."

"We assumed that would be the case. We are prepared for whatever you have for us. Are you ready to go home?"

"Are you kidding? I have been ready ever since I arrived."

"I understand that thought. It's not easy being separated from your wife and other loved ones."

"How is she?"

"She is fine. Anxious to see you but thrilled you will now be home for a while."

"I am anxious to see her too. You know she is pregnant."

"Let's get you back to the base of operations. Then we can drive you to the airport for your flights home to see your wife and future baby."

"That is the best news to hear."

Together they gathered up Jay's belongings. He had collected small stones and several shells during his stay. All of his photos were on the SD card in the camera. His writings were in a journal he had kept.

Jay looked around his living quarters before they left. Everything that he owned fit into the backpack he had. He may have been alone, but they had provided the basic comforts of home in his cabin. There was no TV, no radio. His human contact had simply been that of observing activities on the computer they provided him after his first three months. The first three were to see if he could endure without any human contact. The last three had limited human observance but no physical or verbal contact.

He had survived his time here. He was excited at the end of that tour, so to speak. He wanted human touch after the first three months. Instead, he was immediately shipped off to a remote location for the next three months.

Jay was just thrilled that it was over. Jay packed his belongings in one suitcase and used the other for all the souvenirs he had found along the way.

Two hours after he thought he saw a mirage, Jay was on his way to the airport to fly home. Those in charge of the event were unavailable but would be in touch for his writings and photos. He would take his time on those. Being with his wife was all the therapy he needed.

Overnight on the plane allowed for watching people and hearing the chatter among them. He had missed that so much. He wanted to join it. But even more, he wanted to be in the arms of Carrie. He missed her most.

Eighteen hours after leaving the secret location, Jay was in Carrie's arms at the airport. He never wanted to let her go again. The six months alone had taught him to value his life and cherish those he loved.

Carrie saw a change in her husband even as she drove them home from the airport. She expected such. She hoped it was not too much of a change. She had fallen in love with the person he was when he left. Could she love this new person? She watched him that evening. He walked around like their home was new to him. He remembered where everything was, but he seemed to view it with more passion.

As they lay in bed that night, Jay never let go of Carrie. He had never held her while they slept before. She liked sleeping in his arms. Liked to feel his breath on her neck. Liked her arm across his stomach when she rolled over with his gentle grasp across her shoulders. Listening to him breathe was a much more welcome sound.

The next morning Jay rose early. Carrie found him standing out on their deck, drinking coffee. She poured herself a cup and joined him. In silence, they watched the sunrise.

Life for the two of them was never going to be the same. Jay had changed. Carrie did not realize how much. Jay knew he felt differently about life and living. He hoped he could explain it.

Later that morning, Jay received a phone call from the company that had sent him on his adventure. They wanted to meet with him to discuss his photos and writings. He told them it would be a week before he could go through everything and edit his work for them. They told him they wanted to read the raw writings. Those would reveal his true emotions while he was isolated. The raw words were what they wanted. Jay agreed with the understanding that they would only get a copy of his work. The original was his to keep and edit as he saw fit.

The man began to argue until Jay reminded him that he had not signed any contract giving them rights to his original. And Jay reminded him that he had the right to write his own book. They had the rights to the story, but he could write the book.

The man sighed. Jay was right. They had left that option open to Jay.

Jay scheduled to meet with the company a week later to show his photos.

Carrie took time off work to spend with Jay. She did not want to be away from him. She offered to help Jay look through the photos and read his writings before his meeting. He accepted her offer of the photos but declined her help with his writings. He knew what he had written and was unsure Carrie was ready to read it. He had changed while he was away. His thoughts had drifted over the days, weeks, and months. When he came home, he knew what he wanted. He wondered if Carrie could accept the process he had traveled in his mind.

252

Chapter Forty-Six

Family Isn't Blood

Terri sat in her great-grandmother's rocking chair long after Makenna had fallen back to sleep after her two AM feeding. Her gaze watching this little one sleeping, soon found her with her eyes closed and dreaming.

Makenna was running around, playing with two other children in the gardens. A little boy was swinging high on the double set swing set. Another little girl was playing with a doll on the steps leading to the garden path. The stone path led to the garden gate that stood open. The sun was shining bright. Birds sang as they ate from the feeder and splashed in the birdbath.

Adam woke up and smiled. He knew his wife and child were in the living room sleeping. He rose and tip-toed to the doorway. As he often did at that hour of the day, there he saw pure love. The love of a mother and child. The way life should be.

Sadness crept in and diminished his smile. *The way life should be.* He saw Terri's love for this little one and felt it himself. Thinking that the baby's biological parents could not share this love tore at his heart. How could anyone not feel love for her? He and Terri would give her all the love they could and hope it would have a lasting effect.

Terri stirred and opened her eyes. She noticed Adam standing in the doorway and shook her head. He walked over to her and kissed her forehead.

"You need to come to bed."

"I know. It is hard to put her down when she sleeps in my arms. But, you are right." Terri eased out of the rocker and carried Makenna to her crib. She had already outgrown the bassinet.

After Terri put her down, she joined Adam in their bedroom.

"I know we have not had her with us for very long, but I have been thinking," Adam whispered.

"Oh no. Now what?" Terri cuddled in his arms.

"Have you thought about adoption?"

Terri pulled away from him and looked into his face. "Have you?"

"I have watched you with her night after night, day after day. You have a special bond with her."

"Yes, I feel that too. I know it is more than it should be. I try to remember the truth. We will be giving her up one day. All the ones we foster will eventually return to their original families or to other couples who want to adopt them. Some will move on to other foster families for one reason or another."

"What if this little girl didn't have to go back? Or she could not return to her biological family?"

"That would be different."

"Different in the sense that we would consider adopting her?" Adam asked and raised his eyebrows.

Terri looked at his face and laughed. "You are serious."

"Very serious."

"When the time comes, we will discuss it," Terri said and lay back down, cuddled in his arms. Her smile felt more inside than she allowed it to show on her face.

Terri closed her eyes and drifted back – to her dream.

Adam slept until the alarm sounded. He had an early appointment for a new construction job. He was meeting Donovan and the new client for breakfast. He did his best not to disturb Terri, but she soon joined him in the kitchen while making his coffee.

"You should still be sleeping," Adam said as he handed her a mug of black coffee.

"I know. I am learning to function on little sleep. The life of a new mother, you know." She winked as she walked to the back deck.

Adam joined her for a few minutes. They were silent as they breathed in the fresh air and took their first sips of delicious morning coffee. Then Terri pointed to the backyard.

"We need to fix up the backyard."

"Yes, we do. What do you have in mind to do with it?" Adam knew women enough that they always had something going on in their heads. It may take them a while to say something, but they have it all planned by that time.

"A garden and a play area for the kids."

"Kids? As in plural?" Adam turned and looked at her. He almost choked as he swallowed.

"What? Oh, if we become foster parents to more than one child at a time." She recovered her thoughts.

"Ah, ok." He looked at the empty yard. "We could make good use of this space. You are right."

"Maybe I'll draw something up today. Think we can get Ben to help us create it?"

"I'm sure Ben would love to help. He's great with landscape work. I can build some decking."

"Perfect. I'll call him today too."

"Are you in a hurry? Something I don't know about?" Adam looked at the time on his phone. "I've got to get going. You work on that. We'll talk about it later."

He walked into the kitchen and took his last swallow of coffee. Terri walked him to the front door, and they kissed goodbye. She smiled and waved as he drove away.

Before her baby girl woke up, Terri found a sketch pad and began drawing her vision. The vision in her dream.

She was almost done with it when her phone rang. It was Barbara.

"Good morning. How are you, Barbara?" Terri walked outside so she could talk.

"I am good. How are things going with Makenna?"

"Amazing. She is a joy. I don't get as much sleep as I once did, but the lack of sleep is worth it."

"I am glad she is doing well for you." Barbara hesitated.

"Is there something on your mind? You sound concerned about something."

"As a matter of fact, there is. We have a situation."

"What kind of a situation? Something I can help you solve?"

"I hope so. I need to talk with you and Adam about Makenna's parents. Is he there?"

"No. He is at a breakfast meeting. What's going on?"

Barbara sighed. "I know you are new to being foster parents and was hoping to make your first experience a short one."

"I know. You also know we are in this for as long and as often as you need us."

"That is what I want to hear. Her parents were just sent to jail. They have their trials coming up. Terri, it does not look good for them to be out of jail anytime soon. I will need the two of you to keep Makenna for an extended period."

Terri felt a lump in her throat. She looked at her backyard and thought of her dream. "We would love to keep her long-term. You have nothing to worry about for that little child."

Terri wanted to jump for joy. Her dream may be coming true.

"Thank you so much, Terri. I will need you and Adam to come in, or I can come to your home this evening to do some more paperwork. You are lifesavers for me."

"We will be home this evening. Come on over. I don't know about being lifesavers, but we will do what we can."

They disconnected after setting a time to get together that evening.

Terri walked into her home and into the nursery. Her foster child lay there awake, looking around quietly. Terri picked her up and held her close. Her love grew more each time she held her. She and Adam would do their best to give her the love and the family she needed.

When Adam went home for dinner, he was impressed at all Terri had accomplished. He was also thrilled with the news of keeping their first foster child longer than planned. They could keep her forever if they needed to. Terri also told him that Ben was coming over the next day to discuss her backyard plans.

Barbara knocked at their door soon after they had finished cleaning the kitchen of their dinner dishes.

Adam made a fresh pot of coffee while they talked and filled out the necessary paperwork to keep their foster daughter long-term.

The next day Ben arrived and helped Terri draw up the plans for the backyard transformation. Adam had added his ideas to Terri's the night before. When Terri agreed to the final rough drawing, Ben left to get the estimate ready for them. He said that he could start working on the design once they agreed.

Terri was excited about the changes in her life. All within the last two years. She had made a wise choice when she met Adam. She praised God for putting him into her life. The life she had before was fun and interesting, but she always knew something had been missing. Now with Adam and Makenna, she felt whole. Her life was complete.

Chapter Forty-Seven

Booked

It had taken a while for Bella Rose to become reestablished after Glen and Susan had died and left the Estate to their children. When Susan developed her last will and testament, she only hoped her three children would be able to be successful. Their success rested heavily on finding Andy and bringing everyone together to live near each other. Susan had that honor only briefly with her children. She led such a scattered life. Her childhood was protected early on from the truth of her parents. Although she was very young when things began to change, she somehow remembered the chaos of some of her earliest years living on the estate. She planned to make life easier for her family. Instead, in the end, she made it challenging for them.

Susan's demands for her children had made them each stronger. She had not lived long enough to see the wonderful lives they each would have.

Sara sat in her writing room in her home in silence. Randall was at work. Everyone else was working at the Manor or at other jobs. Sara enjoyed her time alone, reading and thinking about her family in past generations. The journals her mama and grandmama had written, combined with what the other research had exposed them to, brought her family's history to life. Sara found herself lost in the details. Forgetting that she was there to pull out the important details and write a book about her family.

A knock on her door stunned her back to reality. She blinked her eyes and walked to the front door. Peering through her peephole, she saw that it was Steven. She opened the door to let him in.

"Hi. What can I help you with, Steven?" Sara asked. It was not like him to come to her home. They usually saw each other at the manor or when they all went out to eat in town.

"Hi, Sara. I hope you don't mind the interruption. I know you are busy writing and probably hate interruptions."

"That's okay. You caught me reading instead of writing."

"Good. Not that it is good you're not writing, good that I didn't interrupt your process."

Sara smiled. Very few people understood that writing was a process. Most thought it was a simple task, even though most also admitted they could not write a story. Not even a true story.

"Come on in and have a seat. Would you like something to drink while you are here?"

"Thank you. I am fine. I am not planning to stay too long. I just have a question."

"Okay. I'm listening. What is your question?" They had gone into the living room to sit and talk.

"You know Barbara has been busy with the foster care system. She works long hours and then brings work home."

"Yes, I know. Barbara has done some amazing work in her time there. I hear good things about her."

"Moving and connecting her to Ben has been the best for her. I would like to give her a party in honor of her work. And not just for the family but for her co-workers, staff, foster families, and the children."

"That would be amazing. Why are you telling me about it?"

"I need your help to pull it off. I also need to talk to Heather for her help, but I would like to have it at the Bella Rose reception hall."

"Sounds like fun to me. You will need to talk to Heather for an open slot to rent the hall."

"I would also like your help."

"How can I help?"

"Can you do a write-up of her story?"

"Why me? I only know as much as I've been told. You may do better talking to Ben. And you know her better than any of us."

"I do, but I have no writing talent. You have the writing talent. It runs in your family."

"Thanks for the compliment. I would be happy to write something. Will it be read at the event or recorded?"

"I was thinking of reading it. But I need someone to write it for me."

"I can do that. Get back to me when you have a date for the event, and I will be sure to have it done by then."

"Thank you, Sara." Steven stood to leave.

"You have been the best thing to come into her life, you know?"

"She keeps telling me that same thing. She had so much potential when I met her. I could not sit back and not encourage her to fulfill her dreams."

Sara walked Steven to the door and watched him drive away. He was truly a Godsend to her. Sara was glad he was a part of their lives.

When Sara returned to her writing room, she pulled out a legal pad and began to jot down notes about Barbara's life.

Steven stopped at the manor to talk to Heather and chose an open date for the party. He was surprised that Heather had an opening just a month later. He would have to work hard to make it happen by then. But he knew he could do it.

Steven's next stop was to talk to Terri about time off work. He also needed to talk to Adam about music. Terri and Andy about food. And, of course, Barbara's supervisor for information on the foster families and how to invite them.

He had everything set in motion by the end of the day. Including instructions to everyone he had talked to about it being a surprise and no one could talk to Barbara about it. Keeping that secret would be the difficult part for everyone.

That evening when Barbara went home, she sensed something was wrong with Steven. He was quiet.

"Are you feeling alright?" Barbara asked Steven at dinner that night.

"Yes, I'm fine. Why?"

"You have been quiet since I got home. That is not like you. You usually tell me about your day before I get a chance to ask."

"Oh. No, I'm fine. A lot going on today, but nothing to talk about. Nothing new going on. There does come a time when couples must run out of things to talk about, right?"

"I doubt that will ever happen with the two of us. Between my work always having something going on and you always meeting new people at the lounge, I don't see any time when we are quiet."

Steven smiled and touched his wife's hand. "You are probably right. Okay, I will tell you what has been on my mind lately."

Barbara sat up a little straighter. If he had originally wanted to keep it quiet, whatever he was about to say must be important.

"I have decided it is time for us to get a puppy."

"What?!" Barbara stopped everything. She almost stopped breathing. "Where did that idea come from?"

"One of our regulars at the lounge was showing us pictures of his dog's new litter of pups. They are so cute! I just got a wild hair that we needed one." Steven did a quick save with his fake story. It was true about his regular showing the pictures to everyone, but Steven had no plans to get one of the puppies. He knew better.

"You realize the puppy will grow up alone with how we both work, right?"

"I might be able to talk Terri into letting me bring the pup into the lounge."

"You don't want to do that. You will then have your customers wanting to bring their pets inside. That is not a good thing for that place."

"Maybe you are right. You'd fall in love with one of them if you saw them too."

"Nope, not me. It's not that I don't like animals, but I know I am not home long enough during most days to take good care of even a cat. A dog requires more work."

"Okay, I will drop the idea." Steven shrugged his shoulders as if he was genuinely giving in and giving up on the idea.

"Good. Until we are home more often, I don't want to hear about a pet again."

"Okay. So when we are retired, we may get a dog."

"Right." Barbara laughed. She had no plans to give in to the idea, ever.

Steven then changed the subject to discuss their plans for the next day. He had to get his wife away from suspecting anything was seriously being planned in his mind. Maybe this celebration of his wife was more complicated than he thought.

When he was positive Barbara was not looking, he smiled. He had already had so much of it planned. It was already booked in the minds of many who would attend.

Chapter Forty-Eight

Accomplishments of Life

A month later, Barbara got a phone call in the early evening. She was involved with a foster family receiving their foster child. She rarely took a phone call while speaking with the family and child but saw that it was Sara. Sara rarely called her, but it was usually important when she did.

"Hello, Sara; how can I help you?"

"Hi, Barbara. I hate to disturb your dinner, but I need you to come to the hall at the manor."

"I'm not home; I'm with a foster family, but why do you need me at the reception hall?" She was confused. She had rarely been there except for family functions. She could not think of a family function planned that she may have forgotten.

"We need you to come immediately."

"I am in the middle of something; I can't just drop everything."

"Excuse me." Said the foster mother. "Is there somewhere you need to be? We can wait on this?" She motioned around the home and their child.

Barbara covered up her phone. "Are you sure? I don't know what this is all about and cannot promise to come back tonight."

"That is fine. We can reschedule. Go where someone needs you."

"Okay." Barbara returned to her phone. "I will be there shortly. My client is telling me to go. I guess I'll be on my way."

"Okay. Good. We'll be waiting." Sara hung up her phone.

"We?" Barbara asked too late. Sara had already hung up. Barbara stared at her phone. She shook her head as she put her cell phone in her pocket.

"Are you sure you don't mind?" She asked the foster mother and touched the head of the foster child. The child looked so scared. This family was the third one she had been sent to in the last two months. No one seemed to want her. She had been with this family for two weeks, and the foster mother had called Barbara with a few concerns.

"We are sure. We will be fine. We've already touched on many things I needed to discuss about our situation."

Barbara apologized again before she left. She was reluctant to leave. That was not her style.

After Barbara left, the foster mother called Sara and told her that Barbara was on her way. She apologized that she would be a few minutes late but was glad to have helped make sure Barbara was there.

Fifteen minutes later, Barbara pulled up to the reception hall at Bella Rose. She noticed several cars parked around, which was odd from what she remembered about previous special events. She closed and locked her car door and walked to the hall door. It opened for her.

Barbara was met by Steven.

"Hi!" Steven managed to say with a somber face.

"What is going on? Sara called me away from a meeting with a foster family to come here. What are all these people doing here?"

"Come on in and find out." Steven put his arm around his wife's waist and led her inside.

Once inside, Barbara saw the banner hanging across the front.

"Thank you for all you do" was printed across the banner with her photo on the end.

Barbara was still confused.

"My love, I invited all these people here to let you know how much we appreciate all you do. You created a new role for yourself in this field and quickly improved the system. All of us are amazed and proud of you."

Barbara felt emotional. She didn't want to cry, but she was not far from it. This was so touching. No one had been publicly proud of her before. No one had been amazed by something she had done.

"I never knew I had touched so many lives." She said as she looked around. She knew everyone there. Her family and friends she had made since moving there. Then there were the many foster parents who were there, some with their children. She turned as the door opened and saw the foster mother she had just left walk in. Barbara just shook her head and smiled. She realized that their meeting had been a hoax.

Adam started playing some music. Steven walked to the front of the room, captured everyone's attention, and began speaking. He shared all Barbara had done for the foster system in a short time. The foster families applauded her. A couple of the children walked over to her and hugged her.

When Steven finished his speech, he asked if Barbara wanted to say anything to those there. She shook her head. She was not ready. Maybe in a few minutes. Steven then ended his time with the microphone by inviting everyone to enjoy the food. Then he stepped down and walked to his wife. He kissed her on the forehead. She was the love of his life.

After everyone had eaten, Barbara told Steven she was ready to speak. He told her she would need to wait. When she looked up, there was a line of people waiting for their turn at the microphone. She shook her head. How had Steven put this all together, she wondered.

One of the younger girls was at the mic. She hesitated, then spoke. "I want to thank Ms. Barbara for all she has done in my life. I was lost. I was alone. I was scared. My family got taken away on criminal charges, and I was thrown into the foster care system. I had only heard about it before. Suddenly I was a part of it. I did not want to be there. Ms. Barbara met with me and eased my fears. She asked about me. She asked more than just my name and age. She wanted to know about me. She wanted to assure I was placed with the right family. I had previously been sent to live with the Jones family. They were nice, but we did not blend well. They could not deal with me and helped me make the phone call to Barbara. I needed a new foster family.

That was when I met Ms Barbara, and my life was forever changed. I was placed with a family that already had a child. I felt like the fifth wheel. I was different from the rest of them, I could tell. She was just the connection to my placement. One that she would change according to what was needed for the families. Yet, she knew that I was my own person. I felt I did not need anyone in my life. I am so thankful that Ms Barbara saw through me. She knew I was going to be all right. She knew my potential. She saw more than I did. Thank you, Ms. Barbara."

Everyone stood up and applauded her. She was followed by three other young girls and a young man who continued to praise her for placing them with loving families. Then a couple of the foster parents took to the microphone and thanked Barbara for all she had done for them and the changes she was about to make with the system.

It took nearly an hour for everyone who wanted to share how she had touched their lives. She was becoming embarrassed by some of the praises. She felt she was just a woman. She got dressed the way any other woman would. She had suffered her own losses most of her life and risen to become the one who hopefully would change the laws.

Near the end of the evening, Barbara was able to stand and talk. She was tired but did not want anyone to leave without her words.

"Everyone, I am overwhelmed by your words. I did not see this coming. This night has been overwhelming. You have all made it that way, and I am honored. I promise that the work I am doing now is for you and the children. I continue to make changes to improve the system. It still has a long way to go. I will be available for anyone who wants to talk afterward."

She continued to speak. "I want to thank all of you for providing me with the tools, connections, and freedoms to do what I believed needed to improve the lives of these children who otherwise would have no safe place to live. They would end up like I did, in homes that cared only for the money they were making and not the children in their homes. I was blessed to live with one lady who did care. She had circumstances that required me to be moved one more time. That time I was adopted. Most of you know my story. I hope that some of you will be so touched by the foster families that you children will grow up to make your own changes in the world; you foster parents continue to love the children you have been entrusted with to provide a loving home. All of you here, I hope my story and the story of some of these children and parents lead you to want to become foster parents or help the system with donations, and your positive support in spreading the word of what can be done."

Barbara finally ended her unprepared speech with a simple, "Thank you all." She sat next to Steven, who reached over and kissed her as she joined him.

The rest of the night was spent enjoying more food, music, and fun. Slowly people began to leave, and soon it was just family. Everyone then helped clean up the hall and go home for the night.

Barbara felt so blessed and empowered to continue her work for all the children. She looked at Steven. He was her soulmate, there was no doubt.

Chapter Forty-Nine

Discovered

Jay told Carrie that he needed to hide away in his office to review his writings and photos so he could have them ready in a week for the company he was working for. They wanted to feature his experience in the next issue of their magazine. They wanted the raw truth. He wanted perfection.

Carrie walked him to his office and kissed him. She turned and walked away, hearing him gently closing his door, separating them. They had been miles apart for six months. Now they were just feet apart, yet she felt it was more. A sense of loneliness melted around her. She returned to the kitchen, poured herself a cup of coffee, and walked outside to sit on the bench in her flower garden.

Jay sat in his favorite office chair and pulled out his notepad. The first pages were full of words that formed complete sentences. Paragraph after paragraph filled the first several pages. He skimmed over the words. The sentences showed what he experienced in descriptive details that any reader could feel what he felt.

He flipped through the first notepad, picked up the second, and then the third. He watched his words fall. His sentences failing. The showing gradually lapsed into telling. He felt inadequate in his writing. He set aside the fifth pad and picked up the sixth. Words. Just words. No sentences. No eloquent feelings showing what he felt.

He swiveled his chair around to gaze out the window behind him. Propping his feet on the window sill, he thought back to that last month. What was he feeling? What was he thinking about? Why had his writing changed?

He closed his eyes.

He recalled feeling alone and lonely towards the end of his stay. He felt a chill on his arms, recalling the cold breezes as he sat alone in nature. Even now, he could not think about it clearly.

He took his feet from the sill and turned back to face his desk. Carrie had snuck in and placed a glass of white wine on his desk. She had said nothing when she did it and had quietly walked back out, closing his door. She could tell he was deep in thought, and although she would have loved to be a part of his inward conversation, she knew that was between him and himself.

Jay took a sip of the wine and smiled. Carrie knew him so well. He could not have married a better match. She was perfect for him.

He lifted the glass and gazed into the pale gold color of wine that occupied the etched, stemmed glass. He smiled.

Life. Life was good.

He set the glass down and returned to read his notepads. He opened his laptop and began to write. He wanted it all to be perfect, but he began just typing, word for word, what he had written by hand while out there alone. The beginning was perfect.

When he got to the fourth notepad, he leaned back and stretched. An unexpected image formed as he closed his eyes to rest from the strain of computer work. He shook his head in an attempt to erase it. He opened his eyes and looked at Carrie's photo on the bookcase. He picked up the five by seven framed portrait. He realized he was not smiling. He picked up the notepad and continued typing what he had written while away, isolated from everyone.

He stopped typing when he reread what he wrote and knew the words were not the correct ones. He hit delete until the last few sentences were gone. He saved his work and then turned off his computer. He opened the center drawer of his desk to find a pen to mark his place in the notepad. When he reached in, he noticed the back of a photo. He picked it up and turned it over.

His mind drifted back several years to a time before Carrie. There, looking into his eyes, was his first love. The lady he regretted letting go. Terri's photo somehow had survived his moving across the country, his getting married, a new desk, and what should have been put away inside a box lost in the shuffle of life. He turned it over, read the words he had written on the back, and smiled. They were still true. His life had moved on. She had moved on with her life. They both were happy with the lives they lived. As he placed it back under other writing supplies, he read the words again. *"If nothing more, we will always have the Pineapple."*

He closed the drawer, stood, and left the room. He turned the light off on his way, closed the door, and walked to the living room where Carrie patiently had been waiting for him.

He sat next to her and put his arms around her. She bent her head back and kissed him.

"Are you okay, my love?"

"I am perfect," he said. He turned her around to face him and kissed her. He was home. He was going to stay home. Before him was the lady he would spend the rest of his life with.

His writing could wait until the morning. The feature story would get done on time. The story would tell how he digressed in thoughts and became less aware as time passed. It would tell how forming imaginative sentences with the perfect structure gradually dwindled down to just the important words and phrases to barely remember what he did that day. He wrote the names of the plants or the animals but omitted the story behind seeing them in those last days. He digressed further to the point that all he could do was scribble lines in the last few days. Circles even changed to just repeated straight lines.

On the last day, there were no other words written except *home*. All he knew by that point was that he wanted to go home. Now, he was home. And that was where he would stay—with the woman he loved.

For the next three days, he concentrated on writing the perfect article for the feature. He sent it all in, along with copies of his rough drafts. The words were written in longhand. The ones that were not changed or even moved on the page. They just were where he planted them each day. They were the cold hard truth.

Two months later, his story was featured in a worldwide magazine with one of the photos he had taken on the front cover. His name was in bold print. His contact information was inside the front cover to identify him. His name and how to contact him were listed at the end of the six-page story, so people could contact the author—the man who had basically been isolated for six months.

And the man who was about to become a father.

Chapter Fifty

Closure

Terri walked into the café after taking time off when they became foster parents. Since she and Adam had gotten married and learned she could count on her staff and Steven to keep the place in operation, she was comfortable not being there in person. She stayed home when they took Makenna into their home, but once Makenna was a little older, Terri began going in at least once a week or for a few hours several days a week. The café was still her first baby.

Adam arrived a half hour later with fresh coffee from the coffee shop three blocks away. She reached for her cup as Adam pulled it away and kissed her.

"What was that for? Give me my coffee." Terri reached out to grasp her cup.

"That, my dear, was for loving me."

She took a sip of the hot love from within the cup. "Okay. Is today any different than any other day? You never did that switch on me before."

"Today, my sweet love, is the anniversary of the beginning."

Terri took another sip. His words not making sense. She needed more caffeine for that. She tried to think what day it was. What was she missing? She was usually the one who remembered special days in her life. That, she had decided when she was still young, was a blessing and a curse. The good special days were okay to remember. The sad days and bad memories were other stories. Those were ones she wished she could forget.

"Today, I celebrate."

"I don't get it," Terri finally admitted.

"Eight years ago today, I got released from jail. Eight years ago today, I started my new life here in the oldest town in Tennessee. It was the day my life changed and led me to you."

"We didn't meet until a couple of years ago. How could eight years ago lead to that?" As soon as she said it, she understood. Without his release and move to start his life over with a completely new start, he never would have met Terri.

"Ah, I get it now. Yes, we need to celebrate. How about an impromptu celebration here at the lounge tonight? You and others can sing. Others can play what they want. A mixture of karaoke and open mic night."

"I want you all to myself."

"Oh, that sounds interesting. May I ask where we are going?"

"You can ask all you want, but I will not tell."

"You are such a tease. I thought I had married a mature man. One who would not play tricks on his wife but be serious about life."

"Me? Serious about life? I thought you knew me by now."

"I thought I did too; maybe I don't know you as well as I thought.

"I will be back this afternoon to pick you up."

"Don't I need to get changed for this?"

"I will handle everything. Don't you worry," Adam said as he tossed his empty Styrofoam cup into the trash and left the café. Terri tilted her head as he left. He had not given her a kiss goodbye. That was not like him. She tossed her matching empty cup into the trash and turned to get to work. The doors would open for business in less than half an hour.

Late that afternoon, Adam returned with a large bag. He handed it to Terri and asked her to go change. She looked around at her staff and began to protest. Her crew was looking at her, and all of them pointed to the back of the café.

"Go change, young lady," one of them said.

"I'm going." Terri lifted the bag and walked into her private office area.

While she was changing, she heard the volume of the music from the lounge increase. She smiled. Adam's first love, music, was playing his style. She danced around as she got ready for the evening out with her husband.

Adam had assured her that Makenna was with the babysitter for the night, and she was not to worry. They had the security cameras set up if she wanted to check on them at any time.

When Terri emerged from her office, Adam met her and took her hand. He walked her to a table set for them, complete with roses and a candle.

"I thought this night was for you?" Terri said, confused.

"It is, but I can't imagine my life without you."

The night progressed with her staff serving them a special meal Adam had selected. Several people were there singing karaoke. Terri was usually in work mode inside the walls of her business. Adam had made it not seem like work at all. The karaoke didn't stop until after midnight, and Terri loved every moment.

As soon as they arrived home, Terri walked into Makenna's room to check on her. Adam walked the babysitter to her car and told her to text them when she got home. She said she would and thanked him for the opportunity to babysit.

The next day was a day off for both of them. Thankfully Makenna was old enough to sleep in a little bit which gave Adam and Terri time to enjoy morning coffee while they discussed plans for the weekend.

Makenna awoke before they had time for a second cup of coffee. They played with her in her room. Terri laughed as she watched her husband and foster daughter romping around playing. She had the perfect family.

After breakfast, the babysitter arrived to watch Makenna for the weekend. Terri went to finish packing. Adam went outside to clean out the car for their trip.

While Terri searched for a necklace she wanted to wear, she opened the top junk drawer of her dresser. She pulled out her jewelry box and noticed a piece of paper underneath it. She scooted it forward, picked it up, and turned it over.

Her mind drifted back to a few years prior. It seemed a lifetime ago—until that moment.

A photo of her and Jay looking into the camera with the city behind them. She remembered the day, the spot in the vast city, and the motions she had that day. Memories she had put behind her.

She turned the photo face down and saw the words written on the back. "If nothing more, we will always have the pineapple." It was written in Jay's handwriting. Below his words, she had added: "Two unlikely souls, passing in time, touched for a moment, forever a place in our hearts. May time heal as we each grow."

Before placing the photo where it had been, she picked up a pen and added the words. "Healed and Grown." Adam knew all about Jay, but there was no need to remind him by leaving the photo out.

Terri smiled as she closed the drawer and viewed her wedding day's eight-by-ten photo. Her perfect day. She could not have imagined a more perfect life partner for her. And foster dad for Makenna.

Adam tapped on their bedroom door. Terri snapped back to the present and hoped Adam had not noticed.

"Are you almost ready to get on the road?"

"Just about. One more thing to pack, and we can get out of here. You never did tell me where we were going."

"You will find out when we get there," he teased.

Several hours later, they were parked outside their hotel with the beach in the background. Terri had figured out their destination long before they arrived. It was hard not to.

"How did you know I was longing for a beach trip?"

"Oh, a little birdie told me. I know you love the mountains and hiking, but I also know you enjoy the beach air from time to time."

"You are amazing, you know that?"

"Yep. I know," he winked.

The next two days were spent walking the beaches, enjoying the sun, and having all her cares washed away with the tides.

Chapter Fifty-One

Growth

The years were passing by for everyone. The younger children were growing faster than their parents wanted them to. Sara and Randall had a teenager on their hands. Fortunately for them, she was not what most considered a typical teen. Gayle was mature for her age. She had taken on responsibilities on her own and found a part-time job so she would have her own spending money.

Her parents were her inspiration. Sara and Randall were hard workers. Sara was busy writing from home, but what Gayle saw was not that her mom was staying at home wasting time. Gayle saw a woman determined to share their family story. A story that few knew about. The history had been a secret for many years, yet her mother was willing to experience it as she researched and wrote the words. Words that Gayle realized were painful at times. Words that brought laughter but sometimes led to tears. Gayle had also watched Sara work hard running the manor.

Gayle looked forward to reading the finished book, or books to which her mom was dedicating her life.

Sara picked up the mail one day on her way to run errands. Inside was a letter from Gayle's school. Since it was so unusual for this, Sara sat down in her car and opened it. She smiled when she read it. Gayle had made high honors in school. Sara shook her head. Her humble daughter had never mentioned anything about it.

Sara told Randall about it at dinner that night, and they praised their daughter. Gayle shrugged her shoulders and said it was nothing special.

Heather knocked on her sister's door while Sara cleaned the kitchen after dinner. Gayle answered it and invited her aunt inside. A few minutes later, Gayle excused herself to work on some homework. She left her bedroom door open to hear what her mom and aunt might be talking about.

"What's going on, Sis? Is everyone ok?" Sara asked Heather. She could tell from Heather's face that she was not happy.

"I wish I could put my finger on it. That would make it so much easier to handle."

Sara turned and looked at Heather. "What's happening? Is Ben all right? The kids? Talk to me. She dried her hands, took Heather by her hand, and walked them into the living room.

"It's the boys. Marc is acting up around his friends. Maddex has decided he hates every food I try to feed him. I am at a loss. Ben tries to help, but being a male hasn't helped their connection. I have noticed Ben staying away from us longer when he works at the manor or goes shopping for things he needs for work. I don't want to assume anything about him. I know we survived before, but I'm unsure how to handle this." Heather put her hands on her face to stop the flood of emotions.

Sara put her arms around her sister. She could feel her frustration through the tightness in her shoulder. She smiled, although Heather could not see it. She knew what her sister was going through. Her boys had reached a difficult age. Sara did not have the guts to tell her it would get worse in a few years when the boys became teenagers.

"It will all work out. This is just a rough phase for the boys. Marc has been in school, sees how the other kids are, and picks up things from them. He is the older brother and may feel pressured by that somehow."

"How would he feel pressured by being the older brother?"

"Do you ever tell him to do something or be a certain way as an example to his brother?"

Heather thought a moment. "Oh, my. You are right. We have been doing that for years. We never gave it a thought that it would cause stress. Who thinks kids get stressed?"

"I know. It is not something I had ever realized either. I learned it even by having one little girl who has grown up before our eyes. She is amazing, but she had her moments when she was younger."

"Really? Even though she was an only child?"

"Yes. Gayle took it upon herself to act like the older sister to her classmates. She pushed herself to reach high honors, which is more stressful. Life is not easy for kids these days."

"Glad we were kids when life was easier," Heather laughed. I never knew life was so hard on kids now. You are right, though. I need to talk to Ben about how we act and project things around them. You are so smart, Sis. Thank you."

"Talk about stress. I am the older sister here. I know all about the stress of setting the example to my younger siblings." Sara said. To her, it was just life and living.

"And here I am, coming to you for answers." Heather laughed. Her sister always knew what to say and what to do. She never realized it was stressful. She just thought her older sister had all the answers. Heather reached over and hugged Sara.

"Any time, Sis. Any time. I will do my best to have the answers.

Heather hugged her older sister and returned home. She had always admired Sara. It wasn't until their conversation that Heather realized how much pressure Sara was under. She never complained. Heather was going to do her best to ease that for her. She understood now why Sara had stepped away from her constant involvement with Bella Rose.

Sara went back to her writing room to read more of the journals. That was when she heard another knock on her front door. She closed the journal and went to open the door.

Gayle had beat her there and was letting Andy inside.

"Hello, little brother. To what do I owe this pleasure?"

"Yeh, why are you here? Aunt Heather just left." Gayle reacted.

Sara looked at Gayle and wondered why the attitude from her daughter. It was not like her.

"Oh, nothing much." Andy walked in and went to the kitchen.

"Never fails, you head to the kitchen no matter where you are." Sara laughed as she followed him.

"I know. Bad habit from my career as a chef." Andy poured himself a glass of water.

"Something is up. Talk to me." Sara shrugged her shoulders. Her siblings were beginning to remind her of younger days when they came to her to settle arguments instead of going to their parents.

"I just need a break." Andy sat on the sofa in the living room. Instead of sitting back, relaxed, he sat on the edge and leaned forward.

"What do you need a break from?" Sara asked as she sat in her chair.

"Life. Well, not life, really, but everything going on in life. I feel sometimes overwhelmed by three little ones, being chef, and everything going on."

"We all seem to be feeling that at the moment. Heather was just here talking about the stress of all she was going through. I think all of our kids are at stages that cause extra stress. Randall and I seem to be the lucky ones." She looked toward Gayle's room, where her daughter had returned to give her mom and uncle the privacy she knew they wanted.

"You are the lucky ones. Gayle is a dream. Our kids are very needy, or so it seems. They all are great but are a lot of work. We rarely get time alone, let alone time to breathe."

"You both get a break when you are working, but that is not a total break and a time to get away for even a date night. When was the last time you and Karen went out for an evening?"

"Ha! Months. The last getaway was with the entire family."

"Ok." Sara sat up. She had a solution of sorts. Her siblings needed to rekindle their marriages and have a night out without kids. Once again, it was time for her to give of herself for her siblings. Time for her and Randall to watch their nieces and nephews for a night or two. She was not sure they could manage all five on one night.

"Ok?" What is on your mind? A solution?"

"I think so. I need to talk to Randall about it and maybe Gayle for her help, but the truth is you and Karen need a date night. No kids. Heather and Ben need the same thing."

"Just one night"? Andy laughed.

"For starters, yes. One night. The kids are growing up, but you adults are stumped in the growth of your relationships. You are stuck in your routines and caring for your kids and jobs. It is time for a relationship reconnect."

"Wow. You are amazing. That is just what we need – growth in ourselves and our marriages. How did you become so smart?" Andy smiled at his sister and how she had the answer.

"I'm the older sister. It comes with the territory." Sara just shook her head. She had no idea how she knew what they needed. She made it up as she went, just as she always had. They did not need to know that. She liked having them think she had all the answers so easily. Stressful? Yes. Worth it to see them all happy? Of course.

Andy stood up. "When can we plan this date night?"

"Let me talk to Randall and Gayle and get back to you. It won't be too far from now. The sooner you all rekindle and grow, the better for everyone, including your children."

Andy hugged Sara. Where would he be without her? He put his empty glass in her sink and walked to the front door. "Thank you."

"You are welcome, little brother." Sara smiled as he walked away. She closed the door and turned around. Running right into her daughter.

"So, we are all babysitting when?" Gayle put her arm around her mother's waist as they walked to the kitchen.

Chapter Fifty-Two

Changes

After the visits from her siblings and coordinating their date nights so they could watch the little ones, something had been weighing heavy on Sara's mind. It began when she stepped away from her involvement with the estate, then when she listened to her siblings, she thought more about it.

Maybe it was time for a change. A change not only for her but for everyone. Everyone seemed overwhelmed. No one was as happy as they usually were. Something needed to happen. Maybe it was time she went back to work at the manor. Maybe it was time for something bigger to happen. Something she did not want to think about.

One night, about two weeks after her siblings enjoyed their date nights, she talked with Randall.

"Have you noticed a difference between Heather and Andy?"

"I have noticed they are quieter than normal. Seems they are busier than usual. Why, what's going on? I thought the date nights had helped."

"I think they did, but that is only temporary. I think something more is happening, but I cannot pinpoint it. They are not complaining, other than what led to their date nights. But there may be underlying issues or concerns they don't want me to know about."

"Why would they not want you to know about them?"

"Because I stepped away from my involvement with the estate."

"You are still family and may not be actively managing it, but you are still part owner. I think they would want you to know of any issues."

"That is what I was thinking too. I am also concerned it is time for a major change around here."

"With us?" Randall leaned away from his wife.

"Oh, no! We are fine." Sara touched Randall's arm. Things could not be better as far as her thinking. "No, change at the manor. Change for all of us."

"What are you thinking?"

"Ultimately, most drastically would be to sell."

"Sell? Are you serious?"

"I don't know. It will cause a lot of problems for all of us if we sell the property and business. Although it does not make sense to sell the manor and keep the rest, including all of us living here. I am just thinking of the worst-case scenario."

"That would be the worst. Where would we all live? And where would you all work?"

"I know. If we sell, it puts my entire family out. I just know something is going on with Andy and Heather. I had us watch the kids so they could each have some time alone, but I am not sure that was enough, nor what they needed."

"Maybe it is time for another family meeting. A time to just let everyone open up freely, with no judgments from anyone else. Just the freedom to say whatever they feel, need, want, or are going through."

"You may be right." Sara loved that Randall was so wise and understanding. "You are amazing."

"I know," he laughed and hugged Sara.

"I will call Heather and Andy and set up a family meeting. It has been a while. Maybe that is the issue. Not enough family time over the last several months."

"Maybe it is that simple. You can only find out by opening the lines of communication between everyone. Do you want the spouses there or just the three of you?"

"I will ask them what they want. I am fine with you being there, but if they need it just to be the three of us, you will understand, right?"

"Of course. You know I want the best for you and your family. Whatever it takes to have peace and happiness with your family."

I will call them first thing in the morning. Right now, it is our time." Sara put her arms around Randall's neck and drew him closer to her. They kissed as they rose from the sofa where they had been sitting. Slowly Randall took her by her hand and led them into their bedroom. He never would stop loving this amazing woman he had loved all his life and, for the last several years, had the honor of calling her his wife.

Sara opened her eyes to the sun shining through their bedroom window. It was a brand new day. One that had arrived after one of her best nights in a long time. Awaking in the loving arms of the man she loved.

Randall felt Sara stir and pulled her closer to him. He knew she was in for a possible family change today. He did not want any change between the two of them. Not if he could help it.

Sara smiled as she eased away from Randall's arm and got up. She looked back at Randall and winked. Her life was perfect.

Sara reached for her second cup of coffee when she picked up her cell phone to call Heather.

"Good morning, Sis. What's going on?" Heather asked as she combed her hair.

"I thought that it may be time for another family meeting. We have not had one in a while."

"Is there anything important going on?"

"Nothing specific that I know of. However, after talking with you and Andy a few weeks ago, before Randall and I watched all the kids so you could have a couple's night, I sense that you and Ben may have some stress going on that we could talk about. And I feel Andy and Karen are stressed also."

"Wow. Really? You think there is some stress going on?"

Sara sensed her sister's sarcasm. "And it appears I am right?"

Heather let out an audible sigh. "More than you know, Sis. More than you know."

"Okay. I will call Andy and see if he can make it to a family meeting tonight. Will that work for you?"

"As long as Ben can stay with the kids."

"You want this meeting to be for only us three siblings?"

"If you don't mind, I would."

"Fine with me. It will be like the original days."

"Yes, the beginning. When things were simple."

Sara heard Heather's whisper but didn't make any comment about it. "Okay, let me call Andy. I will get back to you shortly."

"Thank you, Sis. I love you."

"Love you too, Sis."

Sara hung up from Heather and immediately pressed the button to call Andy.

"Hey, Sis. What's going on?"

"Wow, you and Heather answer my phone calls the same way. It's as if I never call either of you unless there is an issue."

"Sorry. How are you? Is that better?"

"Yes, a little bit better. However, I just talked with Heather, and we both agree it is time for a family meeting."

"See, there is an issue, but I agree, we could use a family meeting. When?"

"Would tonight work for you?"

"Sure."

"Oh, and it is for us siblings only. Spouses are not allowed, at least not to this one."

"Perfect. See you both tonight." Andy was short with his reply.

"See you then. Love you, Brother."

"Love you too," Andy said and hung up.

Sara stared at her cell phone in her hand. Something was going on with her siblings. Andy's implications that she never called them stuck with her. Maybe he was right. Maybe that was the change that needed to take place. Maybe their issue and stress were with her.

Sara called Randall and updated him on the meeting.

"Something else is bothering you. Talk to me." Randall said.

"I think their issues are with me."

"How?"

"I am not sure. I will find out tonight. And I will let you know."

"Okay. You know I will be here for you."

"Yes, I do. Thank you."

Sara spent the rest of the day preparing to deal with her assumptions.

The siblings met in the kitchen at the manor like they had since they began Bella Rose. Sara smiled as she saw Andy bring over a plate of chocolate chip cookies and Heather pour coffee for the three of them. Some family traditions never end.

"I am glad we agreed to meet like we used to," Sara said as she picked up a fresh from the oven, still warm cookie. "These cookies are the best."

"Is that the only reason?" Andy laughed.

"Of course not. You know that. It is way past due for us to get together with just the three of us. Life has been hectic for us over the last six months or even longer."

"You are so right, Sis," Heather said, taking a sip of coffee. "I think we have a lot to talk about."

"So do I," Andy added. He joined his sisters at the island with his cup of coffee in hand.

"What has been on your minds? Now is the time to share it all. I know I have not been here at the manor for a while now, and I feel that may have been a wrong decision."

"No, that was the right decision for you. At the time." Heather interrupted her sister.

"It may have been at the time, as you say. I think there is more going on than my not being here. Let's talk about whatever you need to discuss." Sara sat back, holding her mug of coffee.

Andy and Heather looked at each other before Heather spoke. "It has not been the same with you not working here, Sis. We miss you being in charge."

"Yes, we seem to be floating along running this place, but there is a vacancy and not in the rooms. A vacancy in family connections."

Sara sat silent.

Heather looked at Andy. She was surprised he had opened with that statement. Heather thought there was more going on with her brother. Maybe she was wrong.

"I agree with Andy. However, there is more. I feel overwhelmed with life in general. The kids, my work, trying to keep this place going and growing. I know we have Rachelle and the rest of our family who helps us, but we miss you, Sis. You are our glue. You keep us together. We need you."

"And there is more." Andy jumped in. "I need a break."

Heather and Sara waited for him to continue, but that was all he said.

"How much of a break do you need? From the chef's work? We can hire someone to help you or to come in and cook for a while." Sara offered.

"A break from everything." Andy hung his head. He hated admitting that he felt that way. He was supposed to be the strong man who could manage it all. Instead, he felt weak, incapable, and inadequate.

Sara looked at her siblings. She set her empty coffee mug on the island and stood up. "Okay. Let's look at what's happening and how we can work together to better ourselves and this place."

"That would be great. What do you have in mind?" Andy asked.

"First, you want a break. It sounds like more than being away from cooking for the guests. Yes?"

"I hate to admit it, but yes. My years of running got reactivated when I went to Seattle a while ago. I loved the traveling I got to do. The trouble is, I do not want to run away from my wife and kids. That is not fair to them. Karen says she understands my need to go away for a break. Or at least she says she does. I hate feeling that need."

"Maybe if you take a week away, it will help you both. Karen will get a break from your stressful feelings, and you will get a break from everything you have been doing for the last several years here. You gave up the life you knew most of your life to be here for our family. You deserve a break."

"Thank you, Sis. I don't want to leave you short-handed here. Who is going to do the cooking?"

"I can call Terri and see if she can loan us one of her cooks from the café."

"Are you sure?"

"I am sure. She is always offering to help our family."

"Okay. Let me talk to Karen and decide where I am going and when."

"I think you should discuss when, but not the where. You want to be as you were when you were on the run. If you plan ahead where you are going and stay in touch every day, that defeats the purpose. That will not ease your desire and need. You need spontaneity again, not a rigid schedule." Heather intercepted.

"Yes, I agree with Heather. You need to get in your car and ride. Then land wherever it leads you each night."

"You two are the best." Andy smiled and nodded his head. They were right. He needed to run, but for a limited time.

"Now, Heather. What is going on with you?" Sara turned her attention to her sister.

"My issue seems so minor now. The life of a parent certainly is not an easy one. The boys are a handful. Between trying to give them all the attention they need, my work doing events at Bella Rose, and helping out generally, I am exhausted at night. Ben is doing his best to help, but our marriage is suffering. So, we have again started couples therapy with Joe to our hopeful benefit. We had our first session two days ago and considering Joe helped us before, we trust he will help us again."

"That is great news. I am glad you reached out to Joe. If I can do anything to help the two of you, let me know."

"Thank you, Sis. We will."

"Now, I want to know what else is bothering the two of you. I know part of it involves me. Be honest. Talk to me."

Heather and Andy looked at their older sister. They had sidestepped reality about her. They needed her at Bella Rose.

"Sis, we miss you. We need you back working at the manor."

"We understand your writing our family story is important, and we want you to continue doing that."

Sara listened as her siblings took turns talking.

"We have devised a solution we hope you will agree to for all of us to be happy."

"Okay. I am listening. If it helps everyone, I'm game for about anything."

"You come back to the manor and work in the office. You can be there when we need you and have the final say in some of the decisions that need to be made."

"That's all fine and good, but what about the writing?"

"You can move your writing into the manor. That way, you can go home, spend time with Randall, and not work so hard yourself when the day is over."

"This place needs all of us to be together again."

"Yes. I agree. We need to change ourselves, grow, and be better for each other and the good of Bella Rose." Sara reached for another chocolate chip cookie. She turned and smiled at her family. The family they were before and would be again.

Chapter Fifty-Three

The Original Returns

"I'm moving."

Randall almost spat out his morning coffee. "What?"

"Oh, No, that's not the way you think! So sorry." Sara reached over for Randall's hand. "I mean, I am moving the location of my writing."

"Whew! You threw me. Don't start a conversation like that!" He took another swallow of coffee and smiled. "What room are you going to use in the house?"

"To the office, in the manor."

"Why? It is quieter here. Are you going to be able to do your writing justice if you are interrupted all the time over there?"

"That's just it. I am also going back to work at the manor."

"Why? Is that what the meeting with Heather and Andy was all about, you wanting to go back to work?"

"No. The meeting was because the three of us discussed what was going on in our lives. I could tell they were stressed over something more than normal everyday issues."

"And they said it was you?"

"Among other things, yes."

"I was wondering when you would go back. They need you there, and you need to be there."

"You knew?"

"I felt it. But I didn't say anything because I hoped you would figure it out over time."

"Wow. I can't believe you didn't say anything." Sara stood up and walked over to the sink. She looked out the window and ran the past few months through her mind. Her husband had ample opportunities when he could have said something. She didn't understand why he kept quiet. She turned back to look at Randall.

"I love you, babe. You are a strong woman, and I knew that in time you would go back, but it had to be your decision or the input of your siblings."

"Did you put them up to all of this?"

"Of course not. You said yourself they seemed to be under a lot of stress. I certainly did not cause that."

"True." Sara nodded her head. "I know you wouldn't do that. I wish you had talked to me about what you saw in me that I did not."

"You look out for other people far more than you look out for yourself. You always have. That is what I liked about you even when I admired you when we were young."

"You saw that in me that far back? You never told me."

"I watched you grow into an amazing person, but you always put other people first."

"Well, I may be doing it again."

"No, you are doing this for yourself. You see the need to help your family, but deep down, you know that it is what you want and need to make yourself happy. I am proud of you."

"Thank you."

"So, if you need any help to move your writing things to the manor, I can help you any time."

"I think I can manage it."

"There you go again."

"What?"

"Being the strong woman and doing everything on your own."

"Ah. Wow. You're right. On second thought, which should have been my first thought, I would appreciate it, no, I would love your help moving my writing to the office in the manor. Thank you."

Randall smiled. He would take this change in Sara. He knew it would not last, but he would take it. Maybe this small change would lead to other changes. Ones that would make life even better than it was. He would take this as a new beginning.

~~~~~~

Andy packed his car the night before he left. He did not want to wake up Karen or the kids when he left. He planned to leave before dawn. His family deserved to sleep in as long as they could.

It had not been easy to tell Karen he had the urge to run again. Even harder to tell her he was going to walk away and leave everything in his life behind him. Even though he would only be gone for a week. It was a week that he would have no contact with anyone. Not her, not his sisters. No one. He admitted he did not even know where he was going. He had no set destination. No plans. Only to pack a week's worth of clothes, fill up his gas tank, and hit the road. He would decide what direction to turn at the bottom of Rose Lane.

They had told Ryan, River, and Ravyn that their daddy would be away for a few days. The kids were still too young to understand any reasoning and would not realize the concept of a week without their father. They may not even remember this time in their lives when they were grown.

Andy gently kissed Karen on her forehead as she continued to sleep. He was going to miss her and his children but leaving was something he had to do. He would be back soon.

At the bottom of the lane, Andy turned left. He heard once that most people turn right when given a choice. He loved that his rebellious old self automatically took control. The next week would make or break him.

Heather woke up early before anyone in her household had stirred. She snuck into her kitchen and made a single cup of coffee. She'd make a full pot when Ben woke up, but one was perfect for her at this hour. She should return to bed for more sleep but knew that was beyond her.

As she drank her cup of coffee, she saw lights shine through her window. She stood to look out and realized it was Andy leaving on his week-long adventure. She smiled and raised her coffee mug to her brother.

Heather admired her baby brother. He had been a rebel as a young man, and again now, but in her mind, that took courage. Being able to run away with no family contact and learn to live and survive. Andy had thrived when he returned home after their parents died. He had made a name for himself. He found his family, and they had found him.

She knew Andy had reached a point in his life that needed to be explored. He felt alone even though he was surrounded by family and friends who loved him. Heather wondered why that need had resurfaced. She wondered if the week would be long enough for him to find himself again. She wondered if, when he returned, he would be different.

She finished her coffee and sat on her sofa. She felt overwhelmed and had stepped out of her comfort zone by admitting it to Sara and Andy. Now she had to work on herself. Having Sara back at the manor would help free up some of her time. She loved her work, and doing the special events, birthday parties, and wedding receptions at the reception hall had been amazing. She met so many new people. Yet, occasionally she felt there was more for her in life. More than being a party planner and helping at the manor. She was also a mother to two little boys and still felt lost some days. She had lost herself in recent years.

Maybe it was time for a new beginning for her too.

Karen opened her eyes and laid her arm across where Andy should have been. When she felt the mattress instead of her husband, sadness crept in, knowing she had slept through his departure. She reached for his pillow and held it close to her chest. This was all she would have of him for the next week. Reluctantly she had agreed to no contact with him while he was gone. It was not the way she wanted it, but she understood it was what he needed. She trusted him and knew he would be back soon. She also knew that he would be a new man when he returned. A man with a new mindset, maybe new goals in life. Mostly, she knew this time away was best for all of them.

Karen heard her bedroom door open, and her oldest two walked into the bedroom. She reached out to them and lifted them onto the bed with her. They snuggled in. She smiled. These kids would keep her mind occupied, that was for sure.

After several minutes, the three of them got up. Karen quickly dressed after sending Ryan and River out to the living room. Then Karen walked to the baby's room and scooped her up. She was the best little girl. Even when Ravyn woke up in her crib, she never cried. She just waited.

Today Karen would treat the kids to blueberry pancakes. A special treat for them all. As she watched her children eating and talking in their own way of communicating, she wondered what Andy was doing or how far he had already driven. Then she wondered what direction he had taken.

Karen jumped when her phone rang later that morning. She knew it was not Andy as she had set a special ringtone for him. Her worst fear was that it was an unknown caller. One with bad news.

"Hello, I am so glad it is you, Larry."

"Hello. Why are you glad it is me? Is something wrong?" Larry sensed something in Karen's voice. Something was off.

"Oh, no, not really." It was obvious that Andy had not told Larry about his journey.

"Not really? Talk to me, young lady."

"Andy is on a trip for a week, that's all." Karen was not sure how much she should tell Larry.

"Why? Another trip searching for a recipe like Terri and Adam's wedding?"

"No. More of a trip searching for himself."

"Again? He has not done that in years. Everything alright with you two?"

"Yes, we are great. He had the urge to run. We discussed it between us, he discussed it with his sisters, and he is on an adventure for a week. That's all."

"Where did he go?"

"You know Andy, he would not tell us. He said he did not even know where he was going beyond Rose Lane. Said he would decide that when he came to the T in the road."

Larry laughed. "Sounds just like the old Andy. I am sure he will be alright. Are you and the kids doing okay? Grace and I can come over to help out if you want."

"We are fine today."

"Okay. That's all I need to hear. I will call again later or tomorrow. If you need anything, and I mean Anything, please call us."

"I will. Thanks." Karen hung up her phone. Then stared at it. Why had Larry called initially? Karen shrugged her shoulders and went back to her kids eating breakfast. They had made a mess on the table. That was nothing new.

Andy looked at the clock in his car. He had been on the road for three hours. It was time for a break. When he saw a rest area, he pulled in and parked in the back under a shade tree. Standing up, he stretched, took a deep breath, and let it out as he bent and touched his toes.

"Wow, you are in good shape," a voice said behind him.

Andy stood and turned to see who it was. He shook his head. "What the heck are you doing here?"

"Me? What are you doing here? It's the middle of nowhere."

"Which is right where I want to be."

"Why? I thought your life was going great after you moved back home to Tennessee."

"It is."

"Then I ask again, what are you doing here? Are you running again?"

Andy just stared at the person in front of him. Why was his past so much a part of his present? Would he ever be able to outrun the life he once lived? "I am here on a week's vacation."

"Alone? That doesn't sound good."

"It is good. But, I am sure you would not understand." Andy spoke his peace and started to walk away. He did not need this in his life. Not this week.

"Sorry, man. I just know what you were like years ago and how you walked away from that life to run home to family. I wish you the best, whatever it is you are going through. I hope you are right, that your life is still good. You deserve it. Again, sorry. I'll leave you alone." The man walked away.

Andy took a deep breath as he walked into the visitor's center. His life was good. He was happy. He turned and watched the man drive away. He hoped he would never see him again. Living with him in Florida had almost broken him. He was lucky to get away. He hoped the man had gotten out of the drugs and alcohol lifestyle.

303

Andy walked around a few more minutes, then drove off. It was his time for new beginnings, a fresh attitude, and finding peace before he went home to his family.

Andy exited twenty miles later and turned right. The name of the town on the sign drew him. He did not know why.

~~~~~~

Sara sat in the office at the manor. She looked around and smiled. Yes, she still felt it. Her parents. They were still there in that room, the manor and her heart. She felt their love and acceptance. It felt right to be back. This was where she belonged.

A knock on the door interrupted her thoughts.

"Come in. The door is open. And it always will be." She added as the door opened. She expected Heather to walk in.

"Hi, are you Sara?"

"Yes, what may I help you with?" She looked up and saw a stranger standing before her.

"My wife and I would like to rent a room if you have any vacancies."

"Of course. Let me see what rooms are available." Sara pulled up the registration site on her computer. The only room left was the first one on the first floor. Sara double-checked the record to be sure. That room was never available. Why was it now? She looked up. "I have one room left. It is rarely vacant, so today must be your lucky day."

"It must be. May we book it for the week?"

Sara doubted that would be possible, but when she looked again, it showed available for the next two weeks.

"Yes, you may. I will need you to fill out this form, and we can get you set up. Let me make sure it is clean and ready for you." Sara spoke as she picked up her cell phone to call Heather.

"Hi, Sis. What can I do for you?" Heather asked.

"I need to know if the first room on the first floor is clean and ready for guests.""

"Sure. It may not have fresh flowers, but otherwise, it is ready. Why? Did you rent it?"

"Yes, just now. We had a walk-in. A man and his wife want to stay for a week."

"That is awesome. Someone who has not been here before?"

"From what he says, this is the first time they have been here. I have not asked any other questions. They will be here for a week." Sara said and hung up so she could talk with their new guests.

Sara took the registration form from the man. She looked at the name and made sure he had signed it. She smiled at him and said the room was ready if he wanted to bring in their luggage and his wife.

He smiled. "Thanks. I just need the key. We have an appointment to get to first. We will be back in a couple of hours."

"That is fine. Let me just show you where it is so you may come and go as you please. This paper will give you all the information you need about staying here." She handed him the paper and stood to lead him down the hallway.

"Thank you so much. We will be back as soon as our meeting is over."

"Glad you have chosen us for your stay. I hope all goes well at your meeting."

"Thanks. It should. Just a bunch of old people meeting up after several years apart."

"Well, I hope your reunion meeting goes well. If there is anything we can help you with, let us know."

Chapter Fifty-Four

Their Story

It only took Sara a couple of days to get back into the rhythm of working at the manor. Rachelle remained working on the major tasks, which gave Sara time to read more of the journals and organize her writing space. She needed to keep it separate from the estate work. Thankfully, the room had enough space once she rearranged a few things.

The morning after their new guest checked in, Rachelle commented that she nor Bob had seen them.

"He did mention that he and his wife had some meetings to attend in the area. Told us not to worry about breakfast or anything for them." Sara responded to her concern.

"Okay. It is just odd not to see any sign of a guest."

"I know what you mean. Most guests here enjoy spending time in the great room in the evening even if they miss breakfast time."

"And most want to get to know us. This couple is unusual. But each to their own."

Rachelle went back to her work and left Sara alone in the office. Sara opened her laptop computer and stared at the blank page she pulled up in her writing software program. She looked at the pile of journals and sighed. She had read all but the last one. She knew more about the history of her family than anyone alive did. Now she needed to write their story so her siblings, friends, and complete strangers would know the details. Yes, that included the secrets. At least most of the secrets. There were a few that she refused to share with the general public. Her family didn't even know all of them. They would when the time was right.

She began to press the keys on her computer. A moment later, she deleted everything she had written as she had changed her mind about how to start their story.

She began again. This time with inspiration, determination, and a flow to the words she never knew existed.

An hour later, she took her eyes off the computer screen. The office door opened, and Rachelle walked in with a fresh cup of coffee for Sara.

"You have been typing away for a while. I thought you could use a drink. I hope the coffee is okay, even though it is mid-day."

"Coffee is fine any time of the day." Sara slid her chair back from her desk and took the mug from Rachelle. "Thanks."

"How is the writing going?"

"A rough start. I deleted the first attempt. This time the words and the story seem to flow. I hope it stays that way."

"I hope so too. I know it will be an amazing story when you are through."

"That is the plan. Well, to at least tell the story, I'm not sure how amazing it will be. We finally agreed it was time to tell the world our family history."

"I am glad. You all have shared so much of it with me. I would love to know the rest of the story, as the saying goes.

"I hope you don't mind, but you are part of the story."

"Why me? Oh, right. I guess I am part of your story. We never would have met if it had not been for your father."

"That's right. And the hardest part is explaining how we are not quite related but seem so close. It has always felt like we are some sort of sisters."

"I agree. You are my sister by another set of parents." Rachelle and Sara both laughed. They continued talking while they finished their coffee.

Before Sara realized it, the day was ending, and it was time to head back to her house. She had put in a full day of writing and felt she had a good start. She went home and made dinner for Randall and Gayle. They asked her how it felt to be writing at the manor.

"I feel a better connection being there writing. I was okay getting organized at home, but I think being at the manor connects me with Mama and Daddy better, and the words flow."

"That is what you wanted," Randall said. "I hope it continues that way. We are both here to support you. You know that."

"And, Mama, if you ever need help with it, I would love to help write it or read your draft."

"Thank you, Sweety. I may take you up on that down the road. Right now, I just want to get the thoughts down and saved in a file."

"I understand that. There is nothing like writing a long essay and then forgetting to save it."

"Sounds like you have done that before?"

"Just once. That was all it took to always remember to save it."

Late that night, Sara woke up in the middle of the night. The urge to write was so powerful she got up, got dressed, and walked to the manor to write. She was still there when Randall walked into the office with coffee and a blueberry muffin for her.

"I woke up this morning, and you were gone. I knew this would be the only place you would go during those hours. I'll let you write while I get more sleep. I hope you don't mind."

"Mind? I am thankful for that. I feel that may happen a lot now that I have to come here to write. I am sure it will fade at some point. Until then, thank you so much for your support in this."

"You will always have our support, Love. Always."

"Thank you," Sara said. "You don't know what that means to me. I don't want to end up like my mother, who thought she could only write upstairs in the secret attic."

"You will never need to hide from us for you to write. I think your entire family can agree to that."

Sara smiled and then thought of something. "What if I do go to the attic to write a portion of the book? Would that be awkward?"

"If you did it every day, I think it would be. Maybe it would be good for the chapter about the time in the attic and your discoveries there."

"I agree. Time will tell if I get that urge when I reach that part of our story."

"Do you know how much I love you?" Randall smiled at Sara. He had loved her from the moment he saw her when they were still kids. He always thought there was too much of a difference between them and their families. As they grew and he moved away for school, and then she moved away when she got married, he closed that chapter of his life. Only to have it reopened when she returned home. He still felt they were too different for a while, so he never approached her. Now he was so blessed to have her in his life. He could not imagine life without her. Their souls, once unlikely to connect, had made a lifetime commitment.

"I think I know. It is just shy of how much I love you." Sara smiled and wrapped her arms around the love of her life."

Several months later, Sara found herself in the attic writing. She had not been sure she would want to, but when the two guests that no one ever saw after they registered with Sara a few months earlier left, it reignited a need for answers. Answers she thought she could only find in the attic. Memories and events she and her family had forgotten – temporarily.

Epilogue

"Glad you were finally able to spend time with us," Sara remembered saying to the gentleman when he told her they had heard about Bella Rose Estate years before.

"My wife and I will not be in your way while we are here. We have a lot of meetings in town and family to visit. You may not see us at all."

A week later, they left, and true to his word, no one had seen them, not even for breakfast.

Heather went to their room to clean after talking with Sara the next morning. Ten minutes later, she was in the office facing Sara. Holding an object up in her hand.

"What is that?" Sara asked when she noticed her sister just standing in silence. Heather's face was white. "Are you alright?"

Heather walked over to Sara and handed her the object as she was finally able to speak. "I found this. On top of the dresser in the room where the ghost of a couple stayed."

Sara stared at the antique key now laying in her hand. One that they had never seen before. Her face was now as white as her sister's face. No words. Her sister may have said it best. Ghost of a couple.

Later that week, the siblings had another family meeting. This time it was for the family and those living near the manor or associated with it. This included Terri and Adam, Barbara and Steven, Rachelle and Bob. When they had all gathered in the great room, Sara began to speak. She told them about their guest. No one remembered seeing them while they were there. Not even Terri or Adam and most of the guests from the manor ate at least one meal at the café during their visit.

Sara asked if anyone had anything to share with everyone. Terri raised her hand slightly. Sara smiled and told her she didn't have to raise her hand to share. "For this news, I might." Terri began. "I just want to share that Jay and Carrie had their baby a week ago. A baby girl they named Tamara."

"What a beautiful name," Heather remarked.

"I agree. When I talked with Jay, he said they would visit Jeff and Angela in about a week or two when the baby was a little bigger and could make the trip."

"That is great news."

"Are you alright with them being here and you seeing them?" Sara asked.

"Yes, Adam and I are fine with the friendship between Jay and me."

No one else had any news to share when Sara asked for it.

Sara then lifted the key for all to see. Silence filled the room. Some understood, and some had not heard the story of the keys. Sara briefly explained the background. She then showed them the basket that held the keys they had found years ago and the key Adam found on the beach. She continued by telling everyone to keep their eyes and ears open for an explanation of the latest found key and about the two unlikely souls that had occupied that room.

As Sara closed her eyes that night, after the meeting, she knew their family story, the mystery, was not ending. It was beginning again. The truth had not all been revealed.

THE END

Until the next book ---

Truth is Key

Acknowledgment

Thank you, Chris Surcey, for showing me adventure during our summer together and giving me a dream come true that was more than what I had envisioned. The West Coast trip was one neither of us will ever forget. It changed both of our lives. Thank you for your encouragement to author this fictionalized story, for inviting me to be your travel companion, and for the initial invitation to dinner. Without them, this book would not have been what it is.

Thank you, Katie (Surcey)Kane, for helping me choose a name for one character.

Thank you, Marion Howell, for your part in my life and all the people I met through you that may or may not have become part of this book.

Thank you, Ellen Peck, Cynthia Risk, and Connie Mulligan, for your feedback along the way or with portions of the writing and blurb.

Thank you, my faithful readers, who stick with me, for your encouragement and enthusiasm for the next book. There are more books yet to come.

And as always, I am grateful for the talent and imagination God gave me.

www.ingramcontent.com/pod-product-compliance
Lightning Source LLC
Chambersburg PA
CBHW030418180626
46812CB00005B/2071